Neil M. Gunn (1891–1973), was born in Dunbeath, Caithness. Gunn was educated at his village school until the age of twelve and at fifteen he became a clerk in the Civil Service, working in London and Edinburgh until he joined the Customs and Excise in 1911 and came to stay in Inverness. Gunn continued to work for the Excise during the First World War in which three of his family lost their lives; his brother and closest friend John, (whose story is told in *Highland River*), was badly gassed.

Gunn married his Dingwall girlfriend Daisy Frew in 1921 returning the following year to the Highlands where he settled down and began to write seriously. His first novel, *The Grey Coast*, appeared in 1926, followed by *The Lost Glen* (serialised in 1928), and *Morning Tide*, a Book Society choice, in 1930. He turned to ancient history with *Sun Circle* (1933), and to the Highland clearances, with *Butcher's Broom* (1934), before calling up his own childhood again in *Highland River*, which won great acclaim and the James Tait Black Memorial Prize in 1937.

Supported by T. S. Eliot and Faber, who had become his publishers, Gunn turned to full-time writing, producing the autobiographical *Off in a Boat* in 1938, followed by another huge success with the epic novel, *The Silver Darlings* (1941). Short stories, plays, articles and more novels followed, most notably *Young Art and Old Hector* (1942), *The Green Isle of the Great Deep* (1944), *The Silver Bough* (1948), and *Bloodhunt* (1952). Gunn's last book was *The Atom of Delight* (1956), an autobiography which reflected on his life-long fascination with the Zen-like and elusive spirit of life, wisdom and delight. He continued to work as an essayist and broadcaster until his death in 1973. The Neil Gunn International Fellowship has been established in his honour.

Neil M. Gunn

~Highland River~

Introduced by Diarmid Gunn

CANONGATE
CLASSICS
37

First published in 1937 by The Porpoise
Press & Co (Publishers), first published as a
Canongate Classic in 1991 by Canongate Press,
reprinted in 1996 by Canongate Books Ltd, 14
High Street, Edinburgh EH1 1TE. Copyright ©
Dairmid Gunn. Introduction copyright ©
Dairmid Gunn, 1991.

The publishers gratefully acknowledge
general subsidy from the Scottish Arts Council
towards the Canongate Classics series and a
specific grant towards the publication of this
title.

The publishers gratefully acknowledge Sarema
Press for permission to reproduce the cover
illustration from the book *Henry Scott Tuke
under Canvas*: Wainright and Dinn © Sarema
Press (Publishers) Ltd, England SM5 4JS

Typeset by Falcon Typographic Art Ltd, Edinburgh & London. Printed and bound in Finland
by WSOY.

British Library Cataloguing in Publication Data
A catalogue record for this book is available
on request from the British Library.

ISBN 0 86241 358 3

Dear John,

This can hardly be the description of our Highland river that you anticipated when, lying on our backs in a green strath, we idly talked the idea over. Certainly it is not the description I anticipated myself. Some ancestral instinct, at first glimpse of the river, must have taken control and set me off on a queerer hunt than we have yet tackled. Or am I now trying to cover up the spoor? You will early recognise that though there is no individual biography here, every incident may have had its double. Some of the characters seem to have strayed in from Morning Tide under different names. I cannot explain this odd behaviour – apart from the old desire to be in on the hunt in any disguise. However, if only I could get you to see the hunt as a poaching expedition to the source of delight we got from a northern river, I feel that you might not be altogether disappointed should you come back (as we have so often done in our time) with an empty bag.

With brotherly affection,

NEIL

Introduction

Dedications are seldom read and rarely informative. The one in *Highland River* is an exception in that it contains the key to an understanding of this unusual book. Dedicated to my father John it talks of a northern river and a poaching expedition to the source of delight. The quest, whether successful or not, seems all important.

As Gunn explains, some of the characters may have strayed in from *Morning Tide*, a novel written six years earlier and set in the same area as that of *Highland River*, the Caithness village of Dunbeath and its hinterland. The central character, Kenn, boy and man, is portrayed in such a way that the reader can be forgiven for thinking that here is a sort of autobiography written in the third person. The book, after all, is seen through the eyes of the young and the older Kenn, an anchor figure in human terms, in the same way as the Highland river fixes the book firmly in the strath of the Dunbeath Water. The book's theme is the intricate relationship between a specific boy and a specific river. Kenn is essentially my father as the fundamental experiences undergone by both boy and man belong entirely to him. The epic struggle between boy and salmon, the horrific experiences in the trenches during the First World War including the final meeting with the older brother who was to be killed shortly afterwards, the graduation ceremony at a Scottish university and the exhaustive debates on the potential of physics in an exciting new world all directly concern him. It says much for the author that he is able to transmute these experiences so effectively and convincingly into the warp and woof of the book. Other relatives or friends could have stepped into Kenn's

personality, including Gunn's youngest brother Alec, by far
the most expert of all the brothers with rod and gaff, but
what is important is that the boy represents an archetypal
boy living in a clearly defined Highland community at a
certain time. It is the experiences of the boy and the adolescent that are retained by the grown up man as both a pool
of strength and a help in a quest for the source of life and
being.

The river is central to the boy's experience. Everything
relates to it. It is his world of adventure and wonder. Even
on stormy nights he can hear the constant, rushing noise of
the river flowing below the village, nights when he feels he
has much in common with all the furry creatures that are
seeking shelter from the elements in their burrows or dens.
Then, there is the well by the river, to which he is often
sent to draw water. It is at the pool near the well that he
triumphs over the cock salmon and as the victor of this
combat ceases to be a child and becomes a fully fledged
boy. The relationship with the mother alters, but she remains
the symbol of hearth and haven and the anchorstone of the
family. 'All the history of her people is writ on her face.
The grey seas are stilled in her eyes . . . quietly against
the quiet trees the struggle of the days lies folded in her
hands.' The allusion to grey seas is charged with meaning as
Kenn's father – clearly my paternal grandfather – is skipper
and owner of one of the boats using Dunbeath harbour. If
the river is central to young Kenn's life, the sea occupies
another dimension; it is about him in the same way as the
sky is above him. It is in his father and it is whence the
salmon come to begin their final journey to the source of
the river. The river and the sea juxtaposed, one personal,
the other elemental – both part of an eternal landscape and
seascape.

The idea of a river and its significance to life is not new.
Wordsworth, whom Gunn greatly admired, writes:

> . . . when the fretful stir
> unprofitable, and the fever of the world,

Have hung upon the beatings of my heart –
How oft, in spirit, have I turned to thee,
O Sylvan Wye! thou wanderer thro' the woods,
How often has my spirit turned to thee!

There are differences here. Wordsworth was not writing about the stream of his youth and the Wye is a mighty river compared with the Dunbeath Water. The northern stream, however, is small enough to relate intimately to an individual life; it is manageable in terms of getting to know it from estuary to source. The Dunbeath Water comprises three distinct stretches. The first links the estuary to the Broch where the Burn of Houstry joins the Dunbeath Water; the second stretches from this confluence to the gorge and the third from the gorge to the source. The boy gradually becomes acquainted with these stretches of river, moving with some trepidation from the lower reaches towards the source.

The word Broch brings to mind an earlier civilization, a Pictish one, that flourished in Caithness before the Vikings began to make their incursions in the ninth and tenth centuries A.D. There are other reminders in the strath of times gone by including the Hill of Peace near the Broch and Pictish houses near the upper reaches of the river. Even the place names reflect the history of the area. The Nordic 'Loedebest' and the Celtic 'Ballachly,' so different in origin, but so close geographically. Kenn is aware of signposts of the past and finds them of greater appeal to his historical imagination than the educational diet offered of the genealogical trees of English Kings or battles fought in distant places. In the same way, geography for him is a greater knowledge of the hills, glens and moors of his own area rather than such a fact that Leicester is famous for the manufacture of shoes. Aids to stimulating this historical imagination take the form of scents and sounds. Among the scents are heath smoke and the smell of the primrose:

Heath smoke is an affair of time; of family of communal
life through immense stretches of time. Its colour is the
bloom of mountains on a far horizon – particularly in
the evening light which is so akin to the still light of
inner vision.

And,

Thus the relationship between the primrose and the
heath fire is not so much a relationship between man
and nature as that relationship at a particular stretch
of time on earth, the stretch which solitary voices
throughout all subsequent ages and races have called
'the golden age.'

From the 'golden age' to the Somme and Ypres – what a
contrast in thought and fact! Yet in the midst of destruction
and slaughter the young soldier Kenn draws strength from
the reservoir of his childhood experiences and never forgets
his Highland river. I remember my father telling me that the
skies about France and Belgium enchanted him as much as
those over his beloved strath and moorland. The constant
thud of the howitzers, for he served in the Royal Artillery,
reminded him of the pounding of the sea against the grey
cliffs of Caithness. Even bird life continued in the copses
and isolated trees of a devastated landscape. Again the
saving grace of a transference of thought from battlefield
to 'golden age.'

Cold and clear and exquisite. Just above the cliffs
Kenn got his intimations of an unknown poetry from
the sea's rhythm, so in the flight of the green linnet
against his northern snow was set the rhythm's line in
an unhuman act.

Such intimations of a Highland paradise were not to reach
Kenn's brother, Angus, in reality, Ben, an older brother of
Neil and John. For him, the present is everything and the
major aim of his existence is to survive at all costs. Among
the costs, alas, is an unwillingness to derive sustenance and

comfort from a Highland childhood. The following dialogue between him and Kenn tells all.

> Kenn turned from this high note and in an ordinary voice, quiet as if he were asking for a fill of tobacco, said to his brother, 'Do you remember that time? They were at the heather burning. We lay for a while at Hawk's Hoe, and then went on and down to Achglas. There was a fish under the water and you make me try to see him in the brown water.' 'Yes,' said Angus. But he did not seem to care about remembering.

Angus's attitude is a death in life, a total abnegation of all that is positive and life enhancing, an abandonment of a search for self fulfilment. His ghastly death a few weeks after the meeting is simply the setting of a seal on a life that had already been extinguished. In contrast, Kenn possesses an inner reserve, a reserve that gives strange poignancy to T. S. Eliot's line from *Four Quartets*, 'The river is within us, the sea is all about us.' Kenn's fate in the War is to be gassed and transported to a military hospital in Leicester, the city in which he had been taught at primary school that shoes were made. No footwear now, but the kindly attentions of doctors and nurses in white coats, an assembly of the heavenly host clad in white; womanhood in its most caring and tender mood. Women again at the centre of things.

With the physical and mental horror of war behind him Kenn enters the realm of physics and imbibes all the excitement of new discoveries in nuclear science. The period between the Wars was an exhilarating period for some, but it had its dangers. The choice of the title *The Waste Land* for T. S. Eliot's ambitious poem is clearly apposite. Modern man had backed himself into a spiritual cul-de-sac or waste land in which no spiritual refreshment was available, since God's existence had been eliminated by reason.

Kenn returns to his Highland river not just for comfort but more to explore the source of his being, of all being. The river is now being looked at in its upper reaches in desolate moorland and near ancient and no so ancient ruins. But the

ruins are the stuff of legend and folklore that constitute a
living tradition strong in his native country. A kindred
spirit, the contemporary Russian writer Leonid Borodin
in describing an idyllic childhood spent near Lake Baikal
writes, 'I'm telling you the legend, and every word of it is
truth, otherwise it wouldn't be the legend. The legend is
the greatest truth of all.' Kenn identifies himself with his
forebears and derives spiritual comfort from this feeling.
He seeks a God not in a Biblical sense but rather in the
form of a Being who produces moments of delight, a stream
of epiphanies that cannot be explained, but just happen.
The pilgrimage goes on and the source of Highland River
is reached. The reader eagerly awaits the final vision from
the older Kenn standing there. But his is unrevealed by the
author, who has taken over Kenn again, and perhaps this is
as it must be. For the hunt is more important, perhaps, than
the revelation. All this adds meaning to that final sentence
of the dedication to my father. 'However if I only could get
you to see the hunt as a poaching expedition to the source of
delight we got from a northern river, I feel that you might
not be altogether disappointed should you come back (as we
have so often done in our time) with an empty bag.'

Dairmid Gunn

KENN MUMBLED AND GRUMBLED and kept his eyes shut, for being rudely wakened out of sleep was a thing that often happened to him. He had been up late last night because everyone had been busy over the departure of the boats in the morning for the distant fishing. There had been such comings and goings and preparations that the excitement had kept sleep away much longer than usual. In this little Highland community young boys were not sent to bed early. Kenn was barely nine years old, and though he might be shouted at to take himself off at ten o'clock, he would often hang out until eleven. Last night it had been nearly midnight before sleep had curled him up in a corner of the kitchen, and his father had had to carry him to bed.

It was only when his mother's voice said something about the boats going away that he knew he must get up, so he muttered, 'What are you wanting?' His mother told him that she wanted fresh water from the well. What an excuse for wakening a fellow! He could almost have cried. And when he did stagger out of bed and found from the greyness of the light that it could not be much more than six o'clock, his vexation became bitter. He stood in his shirt, whimpered moodily as he scratched himself, then slowly pulled on his trousers and his blue fisherman's gansey.

In the kitchen his father and mother were talking. He paid no attention to them, but picked up the bright tin pail and made it clatter against the jamb of the door as he went out.

The dawn air was cold and the touch of frost in the ground was such a shock to his bare feet that he nearly cried out. He should have put on his boots, holed as they were. He hoped his parents were watching him through the window and seeing what he had to endure.

In this mood he arrived at the well, which was at the foot of a steep bank by the side of the river. Carelessly he bumped the pail down on the flat stone, and at the sound, as at a signal in a weird fairy tale, the whole world changed. His moodiness leapt right out of him and fear had him by the throat.

For from his very feet a great fish had started ploughing its way across the river, the king of fish, the living salmon.

Kenn had never seen a living salmon before, and of those he had seen dead this was beyond all doubt the all-father.

When the waves faded out on the far side of the stream, where the bed was three feet deep, Kenn felt the great silence that lay upon the world and stood in the midst of it trembling like a hunted hare.

So intensely did he listen to the silence that he might well have caught a footfall a mile away. But there was no slightest sound anywhere. His eyes shot hither and thither, along horizons, down braes, across fields and wooded river-flats. No life moved; no face was watching.

Out of that noiseless world in the grey of the morning, all his ancestors came at him. They tapped his breast until the bird inside it fluttered madly; they drew a hand along his hair until the scalp crinkled; they made the blood within him tingle to a dance that had him leaping from boulder to boulder before he rightly knew to what desperate venture he was committed.

For it was all in a way a sort of madness. The fear was fear of the fish itself, of its monstrous reality, primal fear; but it was also infinitely complicated by fear of gamekeepers, of the horror and violence of law courts, of our modern social fear. Not only did his hunting ancestors of the Caledonian Forest come at him, but his grown-up brothers and his brothers' friends, with their wild forays and epic stories, a constant running the gauntlet against enemy forces, for the glory of fun and laughter and daring—and the silver gift of the salmon. A thousand influences had his young body taut as a bow, when at last, bending over a boulder of the old red sandstone, he saw again the salmon.

Fear rose at him afresh, for there was a greyness in its great dark-blue back that was menacing and ghostly. An apparition, an uncanny beast, from which instinct urged him to fly on tiptoe. The strength of his will holding him there brought a faint sickness to his throat. He could see the eyes on each side of the shapely head and knew the eyes must see him. Still as a rock and in some mysterious way as unheeding, the salmon lay beneath him. Slowly he drew his head back until at last the boulder shut off sight of the salmon and released his breath.

As before, he looked all around him, but now with a more conscious cunning. A pulse was spirting in his neck. There was colour in his sensitive features and a feverish brilliance in the dark-brown eyes beneath the straight fringe of darker hair. Tiptoeing away from the boulder, he went searching downstream until he found a large flattish stone, and returned with it pressed against his stomach.

When he had got the best grip, he raised it above his head, and, staggering to the upper edge of the sandstone boulder, poised it in aim. Then he did not let it drop so much as contrive, with the last grain of his strength, to hurl it down on the fish.

Though untouched, the salmon was very clearly astonished and, before the stone had right come to rest, had the pool in a splendid tumult. For it was not one of those well-defined pools of gradual depths. There were gravel banks in it and occasional boulders forming little rest pools behind them. There was no particular neck, as the bed of the stream merely rose to let the water rush noisily down and in. The tail was wide and shallow.

It was a sea-trout rather than a salmon pool, as became apparent in that first blind rush, when the fish thrashed the water to froth in a terrific boil on top of the gravel bank, cleared the bank, and, with back fin showing, shot across the calm water towards the well where he had been resting. So headlong was his speed that he beached himself not two yards from Kenn's pail. Curving from nose to tail, the great body walloped the stones with resounding whacks.

So hypnotised was Kenn by this extraordinary spectacle, that he remained stiff and powerless, but inwardly a madness was already rising in him, an urgency to rush, to hit, to kill. The salmon was back in the shallow water, lashing it, and in a moment, released, was coming straight for him. Right at his feet there was a swirl, a spitting of drops into his face. The fish saw him and, as if possessed by a thousand otters, flashed up the deep water and launched himself, flailing wildly, in the rushing shallows of the neck.

And then Kenn went into action, caution and fear forgotten. It was in truth a madness not unlike the salmon's. In his blind panic, the fish had no regard for bodily stress; in his blind exaltation, neither had Kenn.

Less than a hundred yards beyond the shallows of the neck was a long dark pool, and in it lay escape. If the brute had been calm, been travelling by night, it could have made the passage with ease. But now, having lost its head, it defeated itself by its own strength and added to its panic by bashing its nose against boulders.

Kenn approached the scene with such speed that before one toe could slip on slime the other was forward to thrust him on. Landing knee-deep in the final jump, he tore a stone from the bed of the stream and, blinded by the salmon's splashings, let drive.

He missed by over a foot and there followed a jumble in which, in his excitement, he not only threw guttural challenge but lunged fiercely and recklessly, to be left grovelling on his back as the salmon shot downward.

In his leap for the bank Kenn stumbled and was thrown severely. But he had no consciousness of pain; only of loss of time, of awful fear lest the salmon should escape.

And running down the bank it seemed to him as if the salmon had escaped. No trace of 'way' on the pool. Nothing. . . . Was that a swirl—far down? Making his way out of the pool!

On his toes again, Kenn sped downward, came in below the fish, and picking up a stone half the size of his head, went straight to the attack.

The water was now growing narrower and deeper, but it was tortured by boulders and sloping flagstones. The passage to the sea was easy and hardly half a mile long, but Kenn complicated the boulder pattern by adding with violence small boulders of his own. Twice the salmon flashed past him, and now Kenn was not merely wading into the water, but falling and crawling and choking in it, yet ever with his dark head rising indomitably.

An altogether strange and ungainly beast to the desperate fish from the dark continental ledges of the Atlantic, where life had been lived for years in a halcyon calm, and red shrimps had fallen like manna about him, to be nosed and eaten at leisure. If the salmon had an instinct for an enemy at all, it must have been for some animal like the otter, swift and sure in attack and deathly in grip. This rushing, sprawling, stone-throwing inhabitant of another world had fingers that slid off the back like caressing fingers of seaweed. Unable to bite yet pursuing relentlessly. Shake him off! A rush and a heave and the salmon bared his girth on a sloping flagstone. From the bottom, Kenn had raked a stone barely the size of his small fist, but he threw it with all his vigour and it scored a first direct hit by stinging smartly blue cheek against red gills.

Back off the flagstone came the salmon with his nose pointing upstream, and he followed his nose. At the best of times it is awkward for a salmon to go downstream, but upstream, given depth and shoulder room, speed becomes a frenzy. This fish turned it into a debauch and reached the Well Pool like a demented torpedo.

Kenn had chosen his battleground and laid down the conditions of the fight.

And it was a saga of a fight, for of all that befell Kenn afterwards, of war and horror and love and scientific triumphs, nothing ever had quite the splendour and glory of that struggle by the Well Pool, while the tin pail that the tinkers had made watched with bright face from the kneeling-stone and his mother, murmuring in her anger, put last night's water in the kettle.

For Kenn had no weapons of attack other than his little fists and what they could grab from the river bottom; no rod, hook, net, or implement of constraint or explosion. It was a war between an immature human body on the one side, and a superbly matured body of incredible swiftness and strength on the other. In physical length, laid out side by side, there would have been little difference between them.

But neither of them was laid out yet! Indeed so far there had been little more than the courteous slap on the cheek as gage of battle, and it had been delivered by Kenn.

The initial strategy, however, for such warfare was his, not from learning or experience but out of instinct, and it could be summed up in the words 'keep him on the run'. All his tactics brought this about as their natural result, whether he was careering wildly up and down the bank, pausing to hurl a stone, or dashing into shallows to get at close quarters. The frenzy of both had first to be worn down, before the cunning brain could stalk the tired body.

A curious mood of fatalism comes upon a salmon that has committed its life to a pool. Up and down it will go, round this boulder, by the side of that, turning here, turning back again there, but never making any attempt to leave the known ground. No barrage of stones will drive it forth, however successfully timed. The dangers of the shallows are the dangers of the unknown, of death. If the pool be just deep enough a salmon will pass between swimming human legs rather than be driven forth, and in this restless fashion will ultimately tire out its enemies.

But if the Well Pool had not sufficient depth over a wide enough area to permit of this endless swimming, it had on the other hand its own suggestions for escape. The water was amber-coloured, for it was the tail-end of a mighty spate, and drained from peat-banks in distant moors; being for the most part shallow, it had a considerable flow; and the scattered pieces of rock against the ground inequalities offered a tired fish many a natural hiding place.

Indeed several times Kenn had his heart in his mouth when it seemed that the salmon had altogether vanished. In the dark shadow of a leaning stone where the amber water gurgled past, a dark-blue back was but a darker shadow. Then Kenn would spot the tail or the curve of the nose or the pallor of a fin; would be overcome with an emotion keener in its thrust than ever; would back away and hunt his stone. Splash! and the salmon was on its journey once more, betrayed by its great size.

This phase of the battle went on for a long time, until Kenn knew all the resting places and there began to grow in him a terrible feeling of power, terrible in its excitement, in its realisation that he might be successful, and even more terrible in its longing.

There came a time when Kenn, having got the fish resting where he wanted him, went downstream to choose his stone, but no longer in blind urgency. He handled two or three before lifting one against his breast.

The salmon lay by the outer edge of a greenish underwater slab. By approaching it on a slant towards its tail, he could keep its head out of sight. Warily he did this until he came to the edge of the stream. But now he knew that however he stooped while wading in, the eyes would be disclosed. He did not hesitate; he let himself down into the water and, the stone against his stomach, slithered over the gravelly bottom on his stern. It was an autumn morning, after a night of hoar-frost, but when the water got fully about his body he felt it warm. Foot by foot he thrust himself on, until at last he could have put out a hand and touched the tail; and the tail was deep as his face and as taut.

Slowly he reared up on his knees, fighting down the sinking sensation that beset him, his hands fiercely gripping the stone. Anxiety now started shouting in him to heave the stone and be done, but, though trembling, he rose with infinite care, little by little, disclosing the back fin, the nape of the neck where the otter bites, and at last the near eye. The fish did not move. Inch by inch the stone went up until at last his own eyes were looking from underneath it. Then in one thrust he launched stone and body at the fish.

The thud of the stone on the great back was a sound of such potency that even in that wild drenching moment it sang above all else. For the stone had landed; the stone had got him! Spewing the river water forth, stumbling and falling, he reached the bank. Then both of them went berserk.

This great fish had not the slippery cunning, the evasiveness, of a small salmon or grilse. It tore around like a bull in a ring. Kenn began to score direct hits more often. He was learning the way. He could throw a stone ahead; he could madden; he could stalk warily and hear ever more exultingly the singing thud.

The fatal part for a salmon is the nape of the neck. The time came when Kenn landed there heavily with the narrow stone edge; the salmon circled and thrashed as if half paralysed or blinded; Kenn with no more stones at hand launched a body attack and received one wallop from the tail that sent him flat on his back; the salmon was off again.

The end came near the neck of the pool on the side opposite the well. Here the low bank of the river widened out into a grassy field. The tired fish, with pale mouth gaping every now and then, went nosing into shallow water, where some upended flagstones might provide a new and dark retreat. But there was no hidden retreat there and Kenn, well down the pool, waited with wild hope. If it lay anywhere thereabouts until he got up, it would be finished! And it lay.

It actually lay in full view between two stone edges, its back fin barely covered. Kenn hit it as it moved and then fell on it.

His hands went straight for the gills; one found a grip under a cheek, the other, slipping, tried for a hold on the body, and there and then began the oddest tussle that surely that river could ever have seen.

Under the burning grip of human hands, the salmon went frantic and threw Kenn about as if he were a streamer tied to its neck; the upended stones bashed his arms, his legs, the back of his head; the bony cheek dug into his wrist; but nothing could now dim the relentless instinct in him to roll both bodies from the shallow water on to dry land.

And this in time he accomplished. When his hand was shot from behind the cheek it drew gills with it.

The salmon flailed the dry stones with desperate violence, but Kenn was now in his own element, and ever he brought his body behind the body of the fish and shored it upwards, thrusting at the gills until his hands were lacerated and bleeding.

He dragged that fish over fifty yards into the grass park before he laid it down. And when it heaved in a last convulsive shudder, he at once fell upon it as if the river of escape still lapped its tail.

Some two months before, a certain Master Douglas MacQuarry, twelve years of age, son of the sporting tenant of the estate, and duly attended by his gillie, had landed with the customary rod and tackle a salmon of ten pounds. It was a feat of sufficient importance to win flattering recognition in the county press. Kenn's mother had read the account aloud and then she had turned to her son and had said, '*You* would never be able to do a thing like that.' It certainly was not meant as any sort of challenge. It might have been very difficult for the mother herself to have explained the curious momentary feelings that prompted her, perhaps out of some dim half regretful recognition that no son of hers could ever achieve such social renown. From her expression, he had turned away, stung.

And now on this busy morning, angered against him for not returning with the well water, she suddenly saw him rounding the corner of the house towards the door of the back porch, face down, hands knotted behind his head, dripping wet and staggering. The salmon's nose was under his right ear, its tail was sweeping the ground behind. She gave way to him as he lurched in. Releasing his crooked fingers and heaving with a shoulder, he set the great fish with a mighty thump on the smooth blue flagstone at her feet. Then he glanced up at her and in a voice harsh with ironic challenge, remarked, 'There's your Master Douglas MacQuarry for you!'

She looked at the frightening size of the fish on the floor; she looked at her son. His dark hair was flattened to rat tails; his brown eyes were black against the excited pallor of his face; water seeped from his clothes; his body seemed no longer boyish but immature and fragile, his bones thin brittle stalks. Yet there was a flame, an intolerant fighting spirit, that knit him together, and separated him from her in a way that suddenly pulled at her heart.

She looked back to the fish and whispered, 'Where did you get that?'

'In the river.'

'Yourself?'

'Who else?' Did she think Master Douglas MacQuarry had helped him!

'You're all wet. Every stitch of you.'

'Oh a little,' he admitted indifferently. 'I'll go back for the pail!'

At that moment his father came round the house.

'Come here, Davy,' said the woman to him quietly.

The father came up. He looked at the fish; he looked at the boy. 'God bless me!' he whispered. 'Eh?'

'I'll go for the water,' said Kenn gruffly.

'Where did you get him?'

'In the Well Pool.'

'God bless me, boy!'

His father was a great and daring seaman; when he read the Bible and prayed he was a bearded patriarchal man; in danger his spirit flashed indomitable and challenging. Now his features softened in a slow winning smile, touched to the breath of wonder. His son felt it without looking at it, felt it in the breath of his voice, and a weakening warmth ran about his heart.

'Did anyone see you?' asked his mother.

It was likely! 'No,' he muttered.

'How did you land him?' asked his father.

'With my hands.'

His father looked at the hands. Kenn, seeing for the first time that they had been bloodily combed by the gills, put them behind his back.

'And he's wet to the skin besides,' nodded his mother in a rising tone that implied all this was none of her doing. She plainly could take no responsibility for him. The father could do that. This was obviously his son. But in the indifference of her voice that thus rose subtly to match her son's gruff indifference to her, was a curious crushed pride. 'You'll go in and change every stitch on you this minute.'

Kenn paid no attention to her.

'Was there no one there at all?' his father asked in his quiet voice, still hushed in wonder.

'No.'

The man looked at the fish. They all stared at it. It beat everything!

'Do you think,' said the mother thoughtfully, 'that Sans would like a bit?'

As her husband stared at her, his mouth fell open. The movement of a hidden meaning could be felt in the silence.

'I'll go for him,' said Davy, and with his seaman's nimbleness was rounding the back of the house and out of sight before either of them moved.

'You'd better go into the kitchen and take off your clothes,' she said to Kenn; but the reflective kindliness had crept back into her voice, and he did not even answer as he shifted from one foot to another. The pail at the well was forgotten. 'Are you cold?'

'No,' he answered.

'I'll go and get some dry things for you.' Because of the secret thought on her mind, she was now abstracted.

'They're coming,' said Kenn.

Sans, the merchant, was a big broad-shouldered jovial man. The folk liked him because in hard times he gave them credit. The boys liked him because when they proffered a halfpenny for nuts he gave them as many as his fist would hold, and he had a big fist. In this way he was different from other country merchants. And now he came with a smile on his face and his shoulders properly hunched in conspiracy. The sight of him made Kenn tingle.

When he saw the size of the fish, he muttered in astonishment a comical Gaelic oath, then laughed and brought down his hand on Kenn's shoulder. He shook Kenn. He stooped and looked into his eyes. 'Good for you, my little hero!' he chuckled.

'He'll wet your hands,' said the mother.

'I'd like to wet his whistle!' said Sans, and laughed again. 'What's the weight of him, do you think?'

'He's maybe twenty pounds,' said Kenn's father tentatively.

'Twenty! If he's not over twenty-five I'll eat my bonnet!' declared Sans.

'I'd say maybe twenty-two at the outside—no more,' repeated Davy modestly.

'We'll weigh him.'

'No, no, boy,' said Davy hastily. 'Some one might see us.'

Sans looked at him, then turned with a wink to the woman. 'He's hiding his pride fine.'

'Pride indeed!' said she, with high indifference. 'More need to be ashamed of the young rascal. I only hope he'll come to no bad end.'

This verbal art delighted Sans, and, stooping, he caught the fish by the gills. Its burden made him groan.

'Wait!' said the father hastily and he stole to the corner of the house and spied around. Sans' great body shook with soft laughter at this display of anxiety. He winked again. 'Come away, Kenn!' The woman stood watching the three of them slipping round the next house—it was yet little more than half past seven—towards the back door of the merchant's shop.

On the wooden scales used for weighing bags of meal, the merchant laid the fish. 'Twenty, did you say? Very well.' He put on twenty pounds—and pressed the beam—and chuckled. He added the seven weight. Nothing happened. Two more to make twenty-nine. Then, gently, one for thirty and the beam trembled.

'Bless me,' said Davy softly.

'Thirty good,' said Sans.

All three gazed at the salmon. It was a cock fish, fresh from the sea, with the very colour of strength in its scales. Youth's silver sheen had darkened into full-bodied splendour. Even underneath, the white shimmer came from an oozing goodness in the flesh. Strong flakes, that would break on a white curd, and feed hungry men, feed families. No delicacy for jaded palates here. The strength and vigour of the sea; the rush of turbulent waters; the overleaping power.

'Get your knife,' said Davy.

'What for?' asked the merchant.

'Get your knife, man, and hurry.' Davy turned to his son. 'Run you home and change your clothes.'

Kenn went home and washed his hands. The shallow scratches stung, but they no longer bled.

'Your dry things are ready,' said his mother, coming from the kitchen into the back porch. 'You're shivering.'

'I'm not,' chittered Kenn.

'You are so,' said his mother. She skinned the gansey off him.

'I'll do it myself.'

'You'll come and stand in front of the fire. It'll be bad enough if you are reported for poaching without me having you ill on my hands.'

The warmth of the fire in the kitchen was grateful, though he did not feel any discomfort. Cunningly he kept his teeth from clicking. What he had done was still incredible to him, as a memory of some high vision. Yet he knew he had done it. He took his time, and only in his eyes could the shining of the vision be seen. The mother busied herself with the table, the porridge pot, and the kettle.

When he had got his clothes off, she came at him with a towel. But he complained and would not let her rub him. 'I'll do it myself,' he grumbled. She looked at him a moment, and gave him the towel.

'Hurry up, then,' she said.

With a sort of manly reticence, at which she now and then

threw a secret glance, he rubbed himself. Once, gone quite still, she stared out through the window with an odd pensive expression.

Before he was dressed, they heard his father's footsteps come in at the back door; then his voice, 'Are you there, Ellen?'

She went out and closed the door between the kitchen and back porch behind her.

Kenn now strained his ears to hear what they were saying, but his father spoke in a low voice. Kenn knew that times had been bad and that his mother would be left with little money in the house when his father went away, maybe only a few shillings in the purse that was always hidden in the best room. They were in debt to the merchant, and the other day he had overheard Sans himself saying that if he did not get some money in soon, God knew what was going to happen. The words had secretly troubled Kenn very much because, with all the wealth of his shop around him, Sans seemed to Kenn to be in a position of everlasting security. He was not dependent on catching fish like the fishermen, or on the price of calves, like the crofters. He could make decisions as to whether he would give things or not. Kenn had often thought how nice it would be to be Sans, and when a poor person, who had no money at the time, came to get something of which he was in grave need – as Kenn was in need of boots—to hand him a pair, saying, 'Take them. I know you'll pay when you can.'

His mother came in with a fine new pair of boots in her hand. 'See if they'll fit you,' she said, putting them down beside him. She rubbed the feet of a pair of stockings and threw them beside the boots.

He examined the boots carefully. They were wonderful boots. Each had a toecap and a heelcap of iron. Along the outer edges of the sole ran a double row of tackets or studs, but the stud heads were not of the usual round shape, they were squared and thus very distinguished, like those worn by certain gamekeepers and shepherds. No other boy at school had them this shape. Moreover, inside the double row were single rows in a new pattern. It was a fascinating pattern, like what shooting tenants might wear.

He sat down and drew on the stockings, then he tried the left boot first, as grown men did. It certainly was very roomy. He waggled his toes inside it.

'How are they?' asked his mother.

'Fine,' he answered.

His father came in, drying his hands, for he had messed them at the cutting of the salmon. He was quiet now, but underneath the quietness there was eagerness still. He not only asked Kenn how the boots fitted him, but got down on his knees and with strong tender hands felt for Kenn's foot under the leather.

'Are they not too big for you, boy?'

'No,' said Kenn. 'They're just easy.' He tried to shove his big toe forward a bit.

'They're just a little too big, but not much,' said Davy to his wife. 'What do you think?'

Knowing all that had passed in Kenn's mind, she answered, 'They're better to be too big than little, because before he gets another pair he'll have to grow into them. Mind, I'm telling you that!' she warned her son strongly.

'You'll have to go easy with them, boy, and not be kicking stones,' said his father gently. 'Try the other foot.'

Kenn pulled on the right boot. 'It's a tighter fit, this one,' he said.

'I believe it is,' agreed his father. 'Tie them up. Aren't they the great laces, what?'

The laces were made of real leather with wired points. They were greased and soft and supple and left marks in the joints of Kenn's fingers. He could smell the grease off them, as if they had been specially prepared for snow and wintertime.

They were long and had to be wound twice round the tops of the boots before tying.

'Walk up and down and see if they're easy.'

Kenn walked. The boots were awkward and stiff and

clicked on the stone floor like clogs. 'They're fine,' said Kenn in a shy voice.

'Are you sure? Because we can get them changed.'

'No, they're grand.' He walked as if he never felt them on him. 'I'll go for the pail now.'

He closed the middle door behind him and glanced quickly about the back porch. Lifting a cloth, he found that only a small part of his great salmon had been carried back from Sans' shop.

CHAPTER TWO

THE LITTLE HIGHLAND COMMUNITY in which Kenn lived was typical of what might be found anywhere round the northern and western shores of Scotland: the river coming down out of the wooded glen or strath into the little harbour; the sloping croft lands, with their small cultivated fields; the croft houses here and there, with an odd one on a far ridge against the sky; the school, the post office, and the old church, where the houses herded loosely into a township; and inland the moors lifting to blue mountains.

On flat ground by the harbour were the cottages of most of the regular fishermen, but many of the crofters also took part in the fishing seasons, for wealth was unknown amongst them, and poverty had to be outwitted by all the means in their power. Sea-fishing and crofting were the only two occupations of the people, and however the rewards of their labour varied from season to season they were never greatly dissimilar over a whole year or over ten years. Thus in the course of centuries there had developed a communal feeling so genuine that the folk themselves never thought about it. They rejoiced and quarrelled, loved and fought, on a basis of social equality. Even the big farm was absent and so there were no bothies and farm servants, and none of the children that went to school had a father who thought of someone above him as 'the master'. The solitary exception was the laird's farm. It was run by a grieve and had a bothy where two ploughmen from a southern county lived. These ploughmen always referred to the grieve as 'the maister', and this provoked a certain laughing astonishment amongst the children of that place, for the grieve was a cross-grained wizened little man and when he found boys playing about his stackyard or around the steading, he would shout at them in a high-pitched voice. They would vanish as if the devil were after them, and when they had got together again they would mimic him and double up with mirth.

The laird was a being apart, who visited his mansion house only at intervals. He did not belong to them and they never thought about him; for even their rents were collected by a factor who came for the purpose from his lawyer's office in the county town. The people had an instinctive fear of this factor, and always assumed their best dress and manners when they went before him to pay their dues. Sometimes they had not the money to pay and then, after the mother and father had had a long miserable morning together, the father would set out to the hateful meeting. There was nothing in the world, no hardship, no danger, he feared half as much as having to admit that he could not pay his full rent. His legs would feel weak under the burden of shame as he went his way. 'I would rather,' said Davy, 'have the seas breaking in white smoke over me with nowhere to run for.'

Accordingly the laird and his factor were outside the daily run of their lives altogether, and the only real touch with this curious menace or tyranny of the mansion house was found in the gamekeepers.

On this morning that Kenn landed the salmon he was hurrying with other boys of his age towards school, for they had been down to the harbour to see the boats off, and even now, though they were likely to be late, they could not help turning round. Whenever they did this, they immediately began to dispute as to which boat was which, with an assumption of nautical knowledge that in the case of the shore boys at least was not without some real basis, for their eyes were extraordinarily acute and trained in minute distinctions of rig and craft. If a crofter's son put up a denial, he did so for the importance of being assertive and pig-headed or because he liked a fight; though he generally got the worst of such a fight, for the sea bred nimbleness, and swift lashing action.

Kenn had no desire to fight that morning. He was gay and laughed, with a voice as loud as any; but actually he walked or ran with his body wrapping his secret warm inside him. The warmth was a golden mist. The secret sometimes, however, gripped him in a fierce inner twist of happiness, an overpowering spasm of it, and to free himself he would have to shout immoderately, or dash ahead, or kick something with his new boots, or do them all at once.

The other boys noticed the boots, but when they cried sarcastically, 'Look at Kenn with his new boots!', he himself might glance at them and smile as much as to say, 'Oh, them!' but do nothing. Normally he would have retaliated.

Nor was this real acting. For all the boys, in such a crisis as a pair of new boots provided in their lives, acted. The sarcasm was acting. Only with his two or three intimate friends could Kenn solemnly in some quiet place show the boots for examination and discussion. That would happen yet.

Meantime he ran with his companions towards the school and the boots were merely heavy and stiff about his feet but not uncomfortable. As he went, however, his eyes had quick glances of their own for moors and distant hills whence the river came. They were secret glances, almost unconscious; little entranced flicks of vision that caught a loneliness and secrecy and magic, at which in a silent internal way he laughed back. When he gave a short loud laugh, he covered it with a cunning that made him laugh again.

It is difficult to be sure, a long time afterwards, that one actually did experience certain delicate or subtle feelings at a very young age. What established the certainty of this in Kenn's case was the clear memory of a sudden sight of the Well Pool from a turn on the high road to the school. It came upon him with a sensation of familiar strangeness, and he stopped, forgetting his companions, and gazed at it. There was no one there now. The water rushed by. He heard the sound of it in his ears like the sound from a sea shell. The dark spot that was the well was deserted. No living being moved about the banks. The scene was now lonely in a queer desolate way. That he could have hunted there and landed so great a fish so short a while ago seemed unbelievable. Yet he knew he had done it. Inside him was the cry that he had done it. The cry, mixing with the flow and faint roar of the river, so affected him that when his friend Beel shouted in his ear, he jumped.

'What are you seeing?'

His eyes flashed at Beel, then the flash died into a withdrawn glimmer and he ran on, shouting, 'Nothing!'

But the hidden triumph in the glimmer was more to Beel than speech, and so he learned that Kenn had a deep secret.

From the rest of that day two distinct memories stand out. The first was the curious fact that he had no great pride in his boots. They interested him at times; he was aware of them often; but in the oddest fashion he was always detached from them. He would look at them and think 'my new boots', and be not thrilled but mildly amused. He liked this feeling. In the forenoon interval he found considerable pleasure in leaving perfect patterns of all the tackets in a piece of soft clayey soil by the road. Some of the boys catching him doing this scoffed at him, but that merely made him do it slowly and deliberately. He would press his foot down carefully, then withdraw it and gaze at the pattern, his head a little to one side. He did it with such amused interest, with such good nature, that boys began doing it on their own account, and soon it was a game. The square heads and pattern of Kenn's tackets were a deep attraction for all, whether admitted or not. When boys of his own age or less begged him, 'Lift your boots, man, Kenn, and let us have a look,' he would answer broadly, 'Ach, away!' or 'Ach, I cannot be bothered,' and move on. But some of the older boys compelled him to show his soles, and the serious way they then discussed the rows of nails was not unpleasant.

The second memory is concerned with the feeling of detachment from everything that went on inside the school. Even the normal fear—often terror—of the headmaster was subdued to the calmness that comes with convalescence or after a bout of toothache. When the headmaster roared—which he often did—Kenn kept a smooth, cunning mask on.

The roar was inside the school, but the freedom and thrill of life were outside. The master was a roaring lion in a cage. Boys and girls sat there, row by row, in almost sick apprehension lest the lion bite their heads off. Yet Kenn knew that this roaring had no real meaning. It was dangerous, just as a lion suddenly in one's path would be dangerous. But if the lion can be hoodwinked in whatever fashion, how amusing the relief afterwards! For the lion has no bearing on human joy—except in the escape from the brute.

Nor had any of the things the master taught any joy in them. History and geography were both taken that day. The history was concerned with English kings and queens and the dates of battles. There had been the Plantagenets. Now there were the Tudors. That Henry VIII had six wives did not really interest the children. They would have gaped in the same way if he had had six hundred. What was important was the exact number six. A near shot, such as seven or eight, would have made the lion roar.

The geography was an even worse ordeal because, as it happened, they were dealing with that portion of the British Isles that contains great numbers of towns, each with its 'most important industry'. Some of the towns, like Birmingham or Nottingham, had several industries. Kenn's memory was his weakest part and he was capable of transposing small arms and lace with an air of innocent calm.

He got thrashed twice.

His first offence was a state of abstraction that produced a stare, a long, round-eyed stare, lips parted and breathing suspended. The master, having set a task, was walking the floor, with his long, heavy stride, up and down, up and down, the wall behind him, and the rows of desks and heads hemming him in in front. His quick eye caught Kenn's stare and he was just about to shout when over the stare went a faint smile. It was hardly so much a smile as a glimmer that shone in the eyes and brought a warmth to the delicate features; there was secrecy in it and memory and remoteness; yet it was near as a heart-beat and so potent that Kenn's chest slowly filled with a long quivering breath.

The master was a man who must have measured six feet three inches and weighed seventeen stones; he was straight and agile and unthinkably strong; brown haired, with a full, smooth, blood-flushed face, and pale-blue eyes that occasionally had threads in them, though he neither drank nor smoked. He was probably under fifty years of age.

Now as he watched the smile dawn on Kenn's face, the fleshy stentorian abruptness of his expression held, then wavered, and finally passed into a small answering smile, not of reverie or gentleness, but of acute humour. A pucker came upon his face; his eyes glinted. He stopped right before Kenn and in a private voice asked, 'What's the smile for?'

Kenn gave a convulsive start, his eyes shooting to the master's face; then, confused, he drooped over his book.

'Eh? What was it?' The voice was quiet and friendly.

But like some adventuring whelk touched on the raw, Kenn wanted to withdraw out of sight. The only thing he could hide behind, however, was his face, so it produced its dour and hostile shell.

'What was it?' The voice was firmer, but still searching for human contact.

'Nothing,' muttered Kenn.

There was a moment of silence in which the whole room could be heard listening.

'Nothing *what*?' suggested the master.

'Nothing, sir.'

'So you were smiling at nothing?'

Kenn did not answer.

The master's expression hardened. The glint in his eyes became concentrated and hostile. 'So you were smiling at nothing?' His voice had risen. There was a pause, then an explosive roar in which the moment of possible communion was shattered to fragments. 'I'll make you smile at something! Come out here.'

Kenn went out.

Swiftly, with thunderous steps, the master had plunged to his desk and returned with the three-fingered leather strap. 'Hold it out!'

Kenn held his arm the full length and took the regulation three on his palm. They stung with blinding fierceness for the master put all his strength into the strokes. Kenn's eyelids quivered, but he made no sound.

'That may teach you to smile at nothing!' The man's face had become congested. His jacket had got hunched up over his shoulders; he jerked it down as he lurched back to his desk and threw the strap on it.

It was an odd gesture this, of throwing the strap on the desk, as if he now had an unconscious spite against it, or against the moment, or against the boy, or against fate.

Kenn went back to his seat, every feeling withdrawn, and bent over his book.

Anger against the master for a thrashing was no doubt bitter and keen at the time, but it is not consciousness of this anger that remains in Kenn's mind, it is the master's smile.

How time has achieved this trick might be difficult to explain, only Kenn does not consider it a trick at all. He now believes that the *revealing* incident or expression is rarely grasped in moments of stress. Anyway, he can summon up the master's face only in the light of that smile: the living face, fleshy and imminent, with the skin crinkling round the blue eyes as they search out, with understanding, Kenn's hidden happiness.

The second time Kenn got thrashed was for transposing the products of Birmingham and Leicester. 'I'll give you Leicester!' said the master. This time Kenn whimpered, for his palm was swollen and tender, and, moreover, he knew that the master was now being vindictive. The whimper had an angry rebellious edge to it, which the master recognised as protest. This infuriated him. So he made Kenn hold out his other hand, and though he should now have given him only two, he actually put extra pith into a third.

Kenn was broken, but the protest in his weeping voice sustained him in some degree and helped him very quickly to a dour silence. He crept now completely within his shell, and for a little time all the glory of the morning was lost.

But presently, when the master was taking another class, his spirit crept out again, its tender feelers searching the desk beside him, the room, and, lifting a little, the windows. Beyond the windows space rushed away to a blue sky with moving white clouds. His eyes on his book again, Kenn continued to feel this space, this wide freedom, down in the hollows of which wound the river. Listening acutely, he could hear the far cry of the brown water.

The thrashings freed him from this school life and any obligation to the master; made him whole and secret and hostile.

Outside this narrow prison with its captains and kings and their wives and small arms, was the free rushing world of light and earth and water, of which the master knew nothing but of which Kenn knew so much that he could stand up at that moment and tell him something that would astonish him! But he was careful not to smile to himself now. 'Leicester is famous for boots,' he said, over and over. 'Birmingham for small arms.' But Birmingham was also famous for bicycles, hardware, rubber goods, edged tools, and other things including steam engines and buttons. And Leicester had hosiery, and machinery too. It was impossible to get a clear vision of Birmingham and Leicester. And unless Kenn saw a thing he could never with certainty remember it. This was all very trying. Particularly when his mind, like a curlew crying far in on the moor, told him the only thing worth remembering in the world, so important that it turned Birmingham, Leicester, and Henry VIII with his wives' heads to dust, was that the Well Pool was famous for its salmon.

But the master did not tell them of salmon and of pools, of moors and the source of a river, of spawning and the mysterious journeyings of fish in river and sea, of all that passed before their eyes and enthralled them, so that they hunted without food and remembered and dreamed, and built up the stores of vision and happiness on which for ever after they openly or secretly fed.

Nothing of the salmon coming in from the sea, from the

deeps of the sea, the grounds that sloped down, down, down into the black, uttermost abyss.

Yet it was a marvellous conjunction in time that brought Kenn barefoot from his home and the salmon from the Atlantic abyss, to meet by the kneeling stone of a Highland well on that autumn morning. To Kenn it was not luck that had happened to him. All of them talked of being lucky. This was the speechless thing from the realm beyond luck. The wonder of it came upon one with the delight that has fear in it; fear first, like Kenn's fear when the salmon sailed away from the well. Fear of the thing itself and fear of its loss. The awful moment of being caught away into utter loneliness, while the inimical, watchful shapes of nature contrive to present one—with a silver gift!

No wonder Kenn was inclined to fall into a state of abstraction, where story and meaning ran into a silver glimmer, or dropped out of sight altogether, dropped, perhaps, upon some 'continental ledge' of the mind, whence, through aeons back beyond reckoning, it had emerged upon the beaches, the rivers, and finally upon the dry land.

It was a long journey even to the salmon from where the continental shelf gives way to the steep slopes that go down to perpetual night. And a difficult journey, particularly in the early stages of having to make up a reluctant mind. After all, Kenn's salmon had been a bachelor, and had got used to his home comforts. And down on the dark slopes there had been many comforts, including a complete lack of hard work and no silly distractions of any kind. Indeed for the most part all he had to do was to doze on his coral couch and get off occasionally to nose about among the red shrimps and consume them as he felt like it.

It was a sultan's life, made all the more secure and serene in its complete detachment from the offices and excitements of the harem. The salmon is an individualist, and not until he has penetrated straths and moors and mountains, to the remote gravelly beds of a newly born river, does he show a personal interest in his kind. True, his interest then is fast and furious, an expenditure of years of wealth, reckless to the point of death, but such gallantry is somehow what one would expect to find in the nature of this fish.

Down in the deeps, however, it took Kenn's salmon a long time, more than half Kenn's age, to get the call of the river so strongly that he could no longer resist it. Just after he had been a year on the slopes, a little higher up, he had first felt the call of the fresh water. He was then a grilse, but that particular summer season the land weather had been good and the amount of water coming into the sea not great enough to be exciting. Many grilse from round about had set off, but if he noticed their going or their absence, it must have been with a slow shrug of fin and tail as he turned away and went deeper to a new bed. Even the light that had been filtering through from the sea's surface had been too gay, too distracting, and only when the green faded into a luminous blue—the deep blue of a night sky when the moon is felt but unseen—did he regain the even peace and pulse of his ways.

No sea plants grew in these depths; no storm disturbed the perpetual night that shaded from blue to black as the invisible sun arched the sky and sank. Even the sponges and crinoids and branching coral were like bushes that, long ago, had been petrified by enchantment. In their brittle delicacy the enchantment still lingered. The red shrimps which he loved were about him like manna. With their redness he stained his flesh. Yet more than eating, he loved resting. An epicure, a glutton, a sluggard—yet developing a perfect figure, a skin more silver than the moon's, and flesh the hue of a sunset. His growth was the only active thing about him. He had entered the sea as a smolt of a few ounces; and within fifteen months was a grilse of seven pounds. Every year after that he had added four to five pounds to his weight and extra grace and strength to his body.

When the spring floods reached him on his second sea-birthday, he could not be bothered responding. Excitement was a delusion; the urge of sex a snare. Why trouble? He turned his nose away and with a slower shrug of tail and fin sank a little deeper into the abyss. Here he added his pounds in an even greater quietude. Nor could he be bothered sinking deeper when once again with the wheel of the year, the water spoke of distant river floods and mountain spawning beds. Younger fish might rush off to what they considered the adventure of life and love. But the young are notoriously foolish. He found a couch under arching branches paler in hue than a mammoth tusk.

Not until he had passed his twenty-first pound did some climacteric disturb his way of life. He felt it as a shortness in breath and a vague but disturbing restlessness in the flesh. He stood it for a time, but at last it set him moving aimlessly. What if he went deeper still? He almost nosed into the body of a salmon that was sixty, perhaps eighty, pounds. The looming mass of flesh gave him a slight shock, and he turned away and upward.

Perhaps there were salmon one hundred, two hundred, three hundred pounds down where not even the blueness came? They had got over their restlessness and would never more return to the streams where new salmon are conceived. Not only their desire had faded, but their potency. They were in the abyss for ever.

The restlessness increased in him. The water had not enough air to breathe. There was a congestion, a lethargy, in his flesh that for once found no ease in rest.

He might have overcome this malaise and attained complete bachelorhood, the last fever of living gone, if it had not so happened that on dry land there had been great floods.

Through the hollows and valleys of the sea the fresh water penetrated, thinning out as it went, but ever being pressed and increased from behind, until at last its influence touched the gills of the restless fish and they found refreshment therein; and with refreshment, the sting of excitement.

The salmon kept his nose to this new influence, and became as it were polarised by it, and slowly went to meet it. No thought or instinct was needed for this, pleasure only . . . .

And here the grown-up Kenn pauses because it was this very

point of what the salmon may feel at such a moment that first launched him on this search into lost times. Experience has taught him that man thinks he moves to memory or high endeavour or fervent hope when all he moves to is delight. A pleasant sentiment may like to conceive of the salmon as being disturbed by awakened memories of the tumbling waters of his youth, by an exquisite nostalgia, but the naturalist answers that this is nonsense, for the salmon, with his tiny brain, can have no memories, no knowledge, of the road that yet will take him back to the very spot where he himself was spawned. Nor is the naturalist concerned with pricking sentimental bubbles. On the contrary, he finds in the forces of nature that contrive to send the salmon on his journey an ordering of the universe so intricate, so unchanging, so perfect in balance, that its marvel is beyond the comprehension of the austerest poet. That a mere need for extra oxygen should set the salmon's reflexes and fins in motion to an ultimate creative end is a far more astonishing fact than any mere operation of nostalgic memory.

Possibly. Yet Kenn cannot see perfect certainty even here; not the whole truth. The amount of human grey matter that is actively disturbed in weighing stars or in contemplating the processions of universes is very slight. And if a salmon is entirely a creature of reflexes then the way in which every one of them differs in response to the pull of a fly hook is something beyond his comprehension. He has known an eighteen-pounder sulk for forty-five minutes, and a fish of about the same weight break his heart in reel-screaming violence within ten. Yet both were clean run and perfectly hooked. As reflex actions their responses had an uncanny resemblance to human moods.

But in his own case, Kenn is not concerned with scientist or humanist. What he wants to catch inside himself is something very elusive, because it is so imponderable, so without meaning or aim. Yet it achieves a startling reality when caught and held—as it must be and always is—suddenly.

It is a moment of sheer unconditional delight that may not

be described or explained, and that nothing can ever explain away. Delight is here not so much too strong as too uniform a word. For the moment may be troubling in the old panic sense; it may be ecstatic; or it may, by a lure of memory, evasive as a forgotten scent, draw one towards it as towards a source.

The third way is the more readily experienced and understood. Thought of it involuntarily recalls the time Beel and Art and himself, sweating and tired from a rabbit hunt on a broken hillside, were suddenly snared by a honey scent. With no heather in bloom, the scent was inexplicable. In the fitful June air, they got it, they lost it. They wriggled up earthy funnels, over ledges, grasping heather tufts, and occasionally setting a boulder bounding down. The scent was warmed by the sun; had in it a rare entanglement. It smelt brown, the dark brown of the honey of wild bees, the honey that is stored in the tiny round cups, the pale tomthumbs, of the wild bees' hive.

They came to the base of an overhanging rock with a slanting passageway to either hand, as salmon might come to a pool where two rivers meet. Which way now? They had no memory of ever having chosen before. Yet they hardly hesitated, all three going to the left. And if one had gone to the right, he would very soon have sniffed and returned, just as an old salmon has been known to go a short distance up one stream, then inexplicably to return and follow the other that, unknown to him, had been chosen of his brethren for thousands of years.

On a smooth slope where the heath had given way to grass, small white flowers of the heath bedstraw grew in profusion. The boys trod the flowers. Beel grabbed a handful of the flowers and sniffed. 'Ow, this is it!' he cried. 'This is all it is!' He laughed, crushed the blossoms, and threw them from him. The other two tore up handfuls, and sniffed, and laughed too. 'Well, I'm blowed!' They got down on hands and knees and sniffed like dogs. Kenn let his hot face crush against the cooling flowers. 'Boys, isn't it a great scent for such a wee flower?' he said. It was that. But still they were cheated. The small flowers had fooled them. In their astonishment and chagrin, they pulled up handfuls of the blossom and threw them at one another and laughed. They were full of unaccountable merriment.

The impulse that moved in Kenn's salmon as it met the fresh water was equally unaccountable. Its long journey was through a slowly changing blue and not until it came within a depth of six hundred feet did the first tinge of green appear. This represented the coming of light, and light, equally with fresh water, plays its mysterious part in the life of the salmon, whose pilgrimage is ever between light and darkness. At one hundred feet, orange and red, the warm colours, are still absent, but the blue is now irradiated with green, and the eyes that have for so many years known only degrees of shadow, reflect at last a colour like the sky at evening when seen over the ridges of far hills where rivers rise. The salmon is swimming back to the source of its life.

Dark-brown seaweeds appear and soon they stir in languid movement. Many kinds of fish inhabit this world and over-head the water is invaded by swift hunting shapes of bird and animal. Life here is restless and abundant and knows sudden flurries of deathly excitement. But the most exciting thing of all to the salmon is the water itself. For it has been oxygenated into a sparkling wine, a wine that has to be searched out, to be swum into, in a heady, craving sobriety.

The craving goes deep into the flesh, into organs that all its life have lain dormant and undeveloped, and these organs respond and slowly increase, in an awakening to love and generation. An evening tide flows into the river mouth. In the darkness the harbour sways in a brimming fullness. There is quietude along the wall and lights in the seamen's cottages. Unhurriedly, like a wraith in a story, the salmon passes up the harbour and meets at last the fresh water from the distant spawning beds. There as it takes the shallows in the throat of the harbour pool it flashes faint silver against the rising spring-tide moon.

A strange new world, this. The peace, the dark timeless-ness of the sea-deeps, has changed to motion, to rushing sound, to a shallowness that is aerated and intoxicating. From the weight of the Atlantic the body has emerged naked, but with the urge of love as yet no more conscious than the dancing of the stars in the singing swirling waters overhead. Cool and uncoloured, with points of starry fire. And with points of fear, as when the back fin leaves the water altogether or when the shallows grow too shallow and the boulders too weirdly shaped. Slipping around and on, entering the pool with a shake from the shoulders, sailing with cautious exploratory speed where the water deepens, quivering a poised moment before taking the miniature cataract, then taking it not with headlong speed but calmly— ever ready to flash, and leap.

Had there been a huge volume of water, the salmon in an orgy of speed might have travelled miles. But in this tail-end of the great spate, with endless variety of deeps and gravels and boulders, he finds something disturbingly of the end of his journey in its beginnings. After half a mile of it, he swims from the main current into a moving calm, with the caress of gravel underneath and, head upstream, settles to rest.

In this moon-glimmering world, the great stars slowly wheel and wane, and stealing upon the braes and the river-flats comes the grey of the morning. This is a new complication added to the troubling birth of sex and to the lure of the fresh water.

He settles to a deeper rest, but uneasy now, as if the magnetism of the distant hills was growing intermittent and his polarised body was losing its perfect assurance. Things can be seen not vaguely but with a near clearness. The grey gathers still more light. Nothing, however, moves; nothing but the water . . . .

Then something moves, quite close to the river's edge . . . an upright body from that outer world carrying a bright tin pail. The pail fell with a resounding clatter. . . .

But far more startled was Kenn himself when the master's leather strap, rolled into a ball and thrown from mid-floor, landed with a resounding whack on the desk under his nose and leapt against his chest. So deep had been his daydream that he was never able afterwards to tell what he had been thinking about. Young as he was, time had slipped from him and he had got lost.

The leap of his heart actually hurt him, like a blow, and for a moment its beating was painful.

'Bring it out!' shouted the master.

Carrying the strap—most bitter ignominy—Kenn reached the floor and stood before the master. There was quick colour in his cheeks and a stormy brightness in his eyes; his expression was now not only dour but desperate to the point of tears.

The master looked at him and saw the troubling of the spirit. He kept looking. He saw the sensitive lips closing against the surge of emotion. He had only to keep looking and the boy would break down. He wanted to make him break down, not out of any vague sadism but out of a positive desire to get his own back upon the young demons that so often tortured him. Quite suddenly, however, in tones drained to coolness, he said, 'Get back to your seat.' Kenn went. And over the school passed an odd silence.

CHAPTER THREE

FROM THAT DAY the river became the river of life for Kenn. He never approached it but with some quickening of breath or eye. When his years had doubled and he was a soldier in France, he could more readily picture the parts of it he knew than the trench systems he floundered amongst. In zero moments it could rise before him with the clearness of a chart showing the main current of his nervous system and its principal tributaries.

Not that there was any suggestion of undue obsession by it. Quite the contrary. Yet, in one vivid moment, it could produce that brightening of the eye that is more than the smile that follows, intimate and yet aloof, like something half remembered and with the quality of loneliness about it that is perhaps more native to man's essential nature than any other quality, and that visits him finally with a strange new dignity before death.

For Kenn, then, the river was primarily not a concern of the folk who lived near its banks. Its communal importance had little interest for him. In all his outings, by himself or with his companions, the river was an adventure often intense and always secretive. They not only went to cover when they saw the head- or under-gamekeeper, but when they saw crofters or estate-workers. If anyone had offered to tell Kenn about the lives of the folk who lived within its drainage, he would have prepared himself to be polite and listen, but all the while behind the veil of the talk his mind would be quick and sensitive as a trout, or would run past green leaves, full of escape and primordial glee. And this, of course, not clearly or consciously, with, as it were, the visible flash of a salmon leap, but, rather, unlooked at, with the aftermath of the dark swirl and the circles coming lipping up excitingly to the mind he kept hidden.

At such a moment the innocence of the dark eyes, stilled to wonder in the smooth listening face, was a deception so elusive that somewhere within it lay the last truth about life.

Yet how healthy the truth, how remote from sad introversions, for when it did come glimmering up from the deeps to the surface of the eyes and broke, the ripple that spread over the face in a smile warmed the very texture of the skin and made it shy and lovable.

Something of this must have been felt by the nurse who answered his question when he came blinded from the war.

This blinding by gas followed at a considerable interval an incident on the Somme that still makes him smile because, in its cool river cunning, it shows so clearly the effect of his early environment.

There is nothing slovenly in the action of a salmon. By the time Kenn was seventeen, he had almost an instinct for precision. The love of it ran in his blood and guided his hand and strove for clarity in his brain. An unclear brain was far more irksome than a dirty body. Native merit in mathematics and science, guided by his mother's will, sent him in his seventeenth year as a student to Glasgow University. But he was tall and quick on his feet; and though for a time he withstood the recruiting sergeants and the general attitude to one who looked older than he was, yet in the end his sensitiveness could not withstand it, so he said he was eighteen and joined up. He realised how much his mother would be hurt over this, for neither he nor his mother had any idealisms about war. He knew how she would sit in her chair and look into the fire, and he damned the compulsive world in his own mind, and in his own mind turned to her, saying, 'Never mind, Mother.' He could not help this thing. He would go. But she could rest assured he would look after himself. The artillery would probably be the safest place, and in any case, what with his knowledge of trigonometry and physics, it would be a place where his mind might be exercised. Because it would thus have been the most useful place for one with his special knowledge, he expected to find, things being as they were, that it was the one place he would not get into. But actually, being a volunteer, he found no difficulty in joining up as a gunner, and on active service very soon became of great value to his commanding officer. In fact the CO trusted him with slide rule and tables before any officer in his siege battery. As a trained observer and gunlayer he got extra pay, and when it came to a piece of quick important shooting he could be relied on to earn it.

The blowing of gaps in the advancing Germans on that early morning towards the end of 1917 on the Somme was coarse unskilled work, though its sheer devastating efficacy had its fascination, because—apart from the joyous potting of church steeples and such—even observers saw little of the actual results of the gun-teams' labours. On this particular morning, however, precision in its trigonometrical sense was almost entirely confined to the exquisite narrowness of the shaves by which death passed them by or the instant and annihilating manner in which it got them. Escape was a matter of pure chance.

No SOS signals had heralded the German attack. It was a complete surprise and Kenn had leapt out of the trench behind his gun without tunic, hat, or puttees, to see the Germans coming over the crest in front of him exactly as he had once seen winter hares coming in a drive over a ridge at home. He went into action with fear in his throat, the old panic fear he had felt as a lad when the salmon had moved from the well, but thickened with the consciousness of death. It ran through his stomach and into his joints and pitched his voice high. For a little time even his sight seemed uncertain. Actually his physical faculties were too highly co-ordinated, were working with too feverish an activity. But recognition of this did not come upon him until the fear began to fade in the activity; and it faded so completely away that in the clarity that followed there uprose the old note of exultation by the well.

His most dramatic escape was concerned with the rhythm

of mechanical timing. Being short-handed and having many things to look to, he had placed his clinometer between rounds in a small wooden tube-box on the ground. Swiftly he had stooped behind his friend Ned, who was number four on the gun, and come erect again. Ned's body was still standing but his head was gone and up from the neck blood spouted in streams. It fell drenchingly on Kenn. He blinked it out of his eyes and finished his task without a break in the firing rhythm.

It was a perfect piece of timing and it stirred his mathematical bent to abnormal acuteness. He felt the instinct in him to serve every gun, to be at every breech, flashing shell upon shell, ploughing up lane beside lane, until the oncoming grey horde had been blown to smithereens, blown to fragments off the earth.

It was the men of his own battery, however, who were getting blown to bits. Forward a short distance and to the left was a battery of sixty-pounders. The co of this battery could be seen standing on a step in the trench behind, his revolver in his hand, presumably prepared to make certain that there would be no retreat. But Kenn's co was a sufficiently old-fashioned officer to believe that there are times when it is the better part of valour to live to fight another day. He gave the order to put the guns out of action and every man for himself. Kenn was now so determined that the enemy should not use his gun that, after removing part of the breech, he stuck it into a sandbag and then threw the lot into the muddy water of a shell-hole. When he looked up, he found himself alone.

For one moment, in the dawn wind, he faced the oncoming horde, hair and face smeared with blood, shirt wet with blood, and driblets of blood on his boots. In his raked challenging features, his nostrils quivered. The horde was already flowing round the sixty-pounders; he saw the gleam of bayonets. 'Christ!' he cried bitterly, and ground his nails in his palms. He turned and began trotting away. In an instant his human nature came clutching at him, and the trot broke into a mad run.

He was escaping now, running like a hare. They would never catch him, unless behind with a direct hit! His woodland cunning, his solitariness, took command, the inner native self that could never be deceived by the idealisms of war. When an officer brandished a revolver at him and shouted, 'Who are you? Where are you going?' Kenn immediately stopped, saluted, and explained.

'Get over there and help these men carry up their ammunition.'

'Very good, sir.'

He went towards the men, a machine-gun crowd, sauntering like one lost, until he saw he was no longer observed by the officer, whereupon he deflected his course, passed by the crowd, and took to his heels again. But not precipitately now. Very warily indeed. Prepared for any emergency and knowing intimately the lie of the country from his map-readings as an observer. When a second revolver stopped him, his discipline was perfect. He told the officer what had happened. Again he was sent to assist men carrying up ammunition. Again he evaded the task when screened from the officer. He had no feelings of responsibility towards the men. They were machine-gunners. He was number one of a gun team that had done its job and he intended carrying out his CO's order of each man for himself in its literal sense. The thought became charged with a satiric humour. They would have to be pretty smart to stop his escaping now! His eyes, gleaming in this wary humour, were everywhere, and he avoided again being challenged until he was fully five miles behind the front line. Then an officer in charge of a mobile anti-aircraft battery, an elderly, decent man, stopped him, stared at his bloodied figure, and asked for news. Kenn told him how the Germans were coming in the open five miles back. The officer began issuing orders to get ready for retiring.

Kenn waited beside him, and when the officer looked at him again, he saluted and said, 'Excuse me, sir, but could I get some food?'

'Over there.' The officer pointed to his canteen.

Kenn went over and the man in charge gave him all he wanted. He stuffed his mouth and helped the chew with raw whisky. A decent fellow, this batman or whatever he was. Kenn mumbled his news. Told of the order for retiral. 'Look here, I'm in a hell of a mess,' said Kenn; 'all this blood. Have you a coat or anything?' And went on eating. The fellow brought him an officer's overcoat. Kenn tried it on. 'Great!' he muttered, tearing the stars from the coat. This was the best show of luxury he had seen for a long time. Eating still, he found water and wiped his face. It was a real fairy tale, this luck. 'Look here,' he said at last, his jaws aching, 'you've been damn decent to me, but where I'll pick up my own crowd again, God knows. Could you give me a bit of loaf and a drop of Scotch?' The fellow at once gave him a whole loaf and an unopened bottle of Black and White. Kenn rammed them into the pockets of the greatcoat, thanked him heartily, and pursued his way.

It was a great war! No nonsense about it. He could feel the bottle in his pocket and the loaf. No hallucination.

He was getting tired of walking. Why not a lift? He stopped a field artillery man in an empty waggon and asked him where he was going. The fellow said in a Glasgow accent that God alone knew, but he wanted to go to Albert. Kenn said he thought he knew the way. 'Jump up,' said the Glasgow man. Kenn got aboard carefully. 'Would you like a drink?' he asked. The driver looked at him, at the rim of blood round his eye sockets. 'Would I hell,' he replied guardedly. 'But perhaps you don't like whisky,' said Kenn producing the bottle of Black and White. The driver stared at the bottle, then at the loaf, then at Kenn. 'Jesus Christ,' he said. Kenn unscrewed the cap and handed him the bottle: 'A little of it won't really do you any harm.' The driver handled the bottle, looked at the label, then gingerly plugged the contents with his tongue. His eyes rolled and he tilted his head back. It was the first whisky he had tasted since he had come to France. Affection moved him to unwritten oaths. 'We're in no hurry,' said Kenn, tearing the loaf. 'That's the way to Rothesay.' When they struck a main road, Kenn knew it and they headed with certainty for Albert. The first officer he saw in Albert was his own CO, who expressed the greatest pleasure in the meeting. He was fond of Kenn because Kenn not only knew his job but also knew the human art of giving the CO his place in a world of necessary discipline. Kenn had to relate his odyssey. The CO listened to the attempted theft of his best man by two other officers and applauded Kenn's cunning in laughter. It was a pleasant meeting and they set about the re-forming of their battery with the greatest heart.

Only five of the original hundred-odd men were on the battery when some four months later it was assailed by an unexpected attack, this time by gas shells. All at once the quiet little deserted town, into whose wine cellars they had happily dug themselves, became a vomiting, suffocating death trap. The telephone wires ran through sewers to the BC post. In removing the mouthpiece of his gas mask to speak, Kenn had to take a risk with the gas. The discomfort began to express itself in his vision. His sight became blurred and painful. He realised he was going blind and presently had to tell his BC accordingly. He was instructed to report in person at once. But by this time he could see little but a flaming red against the bright gun-flashes, and a gunner had to take him by the arm. His lungs were on fire as if someone had thrown the contents of a pepper pot into them. He began to vomit into his gas mask. Gas shells were exploding all about them as they dodged along. Kenn's right thigh got a kick that paralysed the whole leg. A gas shell had burst almost between his feet. He leant against the wall and tried to keep himself upright. The gunner could do nothing with him now. Kenn pushed the gunner from him, telling him with a gesture to clear out. The gunner realised that extra help was necessary and turned back to the gun. Left alone, Kenn retired within himself, hanging on warily to the knot of his will, inducing the mood of endurance of the sick brute, letting the vomit lie until it belched of itself. The revolving fires of pain were wheels behind which he hid. A long time passed. He realised that something must have happened to the gunner or to the battery. Feeling was coming slowly back into his numb leg, enough to assure him that nothing fatal had happened to it. So much to the good. He would hang on. They might find him yet. He tried his leg. He must keep upright.

The earth began to rumble and a twinge of excitement went shooting through his brain. Field-gun teams! They were clearing out! He had better make a move. He staggered out from the wall, hands up, and staggered back from grinding waggon wheels. Again he sallied and again was repulsed. Damn them, surely there was one decent soul amongst them! The flame of red went from his eyes into his brain. His lungs were a fiery, bloody mist. They couldn't pass him by, they daren't! Damn them, this was rotten! He began going with the sound, staggering drunkenly. A clashing and a clanking and a rearing of horses. He went for it. A hand gripped his collar. He scrambled up and was thrown face down on an elevated narrow structure like a coffin. He knew what it was. For a long time he held on and endured. At the first touch of hands he let go and his eyes and lungs dissolved into darkness and silence.

'Where am I?' he whispered to the nurse.

She stooped to his ear: 'In Leicester.'

There was a pause during which she looked at the face, the bandaged eyes, the bone of the jaw, the sensitive nostrils, and the clear cut mouth.

'Leicester is famous for boots.'

But there was no real articulation in the mutter. Only there was the faintest darkening of the skin like a shy, lovable smile, and a perceptible movement of the lips towards a derisive tilt at one corner.

He had been deaf for a long time, but now listening acutely, he could hear the rumble of the hospital noises like the far cry of brown water in the hollow of a strath.

The young nurse was plainly delighted at this evidence of recovery. She knew now that in time he would also regain his sight (as he did). He was her 'special case'. She had liked his face at the first glance; had secretly been touched to the quick of pity in a way that had disconcerted her Irish eyes. For though she was no more than a 'war nurse', her high-bred spirit had insisted on a perfect professionalism. Yet she could afford to be delighted now, and when she saw the lips move again, she stooped so close that the whorl of her ear touched them.

'Like a sea shell,' was what she thought they said.

A warmth ran from her eyes into her face. She put the spout of the china kettle into his mouth and the sheet up over his face.

CHAPTER FOUR

GOING FROM THE MOUTH to the source may well seem
to be reversing the natural order, to be going from the death
of the sea, where individuality is lost, back to the source of
the stream, where individuality is born. Yet that is the way
Kenn learned his river and, when he came to think of it,
that is the way he learned life.

He started amongst people, without any real consciousness of himself at all except as a small being that had to
be gratified and protected. When left alone, he cried in
fear. Should he suddenly find the house empty, with no
one answering his cry, a curious panic would seize him, and
the stillness of furniture and the edges of doors would gather
an ominous waiting power. It was not what *they* would do
to him, it was that they knew how *something else*, coming
invisible and silent, would. . . . But he always cried out lest
the thing form even in his own mind. He tiptoed the first few
steps with breath held, then broke out of the front door with
a rush. This happened to him for the most part at twilight.

The beginnings of life, then, had little to do with a lonely
individuality struggling to self-knowledge in the wastes.
Indeed he constantly strove to be, and was, carried on the
great human currents of life. And nowhere in his early years
did he find such happiness and protection as where the great
currents found the sea.

All the life of that little Highland world met where the
river met the sea. When the harbour swung to high tide and
the boats came in with their shots of herring, human activity
brimmed over as the herrings over the cran basket when the
two men on the halyard rope, faces to the sky, pulled fist
over fist, in heaving rhythm. Limber men, blue-jerseyed,

with lean belly muscles and slender hips, quick-footed as dancers. And great dancers they were. They could dance in the leather seaboots that came to their thighs, or sway drunken in a public house on rooted feet.

They were all large strong splendid men to Kenn at the age of six years, the younger of them easy-going and merry or quick as a blow, the older men with the beards full of friendly dignity, with power in their hands and looks and in their easy commands.

It was a world of action, of doing. It had the warmth of colour in faces and of flashing eyes. One could rush to it with excitement.

And many a sunny morning Kenn did rush to it, books and school forgotten in the long summer holidays. Other boys met him there, and in the wooden gutting stations they played the rushing corner game on bare feet, while waiting for the boats to come in. At such moments (if there was no new cut for brine to touch) the beatitude of living reached its loveliest peaks. Nor can this be altogether an illusion of the after years, for even then rare things did happen that stabbed and discoloured the mind, and had they happened other than rarely would have left the curious repulsive horror that can so corrosively haunt the memory of a place once unclean.

Even the suggestion of this uncleanness comes to Kenn as a delicate treachery, as a deceitful concession to a fashion of mental analysis. He knows quite otherwise, with the precision of the hidden mind that had to listen to so much that was well-meaning or instructive in the past. The only really unclean things then were unclean words. If a seaman came out with an ugly oath, particularly in the hearing of the women gutters, minds were touched on the quick. Not only the ugliness, but the shame, brought a stinging warmth; and in the man's own immediate reaction was a gawkiness, a half-grinning defiance, that made him smell of the stuff that was shovelled back into the sea with the dog fish.

Quite otherwise was the explosive oath of the fighter. At night, by the public house, terror could run on awful feet and the heavens grow darker with the wrath that at any instant might stoop and strike. Often, however, echoes of such a fight carried over into the daylight a saga quality, and boys might repeat the words of a God-challenging oath with a defiance that, when it could no longer be borne, broke into exaggerated action and shrill laughter.

The wheels of light swung over the harbour bar and out to sea to meet the boats coming in. They would dazzle the eyes and fly away, elusive as the heels of boys on a swing. Sometimes they went bounding like iron girds out of control. It was fun to watch them, to shout with them and run. For the boats were coming in, this boat and that boat, and a word was flung and caught, a word of speculation as to the depth in the water of each boat and the size of her shot. Rivalry and jealous hope amongst the young, not for the material gain of the highest shot but for its distinction, its craft of seamanship.

And the incoming seamen themselves were always quiet, the young men smiling, perhaps, or throwing a wink as they stood in easy attitudes on deck. No one ever called blatantly, 'What have you got?' But when the stern rope was fast, an old man on the quay would say, 'A few scales about you today, Henry.' 'Ay, a few; about twenty crans.' 'Good, though! That was you shot off the Head?' 'Yes.' 'We thought they were your lights. Some strangers amongst you?' 'Ay, some boats from the east side. The news that the herring are working is apparently going the rounds. You'll be seeing a few lights there tonight.' The skipper smiled. For the sea was the common hunting ground of all fishermen.

Meantime the boys had become darting news messengers. The women put on their oilskins and handled their baskets. The curers' men got busy with barrels and salt. The harbour came alive to a fierce activity.

Life was good for everyone on such a morning. Kenn's father would stop, smiling astonishment at the small figure. 'Bless me, boy, are you here?' Whereupon Kenn would shyly run away, happy. The women worked with such extraordinary speed that he could hardly see the knife going into the gut or the herring into its appropriate basket. The women worked ceaselessly, stooping, their heads hooded with shawls, while the men stalked about carrying baskets from the holds and emptying them into the stations, shouting tallies, or shaking nets. The difference between the men and the women was marked. Kenn was a little shy of the women and at home with the striding men.

Not every morning was a successful morning, and the summer herring season lasted barely two months. Often there would be blank weeks, with no more than the odd basket to share out. Earlier in the year there had been the west coast herring season. Round about January would appear the erratic local winter herring. But for the most part winter and spring were spent in the laborious and bitter-cold toil of white fishing.

But always the toil was the toil of men. This was what lingered in Kenn's mind and gave to the men he had known a dignity and breadth which he rarely found elsewhere in after years. In fact it shocks him still to find a man with grey hair a clerk, however well paid and 'responsible', and whether in Parliament or the Cowgate. All black-coated business, all industrial routine, everything that ties man down to safe automatic work, takes from his dignity, his decision by will (not by intellect), drains him of some element of native splendour that is as real to Kenn as his memory of the colour in the seamen's cheeks. Accordingly he sees all the more clearly the need and the reason for the work of co-ordination and administration for which an office stands, and possibly for the mass production which is so comforting a result of intense specialisation. But that does not alter what is to him a fundamental response. And even if the splendour he attributes were only and altogether in his own mind—and at that merely as an exaggerated or idealised boyish memory—yet it could still be enough. Though just at that point he withdraws from the discussion—to listen politely or argue with his tongue.

Nor does the fact that the office and the specialisation may bring comfort and defeat the fear of want, altogether alter his private viewpoint; for somewhere deep in him is a distrust of comfort and a belief in struggle. This may be part of his Calvinistic heritage. For the seamen were Calvinists in religion. Yet he does not quite believe this, because the discipline and austerity, the cleanness and precision of action, arose necessarily from the traffic with the sea. They were the only qualities that could hope to counter the impersonal fury, the impending, curling-over, smashing destruction of the sea. The fury of the wind was the fury of a ravening beast that a man, thigh-booted, must never for a moment cease to stare in the eye. If he carried this discipline over to his God, in greater measure, there was at least a logic in the process.

The nearest approach to this attitude of mind he found in a university lecturer in physics who was also doing research work. He liked this man, his quiet ways, his thoughtlessness of bodily comfort, over against the eagerness, the precision, the unending struggle with his uncharted sea. In an exact sense, he felt at home with him and secretly dedicated himself to the same adventure.

In his reading, Kenn found his moments of greatest excitement those that had to do with scientific discovery: Rontgen playing around with his cathode tube, covering it over with black paper, turning on the current to make sure there were no holes in the paper—and then finding his specially prepared piece of cardboard glowing brightly on the table! And when a friend afterwards asked him what he thought at that moment, Rontgen replied, 'I did not think; I investigated.' This reply thrilled Kenn. Or Faraday pulling out the magnet—and happening to see the needle give a kick: the birth moment of all the electric powerhouses of the world. The thing was so simple, and Faraday so human in not having spotted the difficulty earlier! It brought him near; gave to his greatness something friendly and approachable. He was like one of the old bearded fishermen whom even the young addressed by their Christian names only, unless they were very young when they did not presume to any address at all beyond the courteous 'You'.

Galileo, Tycho Brahe, Kepler, the great Newton, Cavendish, Faraday, Rontgen. . . . They were the men who stood beyond the fishermen in Kenn's growing mind. From the fishermen to them there was a natural progression. And this progression carried with it politicians, lawyers, financiers, shop-keepers, clerks, bosses, factory-hands, writers, as a stream carries all sorts of queer craft and cargo and debris. Kenn has never been uncertain in his developing mind about the values here. He is now sure that they are final and therefore behind all other values that give life its appearance of integrity and charm and sensuous beauty.

To picture it he has only to contemplate a fisherman looking at the sea. The horizon line has darkened, and the smudge of weather has come in over the breast of the waters. There is a spit of rain, cold and ominous. Grey-dark cloud, evenly spread yet moving, communicates a leaden pallor to waves answering a wind not yet fully felt. The day is dying quickly. At home the line with its hundreds of hooks is freshly baited and waiting. In the early black hours of the morning, five of them in one undecked boat are to put to sea for the white fishing.

A seaman's eyes develop a far-sighted steadiness, through which the waves seem to roll and wash.

In this half-light of the world the man seems to become abstracted from all men and takes upon himself the burden of decision.

Kenn is sensitive to false symbolism here, but he knows the man, he sees his face, his eyes, his weathered stone-stillness. All that has happened is that in the acuteness of his vision the inessentials have faded out.

The figure may be ageless, but it is a living figure to whom in time past his erratic emotions were directed: who once, in a bitter cold, took Kenn's hands and warmed them in his hair.

Nor is the decision one of idealism; it is one of bodily need. Back behind the muttering sea are a woman and children and, going and coming, the man himself.

Kenn can wait even now, in his vision, with a curious
excitement, until the man turns from the threatening sea
and in a voice so quiet and natural that it seems half-spoken
to himself, says, 'I think we'll give it a try.'

Such was the harbour and sea into which Kenn's Highland
river ran. There was a string of cottages along the bay. A high
winter storm would carry the spume in at their front doors.
On each side of the harbour for a little way the ground was
flat and green and excellent for ball games when herring nets
were not being dried there. Beyond the green the precipices
started again.

It was a wild coast of gaunt headland and echoing cliff,
and the bay with its river mouth was a break that would
hardly be detected were one standing on some distant head
and looking along the immense sweep of the wall. Here and
there were skerries or reefs where even on fine summer days
the green water broke in foam, and occasionally, in front of
a headland itself, a stack would rise sheer, like a sword out
of the hand of the sea.

A relentless coast, whose typical birds were the cormorant
and herring gull. Kenn thinks of the cormorant as a bird all
sinew and quill whose body could never be killed, however
great the number of hands, large the pile of stones, and
confined the pool. That particular memory of stoning a
cormorant in the river is not now pleasant, rather shameful
indeed, however much a robber of young fry the bird was.
And what a thousand lives the black snakelike body had!
In the end some of the older boys called off the attack, and
Kenn had known a moment of release, though he had stoned
with the best.

Gulls following the herring boats and screaming loudest
when the harbour was most active is not his real memory
of them. They take him back to the cliffs as the cormorants
do to the skerries. Far down against the dank walls the
crying of the gulls was forlorn and cavernous; high-pitched
crying with a resounding resonance; haunted and unearthly.
It rarely failed to catch up his mind in a breathless silence,

in a suspense that dared be no more than half aware of the echoes dying away. The gulls cried like restless spirits keening drowned bodies awash on innermost edges of subterranean caverns. The crying would start slowly, then work up in a moment to a frenzied repetition, the wings of the sound beating ever more piercingly, as if the central throat were grey flexible bone. Once, as he had lain near a cliff-head behind wind-combed grass, a gull had alighted a little distance from him. Its round unwinking eye had had a cold unearthly look.

These rocks had occasional deep coves into which one could pull in a row boat. Some of the coves were multi-coloured, and one had an inner passage of ghostly white. Always something fearsome seemed to lurk in them and, before entering, an urge came to shout to see what would happen. Until one got prepared for it, what usually happened was an invisible wing-beating that brought the heart into the throat. Then the rock pigeons shot out upon the air, swiftly eddying up and away. After that, when the keel grated on the shingle, a boy stepped forth with eyes levelled against the inner gloom. It was an expedition that brought more discoveries than the purely physical, though no name was thought of for them then, nor perhaps ever could be afterwards.

Strength was the keynote of this coast, a passionless remorseless strength, unyielding as the rock, tireless as the water; the unheeding rock that a falling body would smash itself to pulp upon; the transparent water that would suffocate an exhausted body in the slow rhythm of its swirl. There was a purity about it all, stainless as the gull's plumage, wild and cold as its eye. However strange and haunted one's thoughts, they were never really introverted; but, rather, lifted into some new dimension of the purely objective, where internal heats and involutions pass out upon, without tainting, the wind and the sea.

This cool rarefied poising of life upon death had its summer days of exquisite beauty. These days were never sought for deliberately; they came by chance or inspiration.

An urge to bathe, then to follow sheep tracks, to go on
. . . and presently a cliff-top cradled the body under a
sun whose heat was tempered by the sea's breath. There
to lie extended above the uprising floor of the ocean was
to experience the lovely sensation of floating between earth
and heaven, as lonely gulls high overhead breasted the sun
in snow-white arcs. Even the crying of the gulls down in the
rocks grew faint with sunny distance, became the echo of
an echo of something forever lost. Yet not entirely lost, as
if the forlorn wave of the cry had buoyancy in it and bore
the body to far shores of sleep. And the body gave way to
this with wordless bliss, yet upon that bliss nothing carnal
intruded. No hot vision came stirring young flesh to secret
images. How could it, out of that near green and remote
blue sea, out of echoing caverns, out of tides that swung to
the changing phases of the moon?

To Kenn's older mind, these are words of 'poetic rhythm',
to be smiled at with the new critical good sense that mistrusts
their vagueness. Once, in a Parisian dive, where a blind
old man with a face marbled like a Greek satyr played a
piano-accordion and one of the dancing girls insisted on
putting her hand on his knee, he had picked up a copy of
Transition, which opened at a poem by a young American,
consisting of chopped lengths of blunt statement to the effect
that when a man mentioned the word Beauty, he (the poet)
replied s—t, and, when the word was mentioned again, left
the room on the pretext that the man was making sexual
advances. Kenn's laughter had been abrupt. It was not the
genuine intensity of the poet's reaction, not even his state of
mind, sick or sickened, but the utter fashionableness of his
literary attitude that got Kenn. Somehow out of his cliff-top
knowledge he realised in a flash what the fellow would have
to work through before he could regard, say, Keats with less
than a jaundiced eye. It was a moment of revelation.

He may be mistaken, but he sometimes thinks that this
apparently simple matter of rhythm from a cliff was of
more importance in the making of what he looks upon
as his essential self than all the dreadful slum life he saw

in Glasgow—and he saw a lot of it in the company of a
medical student doing his midwifery course—or the horrors
and gaieties of the war years in France. And yet so subtle,
so evanescent were those cliff-top moments, that he was
certainly not articulately conscious of them at the time.

The mind grew murmurous like the sea, had the cliff's
height, the sky's arch, the horizon's far line. The inner
rhythm may have been caused by no more than the quick
wave of the gull-cry or the slow wave of the sea. Yet the time
of his rhythm was different from these and had within it
something that went out and away without end, as if indeed
it were the rhythm that underlay or interpenetrated all other
rhythms, and bore upon it—or was itself—ultimate reality.
The later physicist has found a curious fascination in trying
to realise the terms of this problem.

And as a result he sometimes tries to think of a poetry
almost purely unhuman. Coleridge does not achieve it in his
cavernous *Kubla Khan*.

There is strangeness and mystery here; it is overwrought
with human emotion. It is directed inward and down, not
outward to sea and sky. It does not race in wheels of light
on the waters or pass away on the wind like a murmur.
Its rhythm is the human cry against the dark imprisoning
rock; not the freedom that passes into the sunlight, into
the loveliness that is untainted as the sea, heedless of life
or death, cool, passionless, remaining, and passing on.

CHAPTER FIVE

BUT IF KENN'S EARLY LIFE began where the river was
lost in the sea, his individuality came upon him as he turned
his back on this teeming harbour life and started to explore
the river upwards to its source.

This journey, tentative at first, consisting of little sallies
and retreats, with no conscious aim beyond satisfying the
hunting instinct, became in the end a thrilling exploration
into the source of the river and the source of himself.

And also into the source of his forebears back beyond the
dawn of history. It was remarkable how the races that had
gone to his making had each left their signature on the river
bank; often over and over, as children on gates and walls
scrawl the names of those amongst them who are 'courting'.

On one side of the harbour mouth the place-name was
Gaelic, on the other side it was Norse. Where the lower
valley broadened out to flat, fertile land the name was
Norse, but the braes behind it were Gaelic. A mile up
the river where the main stream was joined by its first
real tributary, the promontory overlooking the meeting
of the waters was crowned by the ruins of a broch that
must have been the principal stronghold of the glen when
the Picts, or perhaps some earlier people, were in their
heyday.

And all these elements of race still existed along the
banks of the river, not only visibly in the appearance of
the folk themselves, but invisibly in the stones and earth.
The 'influence' continued, sometimes so subtly that Kenn
had more than once been surprised into a quick heart-beat
by the very stillness of certain ancient spots, as though
the spots had absorbed in some mysterious way not only

the thought but the very being of the dark men of pre-history.

It required no very great effort to reconstruct what had happened in the comparatively recent times of the Norse invasions, round about AD 800. There were pictures of the longships of the Vikings in the school readers. Round the familiar head, these longships had come with their banks of rowers. The folk had gathered but were afraid of the terrible fighting men, for fearsome stories had been told round the peat fires of swinging iron axes and flashing swords. On the edge of the surf the battle would have been desperate but short. Often there would have been no battle at all, the peaceful pastoral folk hurriedly retiring inland and driving their livestock before them. From their fastnesses they could harry at their will. Anyway, the Norse occupied the flat lands along the lower reaches of the river. The names of their homesteads are in valuation roll and feu charter to this day. But beyond the Broch, no Norse name is known.

A story could have been made of all this for the scholars, but in Kenn's time no teacher ever attempted it. The Vikings were a people like the Celts or the Picts, concerning whom a few facts had to be memorized. But these facts were really very difficult to memorize, because they had no bearing on anything tangible. They were sounds in the empty spaces of history. The Saxons and the Romans were different because so many facts had to be learned about them that they gathered a certain bustling reality. And then there were stories about them, too, human stories, like the one about Alfred burning the cakes or Nero burning Rome. One could see Alfred and laugh and like him. He was the man one would follow on a desperate adventure.

But no Gael or Viking or Pict was ever drawn as humanly as Alfred, and Kenn in his boyhood had certainly no glimmering of an idea of how these three had filled his own glen with peaceful and violent history, with cunning tunes for the chanter, with odd laughable twists of thought, with courage for the sea. And yet in some unaccountable way he seemed to be aware of the living essence of this history without having been explicitly taught it.

He knows this is difficult to maintain, and is ready to admit that a long-forgotten word, a chance phrase—like 'the little folk'—may have been sufficient to set his imagination going. But yet he thinks it goes deeper than this. He knows he has been the subject of 'influences', the nature of which could never have been imparted. And he knows finally that these have given him moments of such exquisite panic, of such sheer delight, that they make by comparison many of the crises of his after-life moments of blunt endurance or of gross joy.

And knowing this, he would like to stop the thickening of his mind, to hunt back into that lost land, where Alfred and Nero, for all that they could be understood, were foreigners to his blood. The mind that secretly quickened before a broch, before a little path going up through a birch wood, to presences not looked at over the shoulder, possessed a magic that it seems more than a pity to have lost. For it was never deliberately induced. It was often feared, and sometimes hated. It was intensely real.

Kenn has a feeling that if he could recapture this he would recapture not merely the old primordial goodness of life but its moments of absolute ecstasy, an ecstasy so different from what is ordinarily associated with the word that its eye, if it had one, would be wild and cold and watchful as the eye of the gull on the cliff-top. Though that is a cold image, conveying only the suggestion of a first momentary aspect, of the initial thrill—before translation takes place.

Can he recapture this moment and the subsequent ecstasy? Is it possible in mature years to thin the lenses of the eye, to get the impulses and responses acting as they acted in boyhood? Has knowledge 'explained' the youthful wonder, and lethargy killed it?

Kenn knows what he is searching for here, and no amount of worldly scepticism or hint of sentimental credulity can affect his purpose. The physicist deals with too much invisible evidence to be put off by a visible attitude.

The adventures of boyhood were adventures towards the source, towards the ultimate loneliness of moor and mountainside, and his own adventure will finally have to take the same road.

CHAPTER SIX

THE WINTER THAT FOLLOWED the landing of Kenn's great fish was a very stormy one. For days on end the sea would thunder on the beach with reverberations that could be heard far inland. Sometimes the sound would play on the ear with forebodings of universal doom, and when the light would go dim in the early afternoon and the drizzle thicken into rain, the misery of consciousness would go cold as the mire the feet sucked out of. An old woman, in innumerable knitted and flannelled wrappings, her shawled head stooping from her bent shoulders, would carry a drop at her nose distilled from misery's final self.

And such old women moved here and there about the little steadings of the crofting lands, or went for 'messages' to Sans' shop, or called upon Kenn's mother to see if there were any fresh fish.

But there were no fish and so the old woman would wipe her nose and sit down and, with nice manners, take a cup of tea and a biscuit from Kenn's mother and sigh a little and say that the times that were in it were bad enough for a dispensation surely. She would shake her head and wipe her nose and settle down mournfully to the goodness of hospitality.

But not all of them got such luxury out of it. Many were cheerful and would face up bravely to the goodness and laugh, shaking their heads, and say they never entered this house but they felt the better for it, and ach! they had to take things as they came and they should be thankful they were as they were, what do you say? And 'Draw in your chair', was what Kenn's mother said to them all.

Down at the harbour the fishermen stood in the lee of the cooperage, taking a turn up and down, peering now and then round the corner into the eye of the weather, discussing whatever happened to arise out of the circumstances of the moment: hard winters away back in their grandfathers' time; the year of 'the great storm'; the strange adventure with the shark of 'Sanny o' Jimak's, now no more'; until someone suddenly said, 'Look! there's the doctor.' And in silence they watched the doctor's figure disappearing in the gloom by their own cottages.

Out of this deep reticence, a man said quietly, 'I'm afraid it's not long Duncan will be in it now, poor fellow.'

And presently another man began, 'Boys, I can remember as if it were yesterday, when he came into the bay there with the first fully decked boat ever brought home to this coast. It was the summer my great grandfather died in his ninety-seventh year—and a great disappointment it was to him for he had been sure of making the hundred of it, but he grew resigned in the end and said it was not for him to question the inscrutable ways of the Almighty. He was a good-living man, but very stubborn. His was the first funeral that I remember on, and so I know where I am, for it was just a fortnight after his funeral that Duncan brought his new skaff into the bay. Oh, there was great excitement in the place. It was a great event. Nothing like her had ever been handled by any of the older men. He had gone west and bought her from the Earl of Mosterleigh who had the estate of Claddich from the Cattach duke. And I have heard him tell that journey itself in a way that would take half the night and you interested and laughing. For he had a fine pride and manners when he was a young fellow. Oh bravely set up and full of spirit, yet never pushing himself, yet there. The Earl fairly took to him; asked him who he was and where he came out of. Then he rang a bell and a butler came in with brandy and they drank together and the Earl receipted the bill in full and handed back Duncan five pounds. But Duncan would not take the five pounds. "No, thank you, my lord," says he. It was not pride so much as just that he didn't like, if you understand me, for well Duncan could have done with the money! But the Earl got the better of him by saying that this was an offering to the luck of the boat—and good luck she had in her day right enough. And then the butler gave him a great dinner, the like of you never heard. And what with the servant lassies an' all—some of them English. . . . But that's another story. All I remember is him entering the bay. I was twelve years old at the time and went out in one of the small boats. Oh, he took a lot of us lads aboard. Man, there was something fine and gay in his nature, when I think on it. We swarmed all over her. Then he hoisted sail on her and before the whole shore began putting her through her paces in the bay.'

'How old was he then?'

'He was just twenty years.'

Listening to this talk, Kenn would so forget the cold, that it would come back on him shuddering to the marrow. His teeth would chitter and he would try to rub his skin against the inside of his clothes.

When the body got as cold inside as the point of the nose outside—not the ears which only got cold suddenly, in frost—then nothing could warm it. You were like the miry earth, the damp air, the raw wind coming round the corner with stinging spots of rain out of the dirty weather that lay on the breast of the sea.

How fearsome the sea looked! It came rolling from under the dark weather, the colour of lead. But how wild and how cold! When the wave smashed against the quay-point, the froth was unearthly white as the gull's feathers, of a coldness more deathly than any snow. You drew your head back into the shelter—that was suddenly like warmth.

And the thunder all the time on the beach, the rush of receding water down myriads of rumbling stones; the creaking of ropes over the harbour wall in the deepening gloom.

The sky came lower; the dark pall of weather crept farther in over the sea, and out of it the ashen waves came curling like snakes, crested snakes, hissing white spume. The weak image is hardly born before it goes out like a spark in the smashing, drowning sea-water, colder than the coldest bone.

There is nothing that man can put up against that, nothing known to him, except death—whose body the sea will take and play with and lick and smash against rock and boulder, and leave finally for its eels and claws to feed upon.

A light appeared in the near end window of the row of cottages. It was not like a star or a Chinese lantern. It was a veiled yellow eye, with something solemn and a little sad about it. Footsteps would be moving behind it quietly, amid the faint paraffin smell, the fustiness of the best room. Yet how the eye commanded the night, how steady it was in its detachment, how aloof from the thunderous activity of the sea. And if stared at long enough it seemed to grow in size, to come nearer, out of the forehead of the night. One had to wink in order to set it back again in the parlour of the little house where old Duncan was dying.

It was a signal, too, for the men to depart for their homes. It would be a stormy morning. There was nothing more they could do. But silence fell upon them and none of them made a move. Kenn could feel the strange wrapt quality of their thought, as if each were swathed in the loneliness of the night . . . or in the mindless calm beyond thought . . . like the bows of their boats.

Presently a figure passed outside, against the light. It was the doctor. In a little while a seaman came down the road towards them and in over the edge of the grass.

'How is Duncan?' asked the storyteller.

'He's very low,' said the man. 'The doctor doesn't expect him to last the night.'

A quiet word or two, and the little company broke up. The tide was ebbing and the boats safe enough until they would see what the morrow brought.

It would be high tide at three in the morning. Old Duncan would go out with the tide.

When Kenn saw that his father was alone, he ran up to him. Their home was half a mile up the river.

'Bless me, boy, are you here yet?' said his father to him. 'You should have been home long ago. Aren't you cold?

What?' He took his son's hands in his own and began chafing them. 'You're cold, cold.'

'Not very,' said Kenn, chittering.

'What?' He pressed his son against his legs and rolled and rubbed him a little. 'Is that better?'

'Yes.'

'What'll your mother say to you, eh?' He fondled him cunningly. 'Now! Give me your hand and we'll hurry.'

His father walked at his usual speed and Kenn trotted beside him, the stirring of warmth making his teeth want to chitter harder than before. But he took care not to let them click audibly. Already his father was not thinking about him. He liked that largeness about his father, the friendly concern that could fondle his body without making him feel he was being treated like a child, the kindness that was not high-toned but wise and warm, and could in a moment be nearer than anything in the world.

As they walked on, his father's head was high up and looking steadily before him. Every now and then his hand gave Kenn's hand a few quick, spasmodic squeezes. It was the hand talking, but not to Kenn, though Kenn was not forgotten. And sometimes the hand becoming conscious of Kenn's hand gave it an extra squeeze all to itself, while the thought up above passed beyond its moment of stress into calm again.

After a time, his father paused and turned to look back at the shore. Kenn gripped his father's hand tight, for it was so gloomy and thunderous now where the sea was that the storm might swell up on great black wings . . . the bitter cold shivered away thought of the wings that death would need to flap into *that* in the pitch blackness of the early morning, as the boats in the harbour, straining most fiercely at their moorings on top of the tide, felt the tide begin to ebb.

The only fixed thing in all that ominous world was the yellow eye of the end window. And it seemed to have grown rounder and more commanding.

'It's going to be a dirty night,' said Kenn's father as he turned his back on the shore again. Then he became aware of his son whom he had forgotten and stooped to him as they went on walking, and Kenn felt his warm breath on his cheek. 'Are you very cold, boy?'

The voice was friendly and loving-kind in the little hollow of shelter. But its smile of understanding, as his father straightened himself, touched a remoteness that is the delicate core of comradeship.

It made Kenn light-hearted and free, made it easier for him to step out, to meet the night on his face, and even to glance down at the river rolling darkly past.

It was swollen with the recent rains, gloomy, and forbidding. Its voice rolled along with it in its stony channel. Its pale froth swirled away like melting snow.

After leaving the harbour behind, one came on the footbridge by which the fishermen crossed over to their cottages along the bay. There was a good pool under the bridge, especially for sea-trout in the first of a spate. With the water a dirty yellow, they could be heaved out of it on a haddock hook at the end of a foot of gut. Above the footbridge the water was broken again for a little distance until it reached two long flagstone pools, not very deep, and fine for sea-trout when the spate had fallen away to its last shade of amber and a fly could be thrown lightly for a quick rise.

One could not have done much there in the way of flyfishing on this night! The flagstone at the head of the top pool was completely covered. The water curved solidly over it, black as tar.

Above these pools was a long broken stretch down which Kenn now saw the river advancing with tremendous force. It had a submerged sound of grinding boulders. It could hardly wait to boil and seethe, but hurtled forward in fluted reckless speed, the thin spray dancing upon it. The look of it made him shudder; and its bitter cold.

The older men often talked of a winter flood as 'snow bree', and for all that a smooth curve of it here and there looked solid as rock, yet Kenn felt that there was in it the thinness of melted snow, perhaps because of the aerated gushes and swirls and eddies.

He trotted a few steps every now and then to keep up with his father. Soon the road began to rise slightly and was defined on either hand by a low stone wall. It now ran through a tree plantation in which the wind threshed uneasily. It was so dark in here that one could not see the walls, only the grey opening in front where the rise ended. The bare branches overhead writhed and flailed, and where two of them had got entangled or forked there was a constant creaking. A curious compulsion came on the mind to listen to the trees. Sometimes the wind in sudden fury tried to flatten them; then it would lift in a sighing moan. The bank on the left hand was growing ever steeper, and the roar of the river down below was a rushing of the unstable earth.

Kenn was glad when they got out of the trees and saw the opening in the wall where one went down to the well.

'The well will be covered tonight,' he said to his father.

'Yes, the river will be right in over it. Are you feeling warmer now?'

'Yes.' He could not see the well, but he threw a quick glance towards the field on the other side of the river where he had carried the salmon.

As they went on in the usual silence, he thought of the well and the salmon.

The silence between them as they walked was full of freedom for the mind. It had no compulsions of any kind. It had the quality of perfect naturalness and gave secretly to the memory then something that it discovered long afterwards and regarded, smiling thoughtfully, as rather rare and lovely.

Out of their comradeship, Kenn's 'Yes' was a polite inaccuracy. Though warmer inside himself, his body was still cold as a sea shell. No exercise could bring a glow to it. He had not the energy indeed for the necessary violence and was holding on to what internal comfort he had until he got home.

As he approached the house he felt shy and a little important because he was coming home with his father. He knew his mother would be wondering where he had been; and as the door opened, the light shone on the embarrassed smile on his face. But his eyes, glistening as with frost, soon saw that there was no one in the kitchen. It was empty and all tidy and swept clean. The emptiness, however, held no touch of panic. It was given over to the flames of the peat fire.

The flames flapped lazily in their own dreamy unconcern. The kettle, swung out a little on the iron crook, had an upward trickle of steam from its spout. Everything was arrested in a mood of quiet reverie.

Kenn went to the flames and stretched his hands to them. His father stood listening on the middle of the floor. 'Your mother must have gone out,' he muttered. Then he turned to his son. 'How's the fire?'

'It's fine,' said Kenn.

His father looked at it. From the white core it flickered to the outer half-consumed circle of black peat upon which the yellow flames did their slow dance. It was perhaps past its best, but until more actual flame had to be coaxed under a pot, it would be a pity to touch it. He stretched out his own hands and rubbed them together in a harsh sound.

'It's a fine thing, a fire,' he said to his son, but thoughtfully, as if he were still wondering where his wife was.

Kenn felt it was a fine thing, but he did not consciously dwell on its wonder. Its reflections, however, played in his eyes and its warmth all over his body. He got down on his knees to get nearer it. Behind him, a wall grew up, shutting out the stormy sea and the dark river.

His father went to the back door and called, 'Are you there, Ellen?'

Outside in the night her voice answered. His father closed the door behind him.

Kenn listened. There must be something wrong about the henhouse. Its door was always difficult to close, the bottom edge scraping heavily against the ground. When it was shoved to, the round stone was rolled against it.

Nothing happened for a little time, then all at once there was a wild squawking. Squawk! Squawk! Squawk!

His father was killing a hen!

The hen would be for the Sunday dinner. He listened intensely.

At last the squawking was over. So the hen was dead. His father would hold up the dead hen by the feet until the flapping stopped.

His mother would not like losing one of her hens.

Quite involuntarily he saw her face by the henhouse door, its calm expression, its acceptance of time and chance. His father and mother stood together and their voices were low-toned in the dark.

Something about them out there in the night affected Kenn obscurely. He stared into the heart of the fire until his eyeballs, glistering, felt the heat. Then he brought his hands up against the heat and lowered his head behind them.

Presently, hearing his parents returning, he got up off his knees, stood back from the fire, and waited for what his mother would say.

CHAPTER SEVEN

THAT WINTER THE RIVER did not freeze. In fact, the quietest pool rarely froze right across, and Kenn had never seen sufficient ice there for sliding or skating. Tobogganing on a wooden board or a rough home-made sledge was good sport often, but the greatest fun was got from sliding. Slides were made wherever there was ice, but the public highway afforded the most cunning ones of all. The rough snowy surface under the rush of feet would turn dark and smooth and slowly extend in length. Boy after boy in the short, sharp run and the whizzing take-off would 'keep the kettle boiling'. When the slide grew very long, it required skill to keep the body from turning round or bumping off into the ditch. Many boys were so expert that they could 'sit down' and go shooting forward as from a catapult. There was always plenty of excitement and shouting, and, because of the need for speed, seldom time for bringing a sudden hot challenge to the satisfaction of a fight.

Yet this gregarious enjoyment, intensely stirring while it lasted, did not make a very deep impression. It was all in a sense a sort of skating on the mind. Rarely did one slip through to be caught in the pool of self. Indeed the craving for speed, for keeping the kettle boiling ever more fiercely, seemed destined to ensure that this should not happen, though why or by whom it might be difficult to say.

Anyway, so strong could the craving become, that only exhaustion or hunger could defeat it, and then on the way home with reluctant joints and a dullness in the mind, there would be about one the sparkles of frost under a clear sky or the whiteness of snow under a moon. Kenn would not consciously see any beauty in this, but he would in an odd moment become aware of the stillness, of the Arctic whiteness, perhaps even stand with mouth a little open, listening for sounds of feet or voices going different ways into the night, or for some unknown sound that might . . . before giving a quick shiver and saying, 'It's cold.'

But always in winter time, whatever the fun or grudging task, there was that opening of the kitchen door to the sight of the fire. Its yellow flame was the heart of life.

The flame of the fire, the light in a window, the flashing beam from a rock: the short story of the journey out of primeval gloom to the occulting austerities.

But in the fire itself the first magic, the laughter, the glowing friendliness. And food.

Food! Hot food. The burst jackets of potatoes steaming upward. The sight drew water through the teeth, and while Grace before meat was still being said, a sly hand would slip forth and steal the king of the ashet. Then another hand, and another; voices raised in querulous protest; the parental reprimand; and each brother surveyed his trophies as the benediction passed upward with the steam.

The stew or the salt herrings or the dried fish would be served out evenly. But when the potatoes elbowed their way through their skins, Kenn and his brothers said they were laughing.

And as with potatoes, so with the crisp heel of a loaf, bere scones with strawberry jam (a reckless extravagance, like sin), liver with onions in the gravy, bacon on boiled cod . . . .

But then Kenn came at these things with hunger. And there are as many varieties of hunger as of potatoes.

There was the hunger of gluttony. Sometimes, fishing in the harbour with herring bait they caught an ugly, horny brute, all mouth and maw. They hated the sight of it so much that they often stuck a piece of cork to one of its gristly horns and let it go. When it got exhausted swimming downward, the cork would bring it to the surface again. Because it was a cruel sport, they jeered at the gluttonous brute excessively.

Between the expectation that came palely by use and wont

at fixed hours and the craving that was a disease, there was a long range of hungers. The cheerful but false hunger induced by strong drink. The jealous hunger like the hunger between dogs. But there was only one perfect hunger; and that was the hunger Kenn knew.

It may be that from this hunger all other hungers arise; that in its state of expectancy may be discovered at least the attitude of all human aspirations, from the voice crying in the wilderness, the knightly vigil of the medieval youth, the elderly vigil of astrologer, alchemist and seer, to the astronomer waiting for a new star to swim into the 'unknown' of his mathematical equation. Wholeness, harmony and radiance were the qualities the ancients ascribed to aesthetic beauty. But Kenn touched this static conception with kinetic craving.

And in its small way, too, his belly, when fulfilment had been wholly achieved, did emulate the rumbles and eruptions of creation; though never with anything approaching the art of his elder brother, who, outside and far from the parental ear, could prolong, vary, and modulate an eructation while holding to an expression of ideal gravity.

Nor would he be in any way impressed by his young brother's mirth, but would wait until Kenn was recovering before once more doubling him up.

Kenn now perceives that Angus must have made an art of it, just as later he made an art of playing on the chanter continuously for twenty minutes without appearing to draw breath. This latter feat was a remarkable one and took him over two years to perfect. The chanter is a difficult enough pipe to blow straightforwardly, but to watch a youth playing marches, strathspeys and reels without an instant's pause in the rush and whirl of notes, is first to be fascinated, then horrified in expectation of the whole body bursting into fragments. The trick of it had something to do with drawing breath in through the nostrils while at the same time expelling it from the mouth, and making of the lungs the bag that in the full set of pipes is held under the arm.

The heart of all this winter life was the peat fire. From

sledging and sliding, from the cold sea, from snaring birds and rabbits, Kenn came back to his home, entered at front or back door, and beheld the leisurely dance of the flames.

His mother presided over this central world with completeness. She was a heavy woman, of easy carriage, with a comely face and smoothly-parted dark hair. The graciousness of her manner came out of a wise kindness. Her presence filled all the house, and Kenn accepted her as man accepts the sun or the storm or, perhaps, God, for Kenn had his little sins of omission or commission to think about, and he would wonder now and then—with an evasive smile—what his mother might say, or do, when he entered at the door.

He could never remember having been kissed by his mother, and certainly never by his father. Any overflow of affection came through the hands or the tone of the voice. None of the mothers in that land kissed their sons. If it were known that a boy had been kissed by his mother, not a dozen school fights would clear him of the dark shame of such weakness. That a toddler of five might break down and weep on his first day at school could be understood and forgiven. But that his mother should have kissed him before he set out was enough to make young men of twelve blame the woman and see in her something weak and trashy.

Nor can Kenn remember having seen his father kiss his mother. When he returned after some two months from fishing the western seas beyond Stornoway or Castlebay, where death hailed him more frequently than any postman, there would be no more than a quiet greeting of welcome in the kitchen. 'You've got back, Davy.' 'Yes. How is everyone?' 'Fine.' 'That's good.' And he would sit down like a stranger returned to his own, and the air would be vibrant with his presence. Kenn, shy, a little overcome, would leave the kitchen and, outside, gape queerly at nothing or start running furiously—but presently find himself by the door again listening to their voices.

Anger, outbursts of temper, fighting were not uncommon, but affection was shy and as invisible as death. Indeed, it was the one quality Kenn never thought of himself as possessing.

He would have been scornful of anyone who might have suggested that he loved his parents. And not unnaturally, for in his continuous effort to win balance and self-sufficiency, his parents were his judges, ready to condemn and—though rarely—to punish.

Yet of all the personal emotions that endure from that time, this silent invisible affection is the most potent.

It comes with some surprise to Kenn now that this should be so, yet a little thought makes him realise that nearly always what ultimately proved to be the memorable things were hardly observed at the time; or, if observed, were turned away from, towards what seemed more attractive or important or full of fun but what is now forgotten.

Is there room for curious research here? How far did the discipline, which Kenn felt as natural because it was part of his social being, strengthen affection? In how much was affection a manifestation, a necessity, of environment—of sea and glen, of struggle and resource, of self-dependence and endurance? Had the vexed factor of race much to do with it? of tradition which anthropologists tend more and more to consider the determining factor in social and therefore personal behaviour? In how far was it purely animal?

The questions can be piled up, and though they may seem dry on the printed page, to Kenn in the inner reaches and penetrations of thought, they are bright with fascination. For two factors of great importance do emerge: the positiveness of the affection itself and its lasting effect on the communal life.

Only when lads like Kenn left the glen was this affection perceived, and its reticence translated into active support of the old home.

The exile from his father's land may duly work up a poetic nostalgia for 'the lone shieling of the misty island', but these physical features, importing in their literal description bodily discomfort, must surely be symbols for something that went very deep.

The son did not love the mother more than the father, but loved each differently in her sphere or his. And the affection, being disciplined and delicate, became part of all the ways of life, in the mist, on the sea, in the shieling, on the river, in sunshine and rain. It went about with them everywhere, because everywhere they went had something to do with the communal life, the centre of which was the home. Ultimately the shieling meant food, the river fish, and the peat-bank fire. The contacts were direct and the results were seen. There was thus about the most ordinary labour some of the excitement of creation. Nor could cold or gloom or hunger or other discomfort completely obscure the sense of family unity in its life struggle; on the contrary, as with all creative effort, the discomforts and setbacks, particularly in retrospect, add some extra quality of fineness or delight.

Not that it worked out thus with all families by all the Highland rivers! But out of his experience, Kenn sees this as the essential social tradition.

During all that winter season the river lay dead. Its waters were always swollen by rain or melting snow and never lost their peaty darkness. Often, on his way to school, Kenn would climb on to the parapet of the bridge and peer down into likely spots in the pool below, but rarely in this close season was the movement of a fish seen.

There was something in the river during these months that was cold and deathly. The path by its bank was miry, the trees looked dead and curiously warped as if the fuzzy lichen was suffocating them. It was difficult to believe that they would burst into foliage again; if some leaves did come, it must be thinly, like an old man's hair. There were broken, rotten branches, brown leaves and bronze bracken heaped and mouldering, yielding mole's earth, withered grass, smooth rocks splotched with thin, grey lichen, flood marks of straws and debris, gaunt upended stones, and in the distance always a bleakness that was unadventurous and repelling. The only thing of colour was the moss and it was green on yellow, soft, damp, and unobtrusively everywhere.

Yet the river had one persistent and even compelling attribute during this time, and that was the noise it made.

Kenn was rarely conscious of hearing it until in bed, but then, just before his going to sleep or in some sudden hush of the night, its sound would rise up upon the world and flood all the hollows of silence with its turbulence. It was the noise of the rushing of all the seas, until in a moment it was the river itself flowing past in the darkness down by the well, the river he knew, but beyond his command now and in league with the elements beyond life.

The snug warmth of the hollow in the bed where he lay all curled up would sometimes induce a feeling of extraordinary glee, so that he would breathe under the blankets and laugh wide-mouthed and huskily. Hah-haa! he would chuckle, gathering all his body into a ball and touching his knees with his chin. Hah-hah-haa! softly, so that no one would hear.

It was great fun to be so safe in this warm hole, while the dark, cold river rolled on its way to the distant thunder of the sea. The roaring was between eternity and eternity, and carried dissolution in its flood. But not the dissolution of rocks, where animals, furry and warm, were curled up in their dens. All things with warm life in them were curled up, like himself, and heard, waking or in sleep, the rushing of the river.

So vividly in the dark could Kenn see a rabbit or a fox that he could put his hand on it, and, as it leapt, smile at its astonishment. But an animal like a wild cat made him stare at its sudden eyes.

The initial picture was always that of coming on the animal asleep, and watching the faint movement in its fur, a fascinating, crawling movement, like the slow ripple he had seen in the warm gut of a disembowelled rabbit.

Not that at such a moment he could picture death. For against the noise of the drowning water, all life was in conspiracy—rabbits, foxes, hares, cats, weasels, deer up in the corries—from beast to beast he would pass, understanding best, however, those that were curled up in a den.

Curled up in a den, eyes closed and noses tucked in, with fur so soft and lovely that a breath would separate it.

The picture made him snuggle in his own den and smell the thick warmth out of his own pelt. And the intimacy of this would induce glee again.

But sometimes he would waken out of a dream right into the roar of the river. The world had dissolved into a rushing darkness. All was formless and engulfing, yet immanent with terrifying shape. Dens and animals were not. Life itself had vanished—except his own, quivering now, knees to chin, in some dread prenatal expectancy.

Yet this fellowship with the wild had rarely anything of nightmare in it. Its birds and animals had some elusive vanishing quality that was not only attractive but stirred in him the instincts of the hunter. The most thrilling sensation as far as the birds were concerned was got from catching them in snares when snow covered the ground.

How quickening the feeling of delight when on a winter morning Kenn awoke and found the world all white! It might have been a paradise, by the eagerness with which he dressed and the haste with which he gobbled his porridge and got ready for school. Not only would there be sledging and snow-fights and games, but also the exciting chance of a half-holiday, for many children had to walk long distances.

But behind all the obvious fun was the bright allure of the catching of wild birds by himself and his brother, or by himself and Beel, or even—and more intensely then— by himself alone.

The snares were of several kinds and all very simply made, such as the slip-nooses of horse hair pegged into a divot on which grain had been spread, or a corn riddle balanced on edge by a foot of stick to which a string had been attached. But as a piece of herring net was easy for Kenn to get, he generally pegged out with short upright sticks a small rectangle over which he spread the net, leaving open the near end of the little chamber so formed. On its floor he scattered a handful of ground oatcake, and then retired round the nearest corner.

Hunger would make the birds adventurous but also suspicious, and alas it always happened that the rare birds were the least adventurous and the most suspicious. Sparrows, thrushes and blackbirds, robins, chaffinches, tits . . . to the green linnet. Sparrows Kenn disliked; thrushes and blackbirds could give sport; the robin was a special bird; some of the finches had bonny colours; so had the tits . . . but the green linnet for some reason was the bird of desire.

Kenn never caught a green linnet.

He is not sorry for that now, because his love for the wild has always been against keeping living things in a cage, and if he had caught a green linnet and put it in a cage his vanity would always have been troubled. Yet he would have liked to have caught one. At the time indeed there was nothing he more ardently desired. Once, unaware of its presence, he flushed a green linnet from the top of the henhouse when his snare was set between the henhouse and the peat stack. Some sparrows had alighted and threatened to enter his little house. He put his head round the corner and hished them away. Then above the flat scurry of the sparrows he had seen the dip and rise of the green bird.

His heart had stood still. The line of the linnet's flight had a beauty that was exquisite and inexorable. It went from him. It passed away leaving the world to the scattering sparrows.

The sense of loss weakened him for a little, until strength returned in a loathing rage against the chirping greedy little brutes now fluffing themselves on the henhouse. If one had by chance flown into his little house, he would have drawn its neck and flung it from him and spat.

The green linnet never came again.

The joy he got in the game, however, had its culminating moment. From his hiding place, he would watch for the coming of a bird. Sometimes when there was nothing doing, he would go away for a walk and come back again, as if something strange was bound to happen when his mind was no longer concentrated on the snare. This feeling that only in such an interval of deliberate forgetfulness would a magical thing happen was very strong.

The bird always came hopping tentatively, warily. It would hop on to the top of the little house, balancing itself neatly on the thin point of one of the sticks, then hop down; hop away and hop back; finally it would hop into the little house, glance to this side and that, peck swiftly and glance again.

Whooping like a Redskin, Kenn would burst from his hiding place, and the bird, overcome by this terrifying sight, would dash away from it into the net at the back, although of course there had been ample time for it to have hopped leisurely out by the open door.

If the bird was a bullfinch, Kenn would have great pleasure in its capture. He would hold it cupped in his hand, the spidery legs between the little finger and its neighbour, and the head and neck showing above the circle of thumb and first finger.

'Look what I have caught!' he would shout, running to find his companions. 'Look!'

And they would come around him and look.

A bullfinch! Many folk put bullfinches in cages. They did. There was this one and that who had done it. Yes, and the bullfinches had lived for years. Fact as death. Will you put it in a cage, Kenn? Give me a feel!

They would stand still, while each one put a forefinger gently on the head and ran it down the back of the neck. This made them smile in a gentle way and then laugh and ask for another feel. Some of them when they touched the bird would have their mouths a little open, the smile queerly arrested, as if they were hearkening for something odd: the sort of expression that holds a boy's face when at last he has climbed within reach of a bird's nest and may put his fingers in over the edge to feel the eggs—*or whatever may be there*.

Meantime Kenn would have the flutter of the bird every now and then within his palm, a strange tickling sensation that went all over him, even to the back of his throat. After each struggle, it would sink its head into its neck and blink its eyes. How small and bright the eyes, how frail and brittle the legs and claws; the twin beaks were delicate as oat husks, and should they peck his skin he would shout 'Oh!' as if he had been mortally wounded and dance about.

The beating of its heart would grow so quick that it was like the pulse of pain in a nerve.

Now and then a boy might press the head hard as he would press a pain in his own tooth.

Until all in a moment Kenn would cry 'Look! Watch!' and with a swing of his arm he would throw the bullfinch in the air. Before their bright eyes it fluttered, heeled over, and was off.

An expression of humour came into the eyes, an appreciation of the astonishment the bird must feel at being thus suddenly freed. 'I bet you he got a fright!' 'I bet you he did!'

And Kenn would be left with the feel of the living bird in his open hand.

When, in his teens, Kenn read that Leonardo da Vinci had gone about the streets of Florence buying caged birds for the pleasure of liberating them, the knowledge excited him to that momentary ecstasy where thought is lost in pure light.

Sudden and profound understanding still tends to excite him in this way. Out of disparate and enigmatic materials or facts, synthesis is achieved, or mysteriously achieves itself, in the mind, and for a moment its ineffable perfection is seen as pure creation. Leonardo, from what was known of him, was no ordinary humanitarian, moved by the kindly sentiment that attributes human feelings to birds, nor was he so introverted that he freed the birds to ease his own pain at beholding them caged, nor could so intricate and profound a mind have found satisfaction in a gesture of vanity. Such considerations are but the starting points of thought, the sticky knots that fix the web to earth.

Kenn's eyes lifted with Leonardo's hand, with Leonardo's face, to the infinite brightness against which and into which the bird flew. In that moment, between earth and heaven, between captivity and freedom, all the restless searchings of the artist were stilled to that poise in which the whole being passes, thoughtless, into the condition of light.

In Kenn's mind the figure of Leonardo is always passing on; through busy streets, amongst magnificent courts, over bridges, by rivers with rocks, pausing in studios to look for a minute at some work, before turning away again on his continuous quest. And the figure, glimpsed as it passes through that renaissance age, has youthful beauty by virtue of some inexorable rightness.

For what attracts Kenn finally in this extraordinary being is not so much that he passed from art to science as that in himself he strove to achieve the ultimate at-one-ment of art and science, the merging of beauty and knowledge in eternal design. And though this he could not do, there is yet about him the air of one going about such cosmic business—and, further, the air of an only one.

Yet, as though the figure can be glimpsed only in that renaissance age, taking from the thronged streets and the palace interiors, from the flesh tints and the velvet shadows, a dimness of atmosphere, like thought in the eyes, there accompanies it on its quest—perhaps 'peoples' it on its quest—'the soul with all its maladies' by which a later writer sought to distinguish the Renaissance from the Greek.

This is something added to Kenn's gesture of throwing the bullfinch in the air! And he can contemplate it with some of the humour and wonder that shone for a moment in his companions' eyes. But even as he does so there may be seen on his face an evasive light, a fugitive smile, secretive as those dark Picts who left, as their record of thousands of years of habitation of that land, his own slim dark-eyed body.

The bullfinch, the clear snow, the smooth outlines, the bright air—the picture in art (for that northland has no art) is pure Chinese. The maladies of the soul and the riches of the body-trappings have nothing to do with it. It is cleansed of humanism, and holds in its untroubled perfection its own eternity.

Cold and clear and exquisite. Just as above the cliffs Kenn

got his intimations of an unhuman poetry from the sea's rhythm, so in the flight of the green linnet against his northern snows was set the rhythm's line in an unhuman art.

When first he read Maeterlinck's play about the blue bird of happiness which the children searched for, he experienced a curious revulsion, a shyness which felt uncomfortable before such innocence and sentiment. This was so purely an instinctive reaction that if he had had to act in the play, or even to live in the social order which produced so credulous a goodness, he would have felt caged. Indeed if there had been any likelihood of such a thing happening to him, he would have turned and taken to his heels.

Leonardo, passing there in the street, he could have followed, secretively, at a little distance.

Leonardo was not after the blue bird of happiness, any more than the Chinese artist.

Kenn does not know what they were after, and wonders sometimes if they knew themselves. But he feels it has something to do with an absolute, like catching the green bird—and letting it go.

CHAPTER EIGHT

THERE WAS AN INCIDENT during that winter that made
a deep impression on Kenn. It had to do with the snaring
of a rabbit, and it is not so much the dramatic interest of
the affair that has lingered in his memory as the insight it
gave him into his mother's hidden mind.

While the snaring of birds was in the nature of a game,
the snaring of rabbits, like the poaching of salmon, was akin
to the deep-sea fishing upon which the family depended. As
a sport it was intensified a thousandfold by the knowledge
that it meant food for the home—at a time when it might
be gravely welcome.

Kenn's immediately older brother, Angus, was fifteen
and the youngest member of the crew on his father's boat.
Kenn would have followed him anywhere, like a dog; and
though Angus was good-natured and kind, he frequently
sent Kenn home when setting out on ploys with youths
of his own age. Sometimes Kenn would be stubborn and
would follow. Angus would order him back. Kenn would
still follow. Angus would hit him. Sobbing, half in rage,
Kenn would persist. Then Angus would give him a proper
hiding, and while Kenn was blinded with his tears, would,
with his companions, take to his heels.

This was the usual educative process amongst the young
of all families.

One Saturday afternoon in early February, Kenn's brother
Joe, who was three years older than Angus, came home for
the weekend. That Joe, who with his natural feeling for the
wild had been an expert poacher, should now be undergoing
the process of conversion to a gamekeeper was the sort of joke
that seemed inevitably right to everyone. Of middle height,

he was broad-shouldered, explosively strong, and lithe as a cat; dark, with a pale skin, deep-brown eyes and a slow attractive smile. At the local Annual Games, he carried off the prizes for jumping. To Kenn, he was heroic.

This Saturday, he sent Kenn for three coils of snare wire, and out of the change gave him a penny to himself. Kenn did not want to take the penny. Joe smiled. Kenn flushed, and, when Joe invited him up to the old barn to help make the rabbit snares, he felt that life was very full.

For each snare four strands of yellow wire were smoothly twisted together by inserting a pencil through the end loop and turning it round and round. With Kenn's help, Joe made the snares very deftly, while Angus cut and pointed the wooden stakes.

When everything was ready, Joe turned to Kenn and said that he had better run home. They wouldn't be long and it was as well not to let everyone see what they were after. 'So off you go, boy!'

The very kindness of the tone overcame Kenn. His heart was set on going with them, his whole being given to it. His lip began to quiver. His eyes filled.

'Away home now, like a good lad! We won't be long.'

Blindly Kenn began to follow them, dumbly, moved by a compulsion he could not control. Often when he had run after Angus he had been stirred by a stubborn rage. There was no rage in him now. He was desperately awkward, ashamed of what he was doing, yet he could not help himself. It was like walking in some dreadful nightmare.

Joe waited till he came near.

'Where are you going?' he demanded.

Kenn hung his head, his body twisting pitifully.

'Didn't I tell you to go home?'

The cold tone and the brown eyes were piercing him. He choked back his sobs.

'Go home!'

He could not move. Joe was walking on again. He began to follow.

Joe waited a second time.

Kenn now knew that he would have to experience the bitter degradation of being slapped by Joe. Yet, like one drugged, he went towards him, and hung his head, his teeth clenched against his sobs, hands and legs writhing slowly.

Some dark power in this persistence came out to Joe and angered him unreasonably. His voice snapped: 'Go home, or I'll welt you!'

But Kenn could not go; he was imprisoned.

Because Joe was only on a visit, there was a reluctance in him to hit Kenn, to destroy his friendly, holiday feeling.

'Ach, never mind him,' suggested Angus with his half-derisive smile.

'Go home, man!' said Joe at last, in a tone of contempt, and abruptly turned away.

Kenn followed, but slowly now, and where the wire fence ran through the park, he stopped altogether. His two brothers never looked back and at last disappeared in the birch wood.

There was little feeling in Kenn now, as if all the excitement of the drug had passed and left only the misery. His sobs were spasmodic, a snuffling of tears in the nostrils. His body felt wretched and pummelled, like miry ground that had been trodden on.

Slowly his fingers, plucking at the wire fence, broke and untwisted a strand. Presently he found himself with about two feet of the wire in his hand, walking back towards the barn. He shut himself into the barn and with a stone began hammering out the little twists that were set in the wire at short intervals, pausing now and then to squeeze the wet sniff out of his nostrils. He had no real hope that a snare could be made out of this rough material. But when at last he had formed a little eye at one end and threaded the other end through it, a very natural noose was the result. It 'ran', too, pretty readily. If the rabbit happened to be going at speed, it would be bound to be all right.

In the drained misery of the body, a small point of warmth began to glow. It was growing dark inside the barn. He looked up at the cobwebbed skylight and heard the quiet of the coming evening. As he listened, something in the silence of twilight, that strange, grey silence that so often had had an air of menace or dreadful loneliness, was all at once if not exactly friendly at least beckoning in some intimate way, like a vanishing face.

He opened the door to the daylight and looked outside. There was no one about. A thrush was singing from the top of a tree in the plantation that separated the old barn and the grass park from the houses. There was a touch of green in the blue sky over towards the west; it shone through the wintry branches, making dark patterns of the bare twigs. In the air was a faint smell of the awakening earth, a wintry premonition of spring, like a scent of distant whin fires, not real so much as remembered vaguely from former springs, and, somehow, from springs going far back into time.

Quietened, he cast about him quickly, and soon had the stake that Angus had started whittling when Joe had said that eight snares would do. With his knife he sharpened the point and cut a little groove for the holding cord. In no time he had his snare all ready. He shoved it up under his dark-blue gansey and, closing the door behind him, set out for the birch wood.

He went warily, along by the edge of the plantation of deciduous trees; lingered on the cart road that skirted the birch wood so that anyone could see he was doing nothing in particular. Unnoticeably the wood absorbed him.

Now he was all alive again. As he stood, listening, he could hear the quick soft beat of his heart against near and distant sounds. Then quietly, taking care not to shake the small brown trees, he set off.

The birch wood covered the winding slope that rose from the flat river lands. Presently, well screened, Kenn stood looking down on these lands, on the river itself with its wooded island and its sluice for diverting part of its water into the mill lade, and, beyond the river, on the green braes that formed the opposing slope to what may in remote times have been an inland loch, bottle-necked where both slopes swept towards each other a little distance above the Well Pool.

Except for one woman in black, carrying a hand-basket

of goods from Sans' shop, no one moved on the path that
followed the river. Carefully Kenn's eyes ran along the
twisting wooded slope looking for the slightest sign that
would betray the presence of his brothers. But the trees
were silent.

He did not know where Joe would set to work, as rabbits
burrowed all along the braes, but he knew one or two likely
places where the grassy outrun was full of tracks and very
suitable for unobtrusive snaring.

Keeping to the birches, Kenn began his trek along the
steep slope. His one fear now was that his brothers might
discover him, and when he trod on a rotten stick he
stopped instantly and listened with mouth open so that
even his breathing might not dull his ears. For it would be
unspeakably humiliating to be discovered by his brothers.
He imagined himself coming upon them as they sat hidden
and silent, and could hear not their anger but their derisive
laughter. Moreover, some instinct told him that when they
did reach the selected spot, they would sit down for some
time to 'feel' the security of the place and ensure they had
it to themselves.

Kenn was soon so strung up that his responses to sight
and sound became abnormally acute. In everything, from
the brown twigs and dark-silvered bark to the freshness
of rabbit droppings in new 'scrapes', was a vivid reality,
with the concealed power to surprise and startle. The wood
had to be watched and its grasp avoided, while he passed
through it. In fact his instincts so possessed the wood that
to this day he can walk through it in his mind and feel the
rough bark, see the crooked stem, slip in the brown earth,
smell its exhalation, listen to its silence, and be unable to
know where his own spirit ends and the wood begins.

When the *thud! thud!* of a stone driving home the stake
of a snare fell on his ears, he drew up instantly, and over
his face went a fugitive smile. He had them!

On tiptoe now, with a glee that held its breath, he threaded
his way until he caught sight of them. Then he wormed
himself into a thicket of young hazel.

They were setting their snares in a grassy bay, a secluded spot, just above the wood. They spoke in murmurs as they examined each rabbit track and proceeded to peg and set each snare. Their quiet movements fascinated Kenn. They were like actors in a play, withdrawn into a world of their own. Once Angus pointed with an eager finger; Joe looked and nodded; and Kenn knew that Angus was indicating a new track, still very faint because untrodden by the many, but all the more likely to be fruitful on that account. Then Joe got down on his knees and while the thud-thudding proceeded, Angus looked round on the world he had left.

When they had set all their snares, they turned and came straight towards Kenn, Joe rubbing his palms with a wisp of grass. 'They should be good for one or maybe two,' Joe said quietly as they reached the edge of the wood and swithered for a moment above the earthy declivity where the bank had recently fallen away. If they came to the left they would pass by Kenn's thicket and certainly see him. It was the direct way home. His embarrassment became acute.

'Ach, let's go down by the Intake Pool,' said Joe. 'I haven't been that way for a long time.'

They swung round and, as they passed away, a pellet of earth the size of a marble, reddish brown in colour, trickled down the face of the bank. So keen were Kenn's senses that he seemed to see it actually rock in the earthy face, as if it were being pushed out by a serpent, and then followed it with extreme attention till it came to rest.

He was to remember that pellet of ground when death and its chances had himself as the thing to be snared.

Now with relief so complete that he became detached in a quiet wonder, Kenn began licking his bottom lip and smiling to himself, while his eyes stared at the tiny spots on the hazel wands. He touched the spots with his fingertips. There was no sound anywhere. He looked up through the delicate tracery of the branches at the evening sky. He turned his head over his shoulder. Shadows were creeping into the wood.

He chose his rabbit run or 'roadie' near the crest of a rise, arguing to himself that at such a spot a rabbit would 'keep going'. He also made sure that he was not covering any of Joe's snares. The sound of the thudding frightened him, for the evening was an echoing hollow. He was in the bottom of this hollow pinning it to the ground. The whole wood was listening. But he got the stake in, covered its head with grass, fixed the inner end of the wire in the slot of the 'stickie', poked the stickie into the earth between two leaps of the run, then smoothed out and tilted up the oval noose of the snare. It looked very well, for all the roughness of the grey wire, and he backed away from it, taking care not to leave his scent on the run. Then he turned and made off with such haste that he was at home before his brothers.

'Where have you been?' his mother asked him.

Out of his trousers' pocket he took Joe's penny and handed it to her.

'Who gave you that?' she asked, accepting it.

'Joe.'

'Are you hungry?'

'Yes.'

He watched her put some milk in a pan. She was going to make milk-brose for him. He loved it, and suddenly felt very happy.

That evening he kept his distance from his brothers. But when, amongst other errands, his mother told him to go to the butcher's for a sixpenny bone, the derisive amusement on their faces was very lively.

'Don't take any sort of bone,' suggested Joe solemnly. 'See there's a good bit of meat on it.'

'Shut up!' said Kenn.

'Quiet, you rascal,' said his mother mildly.

Joe and Angus exhibited all the signs of suppressed mirth. They knew how Kenn hated going for the bone. It was a mean and unlordly order. They opened their mouths and chuckled silently.

Kenn's moody anger increased.

But in the morning when Joe smiled to him in a friendly

way and said, 'What about coming to see what's in the
snares?' he could only turn his face away.

'Hsh!' warned Joe, as they heard their father's footsteps.
It was a cloudy but dry Sunday morning. When the way
was clear, he caught Kenn by the ear and led him round
the corner of the house. Angus was already there.

'Come on, boys!' said Joe, and in an instant all the resent-
ments Kenn had been piling up faded away.

They went through the plantation and, after a little scouting, were soon in the birch wood.

'But if we get any rabbits, what'll we do with them, seeing
it's Sunday?' asked Angus.

'Hide them till Monday,' answered Joe.

'But how could we catch them on Monday without setting
the snares on Sunday?' asked Kenn.

For it was wrong to do anything on Sunday, even to go
for long walks. All work, including the brushing of boots,
was done on Saturday night. Sunday was the Lord's Day,
the day of rest. The folk went outside only to feed the brute
beast or attend divine service. Sunday—or 'the Sabbath' as
the old always called it—was different from all week days.
It was a day of sermons and prayer and psalm-singing and
hushed gloom.

How exciting therefore to be going to visit rabbit snares
in order to collect the fruits of poaching! Could anything be
more awful?

But Joe did not seem to care a bit. And though Kenn
knew that all this was wrong, he did not feel that it was evil.
Joe's easy-going, smiling air was friendly and reassuring.

'That can be settled—when we see what we get,' replied
Joe, with a dry humour that made his brothers laugh.

And all the time Kenn had the extra exciting knowledge
of his own snare. If there should be anything in it! How often
already had he imagined a rabbit in his and none in theirs! He
had said to himself, It *might* be. The end of the world *might*
come tomorrow. No one could be *certain* it wouldn't. But
now all he could pray for was that his empty snare might
not be seen. If it was seen, would he try to look astonished?

His beating heart told him he wouldn't succeed. Joe would only have to gaze at him for a moment and he would go all red and guilty.

He could not stand any more derision from his brothers. And his rough fence-wire! They would rock with laughter. They would roll on the grass, pretending to hold their bellies, even though it was Sunday. Indeed Kenn had the awful feeling that everything was intensified because it was Sunday, could in an instant be more reckless and rollicking.

And then they came to the edge of the wood and looked out on the grassy bay where the snares were set.

In after years when Kenn could deal with numbers and the theory of probability, he once amused himself by stating all the factors, and then working out the odds against his own primitive springe. They were so great that he would not seriously expect anyone to believe what did in reality happen. For as they stood on the edge of the wood, Kenn saw that the only snare with a rabbit in it was his own.

Joe's brows were wrinkled. Angus looked puzzled. So used were they to the wild, that they could at any moment have produced a chart of the ground, of each run on it, and of the precise place of each snare.

'That's not ours.' Joe spoke to himself; looked about him with some consternation, a little anxiety. Then he went towards the rabbit. It was a fine heavy brute and from the full-length throw of its body it had obviously killed itself outright.

Joe stooped to the wire. The incredulous look on his face was grotesque. He turned towards his brothers—and saw Kenn's expression. The amazed exclamation died on his lips.

Kenn was deeply flushed. His eyes and fingers were restless. His smile was evasive and nervous. There was a gulping sensation in his throat. His eyes were deep with light as if drenched with dew.

'You?' questioned Joe.

Kenn made an affirmative sound. Joe sat plump on the ground.

To hide his emotion, Kenn tried to shove back the noose, but it had got too deeply entangled in the fur.

'Right to the bone!' Joe was so astonished he could hardly chuckle. He questioned Kenn; got the story out of him; and then lay back and laughed. Angus laughed too. They teased Kenn. They were delighted with the whole thing.

Kenn could see that Joe was proud of him.

It was a lovely morning. The grey of the sky was a soft spring mist that might part like a veil. The grey Sabbath gloom had vanished from the world. The trees were alive and their breath aromatic. The dampness of the earth was like the wet on Kenn's lips. Birds chirped and sang. He had never known that a Sabbath could be a real day in this sweet, secret way.

It was arranged that Kenn should carry the rabbit into the back kitchen and hide it in a corner. But when this was done, Joe and Angus could not suppress the dangerous fun of going as near as possible to the point of telling their mother what had happened without actually touching it. Their father they took care to avoid.

But from the hints of the night before and out of a knowledge of the poaching ways of her sons, the mother gradually divined the truth. She let it be known that any conduct approaching that which had been hinted at would be unthinkable on the Sabbath day, and that nothing arising out of it could be brought into her house.

'What's that you're saying?' demanded the father, fixing his starched collar, his hair on end.

'I don't know,' she said. 'I don't know what they've been up to.'

'What?' He looked at them suspiciously.

'Nothing.' Joe smiled, turning away. 'Kenn just took us a little walk. That was all.'

His father looked sternly at Kenn. Joe winked to Angus.

'Where were you?' demanded the father.

'Nowhere,' muttered Kenn.

'You'd better hurry up, the whole of you, or you'll be late for church,' the mother said.

And in that moment of time, Kenn knew not only that she was aware of what he had done and was shielding him, but also that when the rabbit was produced on the morrow she would accept it. And there and then was born in him a deep understanding of his mother, of something in her that transcended the religious observances in which she believed, that was bigger than place or time because it recognised the inexorable nature of the needs of daily life.

This impression, felt at the time as something that would free him from unhappy consequences, gathered its mythological value as the years went on, until now he can see her as the mother that abides from everlasting to everlasting.

Throughout that winter—throughout all winters—she was in truth the figure that tended the fire and dispensed life, and must often have created her bounty out of material resources so slender that their management assumed in Kenn's thought an air half-magical.

For he has no clear memory of actual need or want; and certainly has none of the associations that must surely have been born out of destitution. Indeed the material anxieties that his parents must have had seem somehow to have made no impression upon him. Always one had only to ask one's mother for food and the food would be there. Nor was there any pretence or undue concealment indulged in by his parents in the matter of running the home. There is perhaps something a little mysterious in this, and yet he imagines that he understands it at least to some extent. For it was all part of a way of life, in which with the winter supply of a few simple, cheap foods—oatmeal, potatoes, milk, fish—the bodily cravings, keyed by hunger, were met and satisfied, and often so completely that the memory of a meal can take on something in the nature of a pagan mass, where the eyes glance and smile out of the heart of life, the teeth flash, and all the senses are servitors.

It requires little effort of imagination on Kenn's part now to watch his mother after she saw them off to church with their pennies or half-pennies for 'the plate'.

She would stand for a time looking at them to see they were decently turned out; then she would go back into the empty house.

Thoughtfully she would fix the peats on end, until the flame was concentrated under the great black pot wherein the sixpenny bone was giving sweetness to the soup. Always on Sunday there was a special dinner; a heavy dinner, at which they all gorged themselves a little.

From the cooking fire she would go, still thoughtfully, into the back kitchen, there to stand a moment and cast her eyes about.

She is wondering now if the rabbit is actually here and, if so, where. Quietly she moves a tub and a herring basket, stoops under a low shelf, looks behind pots and pans, considers the coiled mass of a handline, and at last lifts the old bag in the corner. She contemplates the rabbit steadily, then puts the bag back, and so deep is her thought now that she goes to the back door and stares out. Some of the hens see her and come scurrying hopefully.

Without looking at them and without any impatience, she shoos them away.

The expression on her face is one of wise contemplation. There is something in it like the memory of a smile or the memory of kindness, but so elusively that it does no more than suggest character.

Her eyes, grey and wide-spaced, are lifted towards the trees of the plantation. Her straight dark hair is parted smoothly midway over her pale smooth forehead, and caught back behind the ears, so that the ears, flat to the head and shapely, are seen. All her features are shapely; and the skin has that unlined fullness that suggests the word comely.

Her heavy body is neither unshapely nor billowing, but is deep-bosomed and solid, and stands with quiet poise.

So vividly does Kenn become aware of her presence that he finds himself looking where she is looking as though he might glimpse the thing she sees. But the trees are quiet, save for the odd notes of birds, little twists of song, like twists of crystal water in sunlight. There is no sunlight, however. Beyond the trees the sky is grey, with the greyness not of wet clouds but of smoke, of distant promise. There is a soft warmth descending from it and penetrating the earth so that life stirs there in its sleep.

That is all she can see, and it is nothing strange. There is perhaps something a little strange in the silence that enfolds everything and that is only made all the clearer for the isolated bird notes and the croaking of a hen. But it is not the sort of silence one wants to listen to, any more than is the suggestion of immense distance in the dark moor-horizon the sort of thing one wants to stare at. For by listening and staring hard enough, one may become a little uncomfortable over one does not know what, as though Something might come quietly up over the hills of space that are also the hills of time, and suddenly be there before one (it being the Sabbath day) like the Spirit of God.

But a glance back at his mother's face and the fear that accompanies every thought of God vanishes. So quiet and contemplative and abiding she is, that from the shelter of her skirts one may brave God and all the unknown and terrifying things that go back beyond the hills to the ends of the earth and the beginnings of time.

All the history of her people is writ on her face. The grey seas are stilled in her eyes; danger and fear are asleep in her brows; want's bony fingers grow warm at her breast; quietly against the quiet trees the struggle of the days lies folded in her hands.

He can see her there in the moment of calm between struggle and struggle; in his generation and in the generation before, and far back beyond that till the ages are lost in the desert and she becomes the rock that throws its shadow in a weary land.

But he does not know what she is thinking.

And yet in the fugitive glimmerings of vision out of which the pattern of thought is woven, he can see himself away down on the field of her mind as a very tiny figure bringing his gift of the rabbit to the store that must never be empty or she and he and all mankind will pass away. And because of the impulse that moves him to do this, and of his love in doing it and his pride, he believes the glimmering spider-thread of his path is essential to the whole pattern, more essential in the ultimate, perhaps, than any observances of church or creed; and profoundly in her, without exercise of reason or logic, he believes his mother apprehends this, and bears the burden of it—as she bears the burden of all mortal things— against the earth and against the sky.

A quiet sigh breaks her abstraction and she turns away among the known things of her household; a short cough behind her closed lips has something in it of acceptance; her lips part in an unconscious 'Yes'; and at the sound she stirs with a practical movement as if about to utter the familiar words, 'Come away, bairns, to your food.'

But the house is empty, and, as the quietude of her mood is still upon her, she goes to the front door and looks forth on the folk going to church.

The church lies beyond the school in the middle distance of the slope of crofting land that rises slowly and irregularly to the horizon some two miles away.

Along the roads and pathways figures, singly or in twos and threes, are slowly converging on the place of worship. They are all dressed respectably in black. She cons their names to herself, for her eyesight is good, and in any case she knows the scattered houses they have come out of. 'That is George Sinclair, and the boy, and the girl Mary—though it seems big for her.' She sees the stocky figure of Alick Manson of the loud voice—with his young family some distance behind him. The shepherd from Bunessan, though far away, can be distinguished by his walk. Little groups from crofting townships on both sides of the strath have their individual characteristics, and she thinks of them in terms perhaps of one or two women who call on her or of a man among them who may drive peats and be well known and liked. Up over the steep rise from the harbour, 'the shore folk' are now appearing. 'There is a good turnout today.' She recognises this figure and that, but is occasionally a little doubtful, and her mind wanders among questions of illness and recovery, and wonders with a touch of pity or of calm acceptance. Her husband and her three sons are getting on towards the school. Her eyes find them now and then with a remote detached pleasure. It is good to have your men folk going quietly to church; to have nothing in the family to be ashamed of. It is the goodness above all for which one should be thankful; for what success or position or worldly wealth can be weighed in the balance against 'a bad name'?

The feeling of this goodness flows over her like soft bright air.

Soon the church has drawn all the dark figures into itself and left the landscape empty.

During the sermon and the singing and the prayers she goes quietly about her business of preparing the Sunday dinner. They will be hungry when they come home and she is glad to have her son Joe with her. He looked well today in his new navy-blue suit. . . .

Kenn wonders now why it is that she rarely went to church—until it occurs to him to consider other mothers of families in the neighbourhood, and to realise, with some surprise, that very few of them went.

The main excuse would doubtless be that they had the house—and perhaps a young child or two—to look after and the dinner to cook.

But he is certain there was something more to it than that, something of age-old custom. She need not go to church and yet no harm will come to her. In man's spiritual aspiration, she is forgotten or ignored. In his ascetic moments, she is seen darkened with passion, soiled with the pain of creation, bearing the burden of sin. So long has she been outside the mysteries and cults and secret associations man has made for his own pleasure and importance, that she is beyond the ethic of each age and every age, as life itself is, and continues as life continues, and endures as the hills endure. Possibly it was some such dim apprehension of her state that made Kenn conceive of her as being from everlasting to everlasting.

And if there appears to be mystery here, in the woman's

own mind there is no mystery. Kenn's mother did not go to
communion on the Sabbath of the Sacrament simply because
she believed she was not worthy. Never in her life did she
sit at communion table, never broke the bread nor drank
the wine. She had done nothing to make herself unworthy.
She was seen in her life as a good woman and without
reproach.

Yet she believed herself unworthy and accepted her condition in the calm spirit with which she had turned away from
the back door and gone to the front to see the worshippers
drawn into the church.

It was a humility that was never confessed, as if the core
of it were a shyness delicate as the compassion of Christ.

Neither, however, did her husband, who attended church
regularly, go to communion. When the tables were being
'fenced' by the ministers, he and his brother seamen remained
in their seats, worshipping with prayer and praise. When
shots of herring had been plentiful and the quays of Stornoway or Castlebay or Wick had been quick with life, they
had looked on the whisky when it was raw and sang and
dared and danced. They knew their lives in the past had
not contained enough solemnity of holiness to justify them
in going forward to the tables. They were in act and fact not
good enough. And should a drop of whisky come their way
at any time they would, God help them, not pass it by.

They worshipped decently and quietly, strong incurious
men, with no envy in their hearts. To this position they
had been called and they would maintain it without fear;
and if their church had been a vessel in distress, with the
bread and wine its cargo, they would there and then have
undertaken to navigate it through the brimstone loch of
hell, and on getting a fair discharge would have set off
again for another shot, leaving respectfully the elders, and
the holy widows, and the old maids to the glory of the
Kingdom.

Kenn has promised himself that sometime he will try to
find out how it came about that Jesus had fishermen for his
disciples; though it may be difficult to contemplate, without

a smile, the Loch of Galilee over against the thunder of the northern seas.

If it may thus appear that woman was outside the mystery, at which her husband at least assisted, the final scene of that Sabbath comes back into Kenn's mind with an odd mixture of amused excitement and reverence.

His mother is sitting in her hard chair by one side of the fire; his father, at the opposite side, has induced a mood of silence and preparation.

'Let us take the Books,' he says, in a voice withdrawn from them. He turns over the pages of the big Bible. 'Let us read the eleventh chapter of the Gospel according to St John.'

When they have all got the place in the small print Bibles, he looks at Kenn the youngest, who starts and hurriedly mutters through the first verse: *Now a certain man was sick, named Lazarus, of Bethany, the town of Mary and her sister Martha.*

In a clear voice, Joe reads the second verse; and is followed, sunwise, by his father, his mother, and Angus.

Now this is the chapter that contains the shortest verse in the Bible, namely, *Jesus wept*. It is verse thirty-five. It has always been a game amongst the boys that it is hard luck to get a long verse or one with difficult names and embarrassing to get one dealing with certain bodily organs or acts. But to get the shortest verse in the Bible is to score.

There was a certain shyness and fear about this public reading. When Kenn had got over his first verse, he immediately began 'counting out' to find the lucky one. Angus, who had been quicker on the count, was waiting for him, and, closing his left eye, shoved out his tongue.

The droll mockery excited Kenn irresistibly. Joe nudged him with his knee. He stumbled so badly over his next verse that his father looked at him. He grew red and terribly confused.

The reading went on. Twice Angus coughed importantly. *And said, Where have ye laid him? They said unto him, Lord, come and see*, said his mother.

Jesus wept, said Angus.

There was silence.

Kenn's mother sat quiet and aloof. She did not even look at her young son. Correction here lay with the man of the house.

Kenn gulped—*Then said the Jews*—and gulped again—*Behold how he loved him!*

While his father was still looking at him, his eyes whipping-angry under ridged brows, Joe quietly read the next verse.

Kenn did not look up. Tears were not far away. Then he heard his father's voice going on as if nothing had happened.

His shame was held by a strange and petulant fear. He could not look up; could not look anywhere. The figure of Jesus, weeping.

Joe had read on to cover him up. And then his father. There was that bigness about them. And though he saw this, he resented it, too.

The reading of the chapter over, his father meditated a little while, then turned to the twenty-third psalm. *The Lord's my shepherd, I'll not want. . . .*

While he read the psalm, the fingers of his free hand crushed audibly against the rough skin of the palm. His voice was charged with fervour, and his head moved as if he were telling the lines to himself in a lonely place.

He finished and there was silence.

The mother was sitting upright in her hard chair, the Bible closed on her lap, her face towards the fire. Without a movement of her body she began singing the psalm.

These first notes of his mother's voice always had a strange effect on Kenn. They were balanced and unhurried; they sang with grace and calm; their rhythm entered his breast, took possession of it on a surging swell, surging upward and out of him, on great, slow, expanding rings, till the floor of heaven itself was circled and sustained.

After a little time, Kenn joined in, his voice moody and muttering, but gradually thinning and growing clear, yet never quite winning free of the jealous burden of self-consciousness. When the singing ended, they all got down on their knees on the stone floor, put their elbows on their chairs, and bowed their heads.

His father prayed for a long time, and he prayed well and fluently and without a pause or stutter. There were phrases that he used every Sunday night; favoured quotations from the Bible were frequent and apt; yet the whole was always a new creation.

It could not be otherwise and come so winged from the heart. In the urgency of his supplication, his voice rose and fell. The power of God was like the power of the sea. He had to navigate the sea, to cry out in the storm, to be quick in his flesh and his spirit if he were not to founder in the wrath to come.

The heart of the seaman in utter humility, open and laid bare, was yet the heart of the seaman who, lashed to his tiller in a winter's storm, fought the real sea with a grim and even exultant courage. There were stories of seas fought through that brought the shiver to Kenn's spine.

The abiding calm of his mother, old as the earth; the cleaving force of his father, like the bow of his boat.

Kenn became aware of the stealthy movement of Angus's body. But even in the very moment of making up his mind that he would not look at him, he turned his head and at his brother's mockery stuck out his tongue to the root. Then, feeling better, he bowed his head again.

'. . . and all we ask is in Thy name. AMEN.'

SPRING CAME IN one morning with a spring salmon. Kenn spotted it from the high coping of the bridge, told Beel, and let all the scholars pass to school. Beel did not believe it was a salmon, saying he thought it was the edge of a stone with green slime. But when they went down to the river they found that it was in truth a salmon. With wings to his heels, Kenn flew home for two hooks.

When he returned, Beel was trimming the second stick. 'You take that one,' whispered Beel, 'and tie on the hook hard so that it won't turn.' When the gaffs were ready, he added, 'I'll take him just below the head—you above the tail. When I say Go!—pull.'

No one was to be seen from under the arch of the bridge. Beel got down on hands and knees. Kenn followed.

Slowly their sticks went out over the fish, touched the water, and sank down, down until the hook was hidden by the curve of the body.

'Pull!' said Beel, and he himself pulled and landed clean on his back, his hook having glanced off the hard scales. While he was yet on his back the fish landed with a great wet walloping on his stomach, and Kenn on top of the fish, his hook still embedded, and the freed stick whacking the stones. Through the tumult, Kenn fought for the gills and got his hold. 'Hit him now!' he cried.

Beel hit him on the back of the head with a stone.

It was a nice fish of about eleven pounds, clean run, a hen fish with a lovely small head. Its beauty, dead, frightened them a little.

Kenn undid his trousers, and Beel, lifting the fish, stuck it tail-down against his bare leg; then Kenn pulled up his trousers over the lower part of the fish and spread his jersey over the top part. From under his arm to his knee the cold wet fish was like a gigantic splint. But Kenn did not feel it cold as he went carefully along the grass, holding it in position by pressure of arms and hands.

'No one would ever notice anything,' said Beel, walking close beside him.

'Are you sure?' But behind their earnest whispered talk, Kenn was exultant.

He had seen the salmon, when Beel had not seen it; he had landed it, when Beel had missed.

They hid the fish among the salleys, and, as they were topping the brae, heard the school bell.

Sweating and breathless, they arrived to find the classroom door closed. Boldly Beel opened it and Kenn followed him across the floor before the rows of scholars and the gaze of the headmaster.

But the bible reading had not actually started. Nothing was said.

Kenn had done his home lessons. It turned out a memorable and blessed day. The way in which Kenn and Beel stuck together in the playground or smiled esoterically to each other across the benches was so flagrantly odious in the eyes of their class mates that a fight was arranged between Jeck Munro and Kenn.

Jeck had all the omens against him, however, including a weak nose. The only science in the fighting game was to stand up to your opponent and hit him hard and as often as possible. Before the engagement had right started Kenn landed full pelt on Jeck's nose. The blood gushed.

'Ah ye big coward!' screamed Martha, Jeck's sister, at Kenn, her blue eyes flaming with fight. She came towards him, one flaxen pigtail whipping round her throat.

Kenn backed away, giving her his shoulder.

Beel raked a sarcastic 'Ho! Ho!' at her. Maddened, she swung round on him. Beel took to his heels, laughing affectedly, leapt on to the wall, pivoted on his chest, and was gone.

Mocking laughter came up over the wall.

Kenn joined him on the crest of the brae and they swayed in their mirth, pushed each other with weak arms, and could be heard a long way off.

They went home together, carrying the tantalising mystery with them. In many a township that night, boys singly or in little groups wondered jealously what it could have been.

In the first of the dark Kenn and Beel squatted among the salleys. The silver had dulled and the fish was stiff as a board. A blackbird scolded in a bush.

In the listening quiet of the twilight, Beel opened his knife and measured the fish with his eye.

There. Or perhaps there. There, say.

He cut through the tough skin, opened out the red flesh, came on the bone. The bone finally cracked and, bloodied from the guts, Beel severed the neat tail portion from the stumpy head. While he wiped his knife and his hands, he said, 'You can spit on the stone.'

Kenn took a small flat stone from his pocket and spat on one side of it. Then he spun the stone in the air and for a moment their uplifted faces were pale in the grey light. 'Dry!' said Beel. The stone landed and rolled downward. They followed it, rooting among the salleys. The dry side was uppermost.

Beel chose the tail. Through Kenn went a bitter pang, and, as they walked back across the river flat, the evening drained thinly away through his fingers.

But he found his mother liked the head portion just as well as the other; to her there was no difference. The neatness, the pretty shape of the tail portion was thus lifted and lost in an ampler good. Kenn felt its further horizon break on him as if he himself had been lifted up.

And so his happiness returned and ran secretly in him again.

As he thought over the day's doings in the nest of his bed, he was full of glee. 'Hah-haa!' he breathed, wide-mouthed; he constricted and blinded himself with his mirth; turned in upon himself like an adder, seeking the central core of himself, so that he might burrow into that, crush his laughing mouth against it, and go blind in the last tension of fun.

Then he drew back, open-mouthed and listening, like a troll, and heard nothing in the world but the river.

Contract and expand, systole and diastole: the river flows. The river! In the night of the world. Listen!

He burrowed again, wrinkling his nose. For it was not the salmon, nor the fight, nor the thousand practical incidents of the past day that reared the fun in him. It was that he had seen where Beel the lynx-eyed had not seen, and had succeeded where Beel the leader had failed.

His own personality rose out of the river within him. He was a little shy of it, as he might be of some dark boy-stranger with a waiting smile.

He turned his head away, silently laughing. In the middle of laughing he fell asleep.

CHAPTER TEN

LOOKING BACK ON HIS CHILDHOOD, Kenn finds, is looking back on a small figure in a sunny valley. The birch and hazel trees that clothe the sides of the valley are in full leaf; the green river-flats, widening and narrowing and disappearing round bends, are moss-soft to noiseless feet. The white scuts of the rabbits disappear in bracken clumps or sandy burrows or up under the foliage of trees. A hawk sails from one side of the valley to the other; inland, a buzzard circles high up over a gulch where rock faces stare.

A shot is heard faintly towards the high ground and the small figure stops and listens. That must be Gordon the keeper working the low ground in towards Con na Craige. Wild cats had been coming in from the Sutherland mountains and he had been setting traps for them. He also had traps for the hawks and the eagles.

All of which meant that Gordon was not on the river that day!

The strath is emptied of his presence, drained of the fear of him, and the little figure takes a small run, full of eagerness and the thrill of freedom.

He wanders, he stops, he peers into pools, he pokes under stones, he examines rabbit burrows, he listens, he looks about him, he wanders on.

From high overhead the river in its strath must look like a mighty serpent, the tip of its tail behind the mountain, its open mouth to the sea.

It is easy at such a thought to mount still higher over the small figure, to rise above the buzzard, and with circling sweep to scan that whole northland.

A thrill comes to Kenn as his eye takes in feature after

feature, the shores of the Moray Firth, with all its villages and towns, every name charged with association, thick with the texture of life, Fraserburgh, Buckie, Burghead, Cromarty (the place of refuge), Tarbat Ness, Dornoch, Golspie, Brora, Helmsdale, and passing away nor'-east through Lybster to Wick.

At a glance Kenn can take in the whole steel-shimmering triangle of the Moray Firth. Each of its sides is barely seventy miles. For its size it is one of the finest breeding grounds of fish—and perhaps of men—to be found in any firth of the seven seas. Since the birth of his grandfather, its story to Kenn is intricate with the doings of men and women, legendary or known to him. The rocks are quiet enough today. Even the headlands are stretched out in sleep. But Kenn smiles, knowing the rocks and the headlands, and that innocent shimmer of the quiet water like a virgin shield!

As he wheels slowly, the great plain of Caithness opens before his eyes and the smile that had been in them deepens with affection. This is the northland, the land of exquisite light. Lochs and earth and sea pass away to a remote horizon where a suave line of pastel foothills cannot be anything but cloud. Here the actual picture is like a picture in a supernatural mind and comes upon the human eye with the surprise that delights and transcends memory. Gradually the stillness of the far prospect grows unearthly. Light is silence. And nothing listens where all is of eternity.

Pride quickens the smile. This bare, grim, austere Caithness, treeless, windswept, rock-bound, hammered by the sea, hammered, too, by successive races of men, broch-builders and sea-rovers, Pict and Viking. Against the light, Kenn veils his eyes, and wheeling round sees the Orkneys anchored in the blue seas with the watermark of white on their bows. Brave islands, he feels like saluting them with a shout.

Westward yet, and the granite peaks of Ben Laoghal, the magic mountain, beckon towards Cape Wrath and the Arctic.

Westward still, and all the dark mountains of Sutherland march on Ben Mor Assynt, beyond which is the Atlantic and the Isles of the west.

Kenn completes the circle and his vision narrows on the winding strath beneath him, upon its skyey thread of water that links mountain to sea, west to east; the strath where all he has seen is given living shape and desire; and suddenly closing his wings, he stoops upon the moving figure on the river bank.

But the small figure does not hear the singing ecstasy in the wings; has no knowledge of the eyes that presently peer at him, noting with scientific care every breath of expression, each detail of the face, the dark hair cut across the forehead, the long thin hands and thin wrists, the bare legs and feet. The eyes are hazel brown, with flecks in them, and—this is surprising but instantly right—full of a glancing light of apprehension.

For Kenn had forgotten the fear, the wonder, the sudden heart-beat, the strangeness, the sense of adventure, the ominous quality in known things when encountered in lonely places. He had forgotten what it really was to be young. He had thought it more carefree and golden, more reckless and laughing and thoughtless.

This young figure is not only intensely but mysteriously preoccupied. For one whole half minute he stands staring at the tip of a drooping twig which his finger nails tear bit by bit. Slowly he turns his head to one side with an odd self-conscious expression, as if expecting someone to come round the corner of the bank.

Is he carrying on a conversation with Beel? Is he the hero in an imaginary poaching raid? What makes the skin—so smooth, so tender—seem suddenly to darken shyly, as if thought had been overheard? The lips part as he listens. Something fainter than a smile quivers in his lashes, and the half minute ends in a quick stepping away.

Kenn watches and follows him, and finds him resting in the shelter of some trees near the Lodge Pool. He is excited now lest he be seen. He has never been so far up the river before. Tentatively he steps out on the smooth green bank to look at the pool.

Kenn waits in the trees watching him with profound attention, for the little figure out there is himself.

It is natural to have a sudden access of love for the little figure, of pity for it, to want to lay hands on its shoulders and whisper, 'Don't you know me, Kenn?' With a smile, for affection was never easy.

When everything is said, that figure and himself are all he can be sure of. The rest, however near and dear, are alien.

Kenn suddenly feels this with extraordinary force. He apprehends its truth in a flash of vision. Green trees shut them off and straths and silence. They are forever isolated. The line between them is their line, and when they take it into familiar places it remains itself.

The small boy is adventuring now along a line—already covered in every minutest detail of thought and deed by the grown man who is watching him. Memory balks at that a little. There are things in it—the hospital voice, 'Christ, mate, you've got an eyeful.' . . . Not only the deeds, though. Not merely the things endured, the things seen, the appalling agonies, the senseless treacheries, the wild brutal fun, not the merely obvious common things, but the things of extreme intimacy, of the innermost spirit, that . . . .

Kenn grows awkward, flushing a little. When he looks for the little boy he is gone.

CHAPTER ELEVEN

AFTER THE KILLING of the spring salmon, a particular intimacy sprang up between Kenn and Beel. There was little personal affection in it. Each was like a dog that will wander away from its home only when it can persuade the other dog to go with it. It was not a friendship so much as a secret league.

As the spring days lengthened, they began to haunt the river and its banks and the wooded slopes of the strath where the rabbits burrowed. The shortness of the daylight after school hours did not permit of long adventures, nor did the season of the year, for the trees were still bare and indeed all nature seemed more sunken in death than at any time during the winter.

This impression of death in the earth is a curiously intimate memory and accordingly one that was probably not consciously observed at the time. From an exciting point of view, it is perhaps a pity that the things which made the deepest impression were hardly noticed. Jealousy, anger, fighting, hours of thrilling interest or bitter restraint, fun and tears and shame—when Kenn slips back he sees that their pattern is superficial, that only rarely—as in the realisation of his own emergent personality after the spring salmon incident—did they make him penetrate the surface to be touched unforgettably on the quick.

When Kenn meets one of his boyhood friends now, a great deal of pleasure and laughter is got out of retailing old, exciting ploys. He recognises the element of pure fun in this and indeed loves it. It can be made, of course, nostalgic and sentimental, and there was a time when he resented this, when his instinct urged an impatient turn-away from the touch

of the familiar hand. But now he does not mind so much
the facile, Do you remember? It may even invoke a 'poetic'
inflection, go a trifle soft and mawkish, and still provide
the substance for a lingering smile, a cool, remembering
humour. And that because, when most pronounced, it is
the froth thrown up by the strange, persistent ferment that
is buried so deep in the tissues of life and that he would like to
search out if he could. This is the indication that the speaker
'remembers'. Remembers what? Clearly not the mere action
which he describes, often so unexceptional that an outsider
would be unimpressed, but a something of background and
heredity, that now imparts even to the memory of the action
an eagerness, an excitement, a mirth, that is the fine essence
of delight.

It is this thing behind the action, this secret moving power,
that Kenn now dimly glimpses. It is the important thing, and
the sentimental froth merely indicates its presence.

There was a sharp spell of snow and frost towards the end
of February. The thaw was dark and raw and colder than
the frost. Everywhere the ground was swollen and here and
there it was spewed up. The effect was as if the earth had
been drowned. Long grey grasses lay flattened against the
washed peaty banks. In fields, by roadsides, on river flats,
were tiny high-water marks of brown leaves, twigs, and bits
of grass—short, nibbled bits as if the deluge had searched
out and dispersed even the nests of mice. The moss was
sodden and dotted with the droppings of sheep and rabbits
in astonishing numbers.

Beads of manure on the drowned land. Bare trees, fallen
branches, rotten stumps with spawn of toadstool crushing
away from the foot, tumbled stones of prehistoric dwellings
grey with lichen, and the bitter rain-spitting wind.

The passing beyond death into disintegration.

The matter that was left was a black infertile ooze into
which Kenn, cold and miserable under the spitting rain,
slowly pushed a pebble with his toe, burying it incuriously,
as if his boyish mind were self-hypnotised.

What pleasure could there have been in this? What quality

at all beyond that of sheer, staring, shivering misery? And when Beel and himself took shelter in a cave or a Pictish dwelling or some dung-smelling byre and gazed out on this dead world, what was it made them feel, at such a time more even than at any other, that they would rather be where they were than in the warmth of a home kitchen? When they jigged about to make the blood flow and stop their teeth from chittering, they sang out in glee. It was at such a moment that they smoked or chewed tobacco or cut their initials in stone or wood.

But mostly they would lean against the entrance wall and stare out and spit (in competition) and talk seriously of what a hero had done in the past or of what they themselves would do to some high pool in the summer and boast and fall silent again, staring at the sodden flanks of the earth.

How insidious the chronic habit of personifying the earth! The mire of negation is a conception not so readily held without some schooling. Kenn can now walk outside any town on a raw February day and have the conception at once. The smallest things throw his mind back to the cave days. Whether it is finally going to be burial or cremation does not much matter, should the mind trouble to debate the point. Both fashions have been in force since the beginning of human time. It does not matter to Kenn now because he understands the mire, or rather because somehow or other his bones and flesh apprehend it. They are privy to it and would rather (social considerations not interfering with choice) pass back into it again.

With understanding has come liberation and friendliness.

And accordingly there is no suggestion at all in his mind during such a debate of the morbid, not even when the debate is solitary.

And the debate has more visual knowledge to go on than has been suggested here, for at this time of the year— the lean, unflowering, unburied time—carcases and bits of carcases are commonly found, each supplying its own abrupt and tragic story.

The carcases putrefy and decay leaving clean bones that

Kenn and Beel may throw at each other in summer fields. Time deals with decay evenly, and all the mess of blood and flesh is resumed into the black aseptic ooze.

Into the timelessness in which the great ball of the earth revolves and circles and drives onward into space, lit by sunlight and moonlight and starlight, towards an end or an endlessness of which no slightest glimmer reaches us.

And so in some way past comprehending, the small boy sticking his toe in the mire of the drowned earth becomes one with the grown-up scientist watching that same earth from an astronomical point above it and wondering, as he stares in front of him, Whither? and, occasionally, Why?

That there should be a thrill for Kenn behind this he recognises as the most subtle of the mysteries. The legendary white flower on the dark root.

Now and then it blossoms into a moment of ineffable delight, and then, in a way felt upon the face, humility is known as the divine name for courage.

The early part of spring was a time of premonition and magic. None of the boys could say who told them that the moment had arrived for the heath fires or 'falishes'. But when the word falishes was spoken, its soft syllables came from some *beyond* of the mind, followed by an inrush of excitement, an impulse to dash off shouting Hurrah! To some such impulse birds on the wing wheel and check, swoop together and fly on.

Between the mill and the Broch, well in from the river on a slope to the right, was a stretch of ground that had never been cultivated. It was too rough even for sheep grazing, and whin grew on it in impassable profusion. In spring the withered undergrowth of the bushes was grey and dry as tinder. When a match was put to it, the flame ran up crackling, spread sideways, and, with the wind, melted inward in a shriek. In a few moments the whole bush was throwing tongues of flame upon the air. But a boy did not wait to watch the spectacle. As soon as Kenn had fired one bush, he dashed with a burning branch to the next. The desire was to light every bush, to light the whole place, to send it shrieking upward in flame, in tearing sheets of flame, to consume it utterly. A madness of competition grew amongst the boys. They rushed in and out the flames and the smoke wreaths, shouting at the top of their voices, boasting wildly, eyeballs glistering, faces scorched, in an orgy of fire-raising.

Sometimes a swirl of flame in an eddying wind sent them staggering back. Lifted heads faced the tremendous crackling, the torn sheets, the inward shriek, and shrieked back, Hurrah!

The fire became a lust in the blood. They danced, throwing their arms about; they leapt daringly through flame on outer edges; they appeared, choking, from voluting smoke. Personal names and challenges went up with the flames, screamed from reddened, stinging faces smudged with soot.

In the end they stood back, exhausted, and gazed on what they had created.

There was no rivalry amongst them now, as though what they had really been challenging was something beyond themselves; and even the names they had cried had been cried at the fire.

Kenn wanted to say to Beel, 'Isn't it a great fire?' but something kept him silent.

They bunched together, their faces lit by the vast glow. In the devouring maw a live rabbit would sizzle like a green leaf. Smoke rose from it in a great twisting column; rose upwards into the air and sideways out upon the crofting lands; hazed the farthest reaches of the upland, darkening them as with the coming of night.

The afternoon was fading into evening. Near the edges of the smoke, above the fields, peewits, like blown pieces of burnt paper, heeled and tumbled.

There are two scents and two sounds that have for Kenn a more quickening response than any others: the scent of the heath fire and of the primrose; the cry of the peewit and of the curlew.

The scent of the heath fire has in it something quite definitely primordial. Involuntarily it evokes immense perspectives in human time; tribes hunting and trekking through lands beyond the horizons of history. Indeed by its aid he can see more clearly how man lived before civilization came upon him than for long periods after it did. It is very difficult to describe this curious responsiveness. The usual associative excuses are here not enough. Many scents and smells were familiar to Kenn as a boy: peat smoke, for example. In truth, peat smoke was far more familiar to him, and had been sniffed daily by himself and his forebears back into prehistory. But when he returns from the coal fires of the south and gets his first whiff of peat, he is not affected in the primordial way. Peat smoke has its own intimate associations; but at the core they are social and have to do with place. Heath smoke is an affair of time; of family or communal life through immense stretches of time. Its colour is the bloom of mountains on a far horizon—particularly in that evening light which is so akin to the still light of inner vision.

It was the evening light through which Beel and Kenn and the others turned away, their muscles drowsy from the frenzied exercise, their minds floating like islands upon a state of being nebulous and intimate and happy. They made jokes and laughed easily. The jokes were against others, not themselves. They were a remembering of awkward gestures, of falls, of surprised yells. They felt an access of affection for those at whom they laughed. Their minds were full of beneficence.

The heath fire and the primrose: the two scents were jotted down by Kenn as simple facts of experience, without any idea of a relationship between them.　And then suddenly, while the mind was lifting to the cold bright light of spring, to the blue of birds' eggs and the silver of the first salmon run, there came out of the tangle on a soft waft of air the scent of primroses.

An instant, and it was gone, leaving a restlessness in the breast, an urgency that defeats itself, an apprehension, almost agonising, of the ineffectiveness of the recording machine. Finally nothing is jotted down and the mind is left exhausted.

It recovers by and by and wonders whether it got the scent at all.

And it is prepared to wonder because of the gleams that flickered over the recording machine. The machine stumbles on in its crude attempts to capture them, for much the same reason, perhaps, as little Kenn, in the winter snows, wanted to catch the green linnet.

But the grown Kenn knows quite exactly one quality in the scent of the primrose for which he has an adjective. The adjective is innocent. The innocency of dawn on a strath on a far back morning of creation. The freshness of dawn wind down a green glen where no human foot has trod. If the words sound vague, the pictures they conjure up for Kenn's inner eye are quite vivid. The grasses and green leaves in the clear morning light have a quality of alertness like pointed ears. And they sway alive and dancing-cool and deliciously happy.

But he cannot steal the elusive scent nor the feel of the five petals, however he crush them against nostrils and mouth. He has very early memories of pulling the flower out of its calyx and nibbling its stem as he often did the stems of clover for honey.

But there is no honey taste in the primrose.

He cannot intrude upon the primrose without crushing and bruising it. He cannot take it from itself. It is at once near as the mind and remote as the dawn vision it evokes.

Its colour, too, has a haunting quality: the primrose yellow which man, dimly remembering through the dark aeons of city civilizations, gets his machines to hammer out into beaten gold.

Thus the relationship between the primrose and the heath fire is not so much the relationship between man and nature, as that relationship at a particular stretch of time on this earth, the stretch which solitary voices through all subsequent ages and races have called 'the golden age'.

Nor would all that have been worth writing about primrose scent had it not, in one of those chance flashes that the mind is subject to, presented a certain kind of evidence of the existence once upon a time of the golden age.

For the heirs of brutal savages, the inheritors of brutish instincts, whence this troubling vision of primrose dawns and wood fires, of fleet running and laughter, whence the mounting effect of it all to a flame-bright ecstasy?

There is no denying that however it comes about, whatever the cause, such a state of happiness is produced. Kenn has experienced it over and over again. He has deliberately gone back to his Highland river to experience it afresh. And the wider his general knowledge grows, the more exacting his scientific researches are, the farther from youth he travels, the surer his responses become.

Further, there is in it all a curious personal secretiveness. This secretiveness is often full of the sliest laughter. It is a laughter out of the corner of the mouth, the corner of the eye, at all that which solemnly in its social toils would deny it. It is the suppressed laughter of a superb, secret joke. And not always suppressed! There are lonely places in the higher reaches of Kenn's river where he need no longer suppress it. Nor does he. Only if he is stalking a salmon in a pool must he close his teeth on a shout—*for fear of the keeper*.

The italicised words let the secret out. They are Kenn's answer to any challenge about heather and primroses being a 'way of escape'.

Of course they are a way of escape! he answers, round-eyed. If a bull is charging me with bloody intent, do I wait until he scatters my bowels or do I nimbly mount the nearest wall? The eyelids quiver with mirth and the mouth turns up at one corner.

For in the high reaches of the river even argument has its own secret delights, quick as a bird-beak, threading roots like an adder.

Nor need there be a living adversary in the discussion, for Kenn can always create one, generally with the guise of a person he knows or has listened to. Not that this is ever deliberately done. It simply happens that the argument is in train, that he is in the thick of it.

And the pleasure is got not by abruptly repudiating social responsibility, but by subtly analysing it in the light of his own secret researches.

For to begin with he knows exactly what the adversary means by 'escape'; what schoolmasters and parsons and statesmen and judges and great landowners mean by it; even what the literary critic looks like when he dismisses 'poetry of escape'—though there is something in that superior expression that touches the spring to involuntary mirth.

But never the mirth of derision. Mirth rather like a clap of wind, cool and mind-searching and prepared at the end with shy—or sly—gifts.

This escape from the human struggle, this evasion of social responsibility, this denial of all the codes!

How it echoes back through the ages, in how many tongues, in how many faces, towards how many ends!

What a subject for a cinema film—from the time when the hunters of the golden age first 'settled down' and started the creation of gods and demons, priest-craft and sacrifice, kings and slaves, right up to the perfect culmination and co-ordination of these elements in the Great War!

Under the gorgeous palaces and solemn temples of the Nile, what milennia of dark and bloody rites! Rome crucifying her slaves, crucifying Christ. Rome of the Inquisition, torturing in the name of Christ. The slave hordes turned into slave armies and wheeled by Napoleons to gut each other on the plains of Europe. The rise of the Industrial Age. Machines as the new torturers and the new war-weapons. The hordes marshalled in millions. High explosive for mangling the bodies. Poison gas for disintegrating the lungs. Barbed wire for exhibiting the spectacle of a slow writhing to death.

And the speaking voices always solemn. The priest of Memphis. Pontius Pilate. Through the Dark Ages the voices come. From eternal damnation we deliver you in the name of God. Prison for Galileo. Fire for the Maid. Famine and disease for the hordes. Kings and King-Emperors. Statesmen. Captains of Industry. Children of the hordes in foetid mills;

women as beasts of burden staggering along dark colliery tunnels.

Voices of foreign secretaries as solemn today as the voice of Memphis. More money. More high explosive. More gas. In the name of Civilisation, we demand this sacrifice. . . .

Nor does all that fine rhetoric (says Kenn to his imaginary disputant) give any real idea of the unspeakable personal abominations, from the filth of sex perversions to the drawn-out mental horrors that yelped—and still yelp—in madness, in madhouses.

It's a far cry to the golden age, to the blue smoke of the heath fire and the scent of the primrose! Our river took a wrong turning somewhere! But we haven't forgotten the source. Why blame me for trying to escape to it? Who knows what's waiting me there?

Smiling, he looks around for little Kenn, his guide—and sees him and Beel standing by the Broch Pool and gazing up the strath. They are afraid to go farther. Afraid of the keepers.

No wonder!

CHAPTER TWELVE

THROUGHOUT THE WINTER an odd salmon in from the sea might occasionally be found as far up as the Intake Pool—but very rarely. It was not always easy to see him. In fact all through the winter months the water, draining from the great peat moors, was discoloured. After frost or a comparatively dry spell, the colour might lighten from porter to a pale sherry and a solitary fish might be vaguely discerned, as Kenn and Beel had already discovered. Long experience, however, had proved that it was no use trying to fish for salmon even as late as the end of March. Whether the odd salmon of the winter or early spring went beyond the Intake was not known, but the general belief was that he turned back to the sea. He came up to have a look round and a glass of porter, and then went back! This, of course, was unlikely. But the high pools, many of them ten to fifteen feet deep, and black as night, did not give up their secrets readily.

With April, however, came a change that was felt rather than seen; a state of expectancy, of vague but disturbing excitement. Kenn knew that if he had been a salmon he would be cutting the water with his nose, exactly as he cut the air when he ran in a sudden burst of speed, letting out a shout at nothing. Beel would also shout, and sometimes they made diving motions with their heads to imitate the speed of fish cutting up through the throats of pools. 'Like that, in a flash!' and they quivered their tails.

But though they went up the river as far as the Broch Pool many times, they saw nothing. Then one Saturday morning Angus said to Kenn, almost casually, 'Coming up the river?'

The Friday night had been too stormy for going to sea,

and the fishermen, of course, never went out on Saturday night. Angus had the day to himself.

It was a day of intermittent sunshine and flying cloud. A bright day, cold out of the sun, but when the body got warmed up it was invigorating. Since the year came in, the weather had been very cold, a biting, wind-driven cold with frost and very little growth. Snow showers were more common than rain, and squally, treacherous weather, had made it a hard season for the white fishing.

A flush of excitement warmed Kenn and he whispered 'Yes', glancing about him lest his mother should overhear and ask him to run an errand. Had this happened, he would have rebelled or cried.

In no time, however, the house was out of sight and Angus was talking in his airy companionable way. Kenn trotted every now and then. At such a moment he loved his brother.

'They're up,' said Angus.

'No!' said Kenn.

Angus nodded. 'The shepherd from Bunessan says they're not many: about a fish in every pool.'

'No!' Kenn did not question the information. It never occurred to him to wonder how anyone could see a fish in any pool. He knew it was true.

'But the best of it is that Gordon the keeper was down about last night warning some of the boys for the heather-burning today—if the weather kept up.'

'Was he? I never heard!'

'Yes. The only thing is that it was raining in the early morning. But I don't think it was an awful lot. And this wind should dry up the heather soon. When we go away up we'll watch for smoke. If they're at it—the river is ours.'

They were now passing above the Well Pool, but Kenn forgot even to glance at the meadow beyond, into which he had carried his first salmon. The river path here left the highway. The miller, a tall thin man, was ploughing in the field behind the mill, which was a high grey building. Its top door was open and they heard the trundle of the hurley on the knotted wooden floor. They did not wish to speak to anyone lest they be asked where they were going. So they merely glanced sideways into the river. The water was still so dark that they could not have seen the bottom even if the wind-ripple had not made that impossible.

'Doesn't look very promising,' said Angus. In his tone was an intimate, enigmatic humour. Kenn smiled.

There was a shallow, gushing flow of water down the cobbled slope of the weir at the Intake Pool. The broad sluice-board had been screwed up to its limit and underneath it the main stream hurtled down and boiled into froth over the last causey stone. The pool itself was circular and deep and whirled with currents. It was impossible to see anything in it, though Angus did for a moment leave the path to peer along the gravelly edge under the low grass bank.

Once they had crossed over the rising ground beyond the Intake, the world they usually inhabited was shut off. On the other side of the river rose steep green braes. On the near side, meadowland was bounded at a short distance by a rocky incline where birch and hazel trees grew. Beyond the trees, on a higher level, crofting land began. By this meadowland the river ran in quiet shallows and Kenn and Angus did not stop until they came to the Broch Pool.

This pool is the meeting of the waters, for the burn that comes in on the right is the river's main tributary. This tributary has hollowed out in the ages a narrow wooded glen. Salmon rarely go up it, though its neck of water in spate must make it difficult to distinguish from the principal rush of the main stream. It is a quiet, lovely little valley in its lower reach, with wild roses and hazel nuts. There are two main pools whose near sides consist of smooth, sloping flagstone, down the green slime of which naked young bodies slide on summer days.

It was on the steep wooded slope opposite that Kenn, out nesting with Beel, nearly trod on the pheasant—the first he had ever seen. Its threshing wings flapped into his face and the mad scream was out of him before he could stop it. But he managed to turn the scream into a shout, as Beel came up, and pointed to the nine eggs. For a long time they gazed in wonder. 'I found it,' said Kenn.

Beyond the flagstone pools, the land lifted to scattered croft houses, an aloof place, with the solitude of the moor coming down upon it. They did not care about adventuring too far there, for the folk and the dogs were strangers, but at times the sheer lure of the water, shallow and warm on summer days, drew them from little pool to little pool, guddling for yellow trout, until their heads rose and their eyes encountered unknown rocks and bushes, and their ears hearkened to a solitary sound and to silence.

This region of the Broch Pool must in ancient days have been of great social importance, certainly of religious importance, and perhaps even more than a local centre of government.

The tongue of land between the streams rose abruptly to a promontory on which the ruins of a broch indicated sufficiently the nature of the structure. A round circular building, at one time probably about fifty to sixty feet high, it still has the single small doorway through its twelve-foot-thick wall, and the chamber in the wall on the right hand for guarding the doorway. Inside, too, one may enter a beehive room also in the wall, almost opposite the doorway. In this beehive chamber Kenn and Beel would sometimes find themselves, and young as they were, the cunning manner in which the stones gradually overlapped to meet in one round central stone overhead, without the whole falling, never failed to impress them. There was no mortar, no supporting pillars or stays; only an immense weight pressing down on these overlapping stones. Yet here was the room now as intact as it had been at the height of the Roman Empire. The great wall had tumbled in ruins, but this little room was as it had been in the days of Christ. The stone shelving still stuck outward and deep in the earth sea shells could be found.

When Kenn and Beel crept in through the little door and stood in the gloom, they were vaguely disturbed as if the little door telescoped backward into a remoteness that at any moment might come up at their elbow.

Neither would care to enter the place alone nor to linger there. The stones were so near, the entrance so small. From two thousand years back time's fingers could touch them in less than an instant. More than once, indeed, Kenn almost felt that touch, jerking his shoulder and body from it and smothering it behind him with a cry—a cry, not necessarily, and never quite altogether, of fear. Accordingly, Kenn has little difficulty in finding a certain sort of meaning in phrases like the 'illusion of time', or 'two thousand years are but as a day'. A day? Less than a moment! Instantaneous, in fact. In sober truth, Kenn has occasionally had an impression of very nearly visualising the fourth dimension. This is abstruse and, if one likes, absurd, for it is as needless to visualise the fourth dimension as to visualise music. Yet the idea of visualising the fourth dimension has a strange thrill in it. Kenn is not only sure of this but certain he knows the *kind* of thrill; can, in short, very nearly leap into what happens, and if there is no sense in this there may be a rarer nonsense, eddying around and away with an invisible smile. Kenn's forebears got off a path to let an eddy of wind pass on its spirit feet.

Opposite the Broch, across the tributary, a high knoll rises abruptly from the meadowland. This must from very early times have been a religious centre of importance. A story is told of a cemetery between the knoll and the pool being swept away by a tremendous flood which hollowed out the graves and carried off the dead. Kenn once heard old James Dallas call it Chapel Hill, though no religious ceremonies have taken place on it within traditional memory. A broad, high, lichened wall runs from the knoll towards the river. Evidence of other walls implies that at one time this holy place was protected against its enemies. And perhaps not human enemies only, for wolves roamed the land centuries after these walls were built. On its flattened crest Kenn and Beel had already found two round circles of stones lapped over by moss and grass. They were interested because the circles looked like the foundations of little round houses, about the size of the beehive chamber in the Broch. The boys had never heard of the Culdees; nor for that matter of the Ninian who spread the gospel a hundred and fifty years before Columba came to the West. Of Columba they had heard, but as a name out of the Bible and therefore unreal. Of the immense stretch before the early Christians, they knew nothing at all. True, in a school reader there was a picture of a wicker cage containing young men and women being offered up in fire as human sacrifice by the Druids. But it never occurred to them—or to their teacher—that Druids in the heyday of the Broch may have sacrificed on this very tor—and possibly over a longer period than Christians have broken bread. Though why, of all practices, select this peculiar one of burning the living? After all, very little is positively known about the Druidic practice, and that mostly from a Roman or two. And at least it is known with certainty that the Romans crucified slaves in companies and enjoyed the sport of throwing Christians to the lions. Is it possible that a couple of thousand years hence, school readers will picture a young woman of France going up in flames or an old woman of Caledonia having a needle shoved well into her by a zealous Puritan anxious to prove her a witch, as evidence of the practices of a religion called Christianity before the great Poison War blotted out the civilization of that particular era?

But in the vast stretches of time before the Druids, before the men who built the brochs had landed in this northern land, what people, with what conceptions of life, peered for salmon into the dark waters of the Broch Pool, as Angus and Kenn peered now?

Kenn imagines that he knows them. They run before his inner vision. The knowledge is secretive within himself. Abrupt laughter, touch-and-run merriment, and cloud-shadows and wind on the pool.

He may well turn round startled as Druid and Christian and Viking draw nigh and, exhibiting new and terrifying qualities of human blood-lust and greed, set upon one another and fill the pool with corpses.

The Broch is there in ruins, looking across at the ruins on the religious hill, but salmon are still in the pool, and

Kenn and Angus, like incarnations of the pre-Druidic age, are peering in the dark wind-rippled water.

They don't stay long, for civilization is still too near. The Broch farm steading is on the upland by the wooded slopes of the tributary. Across the river, the crests of the green braes have fallen back and invisible eyes may be peering through grassy tussocks. They cross the footbridge over the tributary and, swinging left round the Broch promontory, enter the strath.

It is a lovely strath. The flat river lands widen and narrow, the path goes by and through hazel woods where nuts ripen in harvest weather, discloses sudden meadows where rabbits look and vanish, swerves round and on, but ever holds by the river. The slopes that shut out the strath from the moors are steep and wooded to their summits.

It is not a glen of the mountains, craggy, stupendous, physically impressive. There is nothing here to overwhelm the romantic mind. Its beauty is an inward grace in oneself akin to what is indefinable in the memory of a masterpiece. Beauty, intimate and secretive, has a lingering, lovely mirth; at the core of it, hope and fulfilment meet and tread a measure; while heads turn with glistening eyes to look for any or no excuse to laugh. In some such mood the Creator must have looked upon his handiwork and called it good. Kenn has long suspected that at the core of goodness there is neither solemnity nor observance, but only this excitement of a perfect creation.

Some little way above the Broch Pool and across the river are the ruins of a mill. At one time all the principal roads and main centres of population were inland. The folk of the straths and glens were a pastoral folk, rearing great numbers of black cattle and small native sheep and ponies. In the beginning of the nineteenth century, the landlords began to see that they could make more money out of letting this land to large sheep farmers from the south, so they set about clearing the folk from their ancestral holdings, burning them out of their homes in circumstances of dreadful brutality. The Vikings trusted to their own fighting courage and were often beaten. The modern landlords trusted not only to the power of the church and state behind them, but to their privileged position as chiefs of their clansmen. It was a betrayal impossible—perhaps unthinkable—to Viking or Druid: and, bewildered and broken, the people were driven to the seashores without lifting a hand in their own defence. There was no question here of lack of courage, for at that very time men from these glens were winning renown in the armies of Britain in Europe, Africa and America. In their act of betrayal, the chiefs risked nothing—and won everything. In the cowardice of such safety there is something even more loathsome than in the act of betrayal. Yet the chiefs did risk something: they risked any spiritual reason for their existence and lost it for ever. And it is only because of the ancient link between betrayer and betrayed that clansmen to this day remember the Highland clearances with a revulsion of shame and bitterness. Time will yet set it back among all the other betrayals of mankind by priest or ruler, and only the ruins of some old mill may draw a glance from bright, hastening eyes.

Herded along the shores, the folk began harvesting the sea, and the great fishing industries of the Moray Firth started to grow. The chief still pursued them with land rents and fish tithes, but the folk built their little fishing villages, their boats and their harbours, their churches and their schools, their coastal roads and bridges, until—for example—there came to be more Sutherlands in the creeks of Caithness than ever inhabited Kildonan.

By the ruined mill, the long strips of meadow were being ploughed as Kenn and Angus passed—the last cultivated land in all the remaining miles to the river's source. The two horses and the red-bearded man went so slowly that to the lads in their excitement was conveyed a feeling of such remote loneliness, that when the plougher suddenly called 'Hup, there!' they both laughed. Kenn has never forgotten that momentary glance at the horses, the tall, stooping figure with the red beard, and the newly turned earth. The mill ruins, the absence of any other living figure, the whiteness of the silent croft house. The slow movement of man along the frieze of time.

An overhanging branch snicked off Angus's cap. Kenn picked it up for him. As they emerged from the low archway of trees, bare springy turf ran back to the brae-foot on their right hand. Two rabbits lifted their heads, looked at them, and then very leisurely hopped up the brae under the trees. The leisurely action seemed in the nature of a derisive challenge and Angus nodded. 'You wait!' Their expressions quickened with good humour.

As they lifted their faces to the strath, however, their whole attention was held by a view of the landowner's shooting lodge, about a mile distant, set on a wooded crest and directly commanding the river. It would be inhabited at the moment only by a housekeeper, yet the boys could never rid themselves of the impression of its windows as eyes.

They went on calmly and, just before gaining the shelter of trees again, were vouchsafed a vision of glory. In front and high up on the right, there uprose from the sombre birches a golden-green fire. They had seen willow-catkins before many a time, but by some trick of the strong, sweeping sunlight, the exotic blaze was such that they debated what tree it could be. But not very ardently, for the burning bush was no more than something added to their own excitement. The secret spirit of the wood surprising but encouraging them with a voiceless shout! The catkins of the hazels, their flame blown from them, drooped like pencils of brown ash. A few withered nut-clusters were still on the boughs, reminding them not of a past autumn but of an autumn to come, for youth's memories have always this happy trick of living in the future. Across the river lay the blackberry flat and beyond it on the hillside the most famous of all spots for blaeberries. A dozen rabbits hopped towards their burrows.

'Nobody has been here for some time,' said Angus. 'That's plain.'

'Yes,' said Kenn. 'Look!' A white scut disappeared under the trees on their right.

They nodded knowingly. Kenn took a small trot to himself, for their pace had been quickening. They went on in silence. The path gradually rose and dipped sharply, the steep wooded slope coming in against their right shoulders, before it fell back again as they emerged once more upon grasslands varied with tree clumps and bronze bracken.

They were now in dangerous territory. The lodge was in full view on the opposing wooded crest where it curved inwards towards the river. On their right, hidden by an upsloping walled plantation of trees, was the gamekeeper's house and dog kennels.

'What about having a look at the Lodge Pool?' suggested Angus.

'What do you think?' agreed Kenn.

From the Lodge Pool, the ground rose in two terraces to the walled plantation. The brae-face between the terraces was wooded, and into it Angus slipped, followed by Kenn.

The pool, lying directly under the steep slope on the opposite side, was screened from view of lodge or keeper's house. Angus and Kenn stepped out from the trees and over the narrow stretch of level turf. It was a long, deep pool, favoured by salmon, but at the moment so dark that its bottom was quite invisible. 'Out there,' whispered Angus, pointing towards a ledge of rock, 'is where they lie. I wouldn't mind betting you there's more than one in it just now.'

Kenn could see that Angus had come out of a sheer need to have a look at the pool, and not with the intention of doing anything. There was a memoried glistening in his eyes, his mouth was open slightly in that curious expression of hearkening to inward thought and the outward world at the same time. He beckoned Kenn with his hand and they went back to the trees.

'Did you ever hear the story of Lachie-the-Fish, Beel's brother, who's now in Australia, and the seven salmon?'

'Yes,' said Kenn.

'This is where it happened. There were seven salmon in

the pool there and he got them all out on the off side. When
he had carried them over to this side, he couldn't resist the
temptation of looking at them. You know. He wanted to see
them, just to see them all in a row.'

'I know,' said Kenn.

'Well, that's the grassy bank where he laid them out, side
by side. Seven of them. Side by side. Bonnie. Well, he was
looking at them and looking at them, when he heard a stick
crack just there and who should come out of the trees but
Gordon the keeper.'

'Lachie must have got an awful fright!'

'He never moved. He stood like the one that was turned
into a pillar; stiff, boy, as stone. And Gordon came down,
slowly down with his back to the river and his eyes on the
trees here where his spaniel was hunting out the rabbits. If
he had turned his head even half over his shoulder he would
have seen Lachie and the seven salmon. But he kept walking
sideways with his face towards us and his back to Lachie,
slowly, step by step, following the dog; slowly down past
us here, and over round the bend there, and out of sight.
The dog never put up a rabbit. And Lachie never moved.'

This true story was one of sheer marvel for Kenn. Its
nightmarish quality of suspense even now held him spellbound.

'And the joke of it was,' said Angus, 'that Gordon wanted
to catch Lachie more than any other living man!'

'Lachie must have been great,' said Kenn.

'He was,' said Angus. 'Come on.'

They soon reached the bridge that spanned a longer and
deeper pool, but Angus resisted the temptation to look
into it, for now they must go more warily and casually
than ever.

Ahead the sides of the strath slowly converged on a deep,
rocky gorge. Had it been summer weather, they could have
gone up through the gorge, springing from boulder to boulder in the bed of the stream, but there was too much water in
the river for that now. So presently they climbed up through
birch trees and came out on the moor with the giddy bank of

the gorge a little below them. Legend had it that once upon a time a man pursued by his enemies had leapt from precipice to precipice clean over the gorge and landed safely.

He must have been a greater jumper than any ever seen at the local Games. There was enough in Angus's murmured joke to defeat the faint sickening sensation Kenn experienced as he glanced down over the bald head of the rock.

Altogether the feeling of insecurity was now at its strongest, for though Kenn had more than once come in sight of the gorge he had never before climbed on top of it and seen the world that lay around and beyond. Behind, the keeper's house on one side of the strath and the lodge on the other were startlingly visible; and beyond them croft houses on wide sweeps of land disappeared like toy cottages towards the sea. There was no sign of life at all about the lodge. And actually neither men nor boys moved about the keeper's house.

'It looks as if they've gone to the hill right enough,' said Angus, as they snuggled into the long heather. They turned from the known world behind and faced the moors. But there was no smoke of heather burning as far as the eye could see.

And the eye could see such distances that here and there a glimpse of moor crest looked like a delicate pencil-shading against the remote sky. The hills were low and long and sinuous; spinal elevation of the backs of moors rather than hills. And all in the one shade of dark brown.

The immense distances drew Kenn's spirit out of him. He had come into the far country of legendary names. As Angus murmured them, pointing from under his nose with the heather stalk he nibbled, his excitement went out from Kenn like heat vibrations from a moor, and left him exposed to the feel of hidden watching eyes; and yet, for that very reason, his brother's companionship deeply warmed him. It was like snuggling into his own bed, but immensely more exciting because of the companionship and of the peril (vastly exaggerated in his mind) in which they lay. And from this nest of insecurity and affection, he gazed away towards the moors and crests that for so long had been names with the remoteness about them of names in Judea but far more intimate and thrilling because they were used by grown men he knew. This far country was the country that he had hoped one day to see. And the day had come.

Through this world of slow-rising moors, the river ran. Its strath, however, was now growing shallow, the slope of trees on the right less steep and less high, and the wide grey-green flat land had the bare loneliness of a place haunted by peewit and curlew.

'Do you see the ruins yonder at the upper end of the flat?' asked Angus. 'Well, it's just beyond, where the brae comes round to the river, that Achglas Pool is.'

'Is it?'

'Yes. That's our only hope. Not really that there's any chance at all. But we'll have a look.'

'What's the ruins of?'

'Och, some old croft houses. They used to plough up the grassland down there. Do you know how I know?'

'No.'

'Well, do you see the shallow hollows in the ground at a little distance from each other, as if someone had been cutting broad straight swathes? That always shows the land was once cultivated.'

'I didn't know that.'

'Yes. Now if you look straight over Achglas and away beyond it, do you see a short white wall?'

'Yes.'

'That's the burying ground.'

Kenn kept gazing at the ancient place of the dead. In all the vast world in front of him only one human habitation was visible. It was a shepherd's cottage.

'It's lonely there,' said Kenn.

Angus looked at him. 'You wouldn't like to live there?'

'No.'

'Would you be frightened of the graveyard at night? Think of the old fellows with the beards coming out of it!'

'Would you be frightened?' asked Kenn.

'I don't know,' said Angus, with a slow smile. 'I have passed it at midnight. You will pass it too.'

Kenn began smiling also, but awkwardly, his eyes all troubled light. He would pass it, too, himself, at midnight.

'Who are they?'

'Who?'

'Buried there.'

'The folk who lived here long ago. They lived in the ruins there, and in other ruins you'll see. They poached the river many a time, I bet!'

Kenn's awkward smile deepened, for he could not see them poaching the river. They were too old and bearded for that. They were men of the heather, out of the solitary moors, out of the past. When Angus looked around him, Kenn looked quickly too. 'Did you hear anything?' he asked.

'No. Did you?'

'No. I thought you had.'

'No, there's not a soul about. If they've gone to the hill, their smoke should be showing soon. The low-ground smoke, I mean.'

'Where's the high ground?'

'Away miles beyond the burying ground. Do you see that long, low hill against the sky, like an animal lying flat with a great waggle on its tail?'

Angus told him of the distances his own squad of burners had gone last year. Told him stories of the fires and of the gillies who controlled each squad, how one gillie had nearly gone mad when the fire was getting the better of the lads, and had himself lashed into it like a demon. 'You're big for your age. You'll be able for the low ground yourself next year.'

'Do you think so?' asked Kenn shyly.

'Yes. Why not? And then two-and-six for one day. A whole half-crown. It's good pay.'

'It's a lot of money,' said Kenn. While he was lost in contemplation of this wealth, Angus caught his arm.

'What?' whispered Kenn, flattening.

'The peewit.'

They saw the bird wheeling and diving and heard its sibilant cry. *Pee-z-wit!* It was tremendously excited.

'Must be a weasel or something,' murmured Angus at last. 'Couldn't be anyone in the trees—unless he's been there a long time.'

They watched the bird and the trees. Its anxiety grew less fierce; its cry more drawn out. Angus caught Kenn's arm again. 'Look!'

Over the ridge to the right of the burying ground a drift of rising smoke shadowed the sky. The first fire by the heather-burners!

Kenn looked into Angus's face. It was smiling with that humoured uplift at the mouth-corner that was somehow so personal and friendly. Angus's bright eyes met Kenn's and he nodded. 'Come on.'

When they reached the shelter of the trees, Angus set off quickly along the ridge of the wooded slope. Kenn could see he was not going down to the river level until he had investigated the peewit disturbance.

But when they arrived at the approximate place, they could find no trace of any living thing. Even the peewit had vanished. As Kenn looked about him at the trees, and rocky outcrops below, and thickets of young hazel, he realised how easy it could be for anyone to hide, for a flattened body to shove a grey face round a greyer boulder.

Angus shook his head, then beckoned with it. He was satisfied there was no danger.

They went down the wooded slope in a long slant and ultimately came out on the river land by the cottage ruins. They laughed silently at one or two bolting rabbits. A good sign! The laugh vanished as a curlew got up and woke the whole place with its long cry. Two peewits got up. The double cry of the curlew fell away with the falling land into the fluting, tremulous whistle.

'Enough to make you mad!' muttered Angus. But when they pulled up in the neck of trees beyond the flat, he said derisively, 'Doesn't matter. Not a soul about.' Then he stood listening, until the cries of the birds had passed into silence.

He went on a little way and stood again. 'That's Achglas,' he said, nodding to the pool below them. 'We'll sit here for a little.'

They sat on the edge of a narrow, stony pathway that slanted up through the trees. There was no hurry. Listening acutely, Kenn heard the soft thud of his own heart.

It was quiet and grey and alert here. *Spink!* said a chaffinch above them. *Spink! Spink!* He had never heard the note so detached and clear. In the sheltered strong sunlight, it was like a sound in another world, or, rather, the world just beyond the known one. The note was not clear, was sibilant a little, like the cry of the peewit, yet it was round and bright with happiness, and hopped from branch to branch like a coloured bubble.

He hardly listened to it, his eyes were so avid for the river, his ears for other sounds.

Though the hazels and birches were not large trees, they were old and twisted and tufted with lichen. They reached down and near; they stood back leaning secretly together. The wind higher up sifted softly through thin twigs. Outcrops of grey rock were patterned with smooth lichen. Rotten stumps and dead branches had yellow moss growing on them. Last year's nuts were in the dead leaves under Kenn's fingers, as he turned his head to look up into the brae-face.

The two sides of the strath narrowed at this point before falling back again. The near side of the pool was solid rock which the water hit as it entered before swirling out into a round basin with a stony beach on the off side. It was not a large pool, but it was deep and, as the boys saw, impenetrably dark.

'Black as peat,' said Angus, with his friendly smile, when presently they stood on the low rock scanning the water. Then he glanced quickly over each shoulder and stepped down to a narrow ledge. Though only some eighteen inches broad and not nearly his own length, he yet managed to curl up on it and peer down into the dark current. As he lay there, his nose in the water and his cap held in his right hand close to his head, with its snout lipping the water, Kenn wondered how on earth he expected to see anything, for the ledge in the pool's throat lay at a slant to the incoming dark current which flowed past at some speed carrying continuous legions of round white foam petals.

But he wondered with the excitement that knew Angus was not going through this performance for the fun of it. This was an example of that secret knowledge of the river which he himself hoped yet to attain; the knowledge that finally got into the bone and remained there for ever. Without this knowledge, all talk of loving a river was so much sailing froth; pretty, and to be smiled at in that pleasant, derisive way Angus had at times.

Angus was now lying still as the rock itself. Kenn glanced about him, holding his breath to listen. Angus lifted his head and slowly turned up his face. The water trickled unheeded from the hair on his forehead and from his nose. He was smiling. 'A beauty!' he said, in quiet tones, and levered himself on to his feet. As he squeezed his hair and his nose, he looked about him. 'A fine fish—about ten pounds. And clean.' He vaulted up beside Kenn.

Presently he got Kenn down on the ledge. 'Wait a bit.' He glanced at the sky. 'You won't see a thing unless you get a beam of sun. When you lie down bring your eyes close to the water. Make a shadow with your bonnet and look down the shadow. Keep staring down. He's about six inches out from the rock and his body moves from side to side a little with the current, a very slow waggle like a clout in a stream. . . . Now! I'll hold your jacket.'

Kenn got down and Angus directed him into position. But though Kenn stared earnestly, he could see nothing but the dark-brown water, foam-patterned, flowing immediately under his eyes.

'Keep the foam off if you can with the edge of your hand or the snout of your bonnet. Make a sort of calm water and keep on staring straight down. I'll hold you.'

The brown of the water beneath him became all at once irradiated with sunlight and Kenn realised that he was staring into depth, a brown depth full of myriads of specks of matter. Far down the specks ran into a treacly thickness. Stare as he liked he could not see the bottom, could not see any shape, could distinguish nothing at all beyond a tiny pale fleck that disappeared even as he looked at it.

He hated having to admit defeat. 'I cannot see him,' he said at last, wiping his nose slowly.

'Did you see nothing at all?'

'No. There was a wee little white thing—'

'That's about his back fin,' said Angus. 'Down you go, you've got to learn to see him.'

Angus's tone was eager. Kenn was his partner, had to be initiated. With a quickening in his breast, Kenn got down again. And this time all unconsciously he guarded the foam away with his whole forearm. He flicked the flowing water with his lashes. He stared until the depth ran a golden brown. He saw the tiny fleck again. It wavered towards the rock and disappeared. It came again. It disappeared. The whole depth vanished and came again—and suddenly for an instant a dark shadow the length of a sea-trout wavered beneath it. Then it was gone.

Kenn reared up, the water running from him unheeded, and looked doubtfully at Angus. 'I thought—something like a trout.'

Angus nodded. 'That's him. Ten pounds. Maybe twelve. And clean run.'

'Was that him?'

'Yes. Great, isn't it?'

'Yes,' said Kenn on a solemn breath, and was aware of a lovely light-heartedness in life; saw it sparkle in Angus's eyes; and climbed up and sat down, tremulous a little and weak.

'You go down round the corner of the trees there and see if there's any life on the flat. Then go up through the wood to the top. By the time you're back, I'll be ready.'

The tremulous feeling merely made him noiseless and extraordinarily nimble. He felt light as air; swung under the branches, round rocks, paused, slipped away, listened, stood for a long half minute screened by a birch, gazing down the flat, saw a rabbit hop from its burrow and cock its ears, began to climb, holding his breath till it came out of him in little gasps, wondered what signal he would give if Gordon stepped out beside him—from round that rock; went round the rock, waited till his heart eased and his mouth grew moist again, and finally stood among the last of the trees on the crest and followed the moor road till it vanished beyond the burying ground. He descended as noiselessly as he had gone up and while still some distance above the pool saw Angus tying a large cod-hook to the end of a hazel stick. The funnel in the trees down which he looked isolated Angus with startling clearness. His slightest movement, his absorbed expression, the stick, the hook, the shake of the white line—everything was so vivid that Kenn had a momentary sensation of prying. With a hawk-like movement, Angus glanced over each shoulder, then put a loop over the hook and pulled it tight, satisfied no human eye was seeing him.

For a moment Kenn could not move. How easy it would be for a keeper to lie low and then rush out and capture at the critical moment! But what held Kenn was something deeper than that; something not of thought but of vision. Down this arrested moment of time, he himself was the Invisible Watcher, and held all the security of the position, like God or Death. Not, of course, that any such image touched him then. But he remembers now the distinct impression of security and of prying, of the moment as one of extreme clarity like time held spellbound. A faint warmth of shame came out of the prying. Were he God or Death, to have advanced on that bright living figure would surely have broken his heart.

Actually he advanced so quietly that Angus looked up with a start, lowered his eyes, and swiftly, as if he'd caught or missed something, looked at Kenn again.

Kenn shook his head. 'No one.'

'Come on then. You stand here above me. When I hook him and lift the stick up, you grab it and heave. If I wait till I get up off my belly, he'll have got a grip of the water and tear off.'

Carefully Angus explained the situation and pointed to the ledge on to which Kenn was to heave the fish. 'Jump on him then and hold like grim death.'

Angus was now nervously alive and keen, with the joy of battle in him. He took off his jacket and turned up his right sleeve. 'Here goes!' and he flashed a smile.

Flat on the ledge, he shadowed the water with the cap held in his left hand, while slowly he sank the stick. Kenn watched it go down, down, at arm's length from the rock but coming in gradually. He could see the wobble on it set up by the current. The hand touched the water and remained there. He had got bottom. Slowly the hand brought the stick nearer, still nearer, inch by inch, until it rested again.

Kenn took a swift glance at the ledge of rock. He would have to stoop swiftly, catch the stick, and heave.

Angus now seemed to have got frozen to the rock. He was taking a terrible time. Suddenly he wriggled as if forcing his body down through the rock to see better; then lay motionless again. The blood was congesting his features. At last Kenn saw the right hand grip, felt the pause, and crouched.

The strike was swift enough, but no stick handle was thrust at Kenn.

Angus pulled the stick clear of the water, and with intense dismay said, 'I missed him!' Dismay passed into anger. 'I missed him!' He stamped about the rock. What a fool! What an idiot! 'We'll never get him now though we wait till the crack of doom!' He spoke out loud. He did not care who heard him. What did it matter? The one and only chance on the river today!

He rapped out short sentences. Had lost sight of the hook. Difficult to feel the touch of the fish. Strong current. Rumble on the stick. Had felt something once—twice—then timed for the third touch and struck. While speaking he had got down on the ledge again, and rose with wet face. Nothing! What did one expect? Kenn asked him where the fish was lying now.

'Out there, and he might as well be in the Atlantic. Come on! We'll put the fear of death in him.'

They heaved great stones into the pool. The noise was terrific. When the water had settled, Angus got down on the ledge again, but the fish had not come back. They searched the throat, poking under flags, slashing the running water. But they saw nothing. 'He may be swimming about.' Angus stoned the pool once more; then they both withdrew on to the rocks above.

As they lay together, Kenn listened to Angus describe at greater length exactly what had happened. They could not tell each other enough about it.

It was a great pity!

A wren, no bigger than a curled brown leaf, landed on a stunted willow, and let out a song of astonishing fullness and power. *Spink! Spink!* came from the branches higher up, and from the trees rounding towards the flat descended a song of clear single notes, a slow-tumbling sunny cataract, with memories floating in it.

'It's fine up here,' said Kenn.

'Great getting away, isn't it?'

'Yes.'

'You can see the smoke yonder against the sky. They're hard at it!'

Kenn smiled too. 'When will they be coming back?'

'Not till four or five o'clock. And it can hardly be one yet. Not much more.' They both looked at the sun in the cloud-moving sky.

'Quiet up here.'

'Yes,' said Kenn. 'I have two wrens' nests.'

'Where? . . . Have you a robin's?'

'Yes.'

'In the serpent grass behind the mill?'

'Yes. But I think I have another one making.'

'If it's in the grass ditch in the park it's a yellow yarling's.'

'I have that one already and two more—all with eggs in them.'

'I'll tell you one you haven't got?'

'What?'

'A blackbird's.'

Kenn rolled over with mirth. Even little boys had a black-bird's nest. 'You'll be saying a sparrow's next!'

They recalled the walk last Sunday morning and the return with eleven peewits' eggs for breakfast. Kenn had eaten two hens' eggs and two peewits' for it had been Peace Sunday. Joe had been at home and there had been much secret fun. It had been exciting, spread out and breasting the fields in the windy morning. And their parents had not said much because there was a long tradition behind the gathering of the peewits' eggs for this festival. Their mother was always at her best when there was plenty to give away. She had the overflowing hand.

Happiness was crawling in their flesh again. 'Let's have a look,' said Angus. 'You never know.' From nibbling odds and ends, the taste of the earth was in their mouths, in their blood. They felt secure from fear, snake-quick under it.

Angus stepped down the rock deliberate as a dancer, and subsided on the narrow ledge, and laid his forehead on the water.

Kenn glanced about him, along the crests, the flats, at Angus, and then swept the pool. It would be fun if he saw. . . . His heart gave a quick turn over as if the dark edge of a stone in eighteen inches of water near the other side of the pool was the salmon. It was just the shadow of a stone-edge. It was the length that deceived. The length was just about right. . . . It really was awfully like it.

Angus uprose, his face dripping. 'Nothing. Rotten, isn't it? What are you looking at?'

'Nothing. It was just that out there—look.'

Angus came beside him. 'Shut up!' he said in a hushed voice and hit Kenn in the ribs with his elbow. 'Shut up your mouth!' He looked about him; picked up the stick; began tying on the hook. 'A blind man couldn't help getting him there.' He was charged with a tremendous excited gaiety. 'Can't you see his head? He's facing *down* the pool.'

The dark outline of the fish came into focus against its

blurred background and Kenn said, 'I thought all the time it was him, but I was frightened to say.'

'You're getting the eye.'

Kenn was quivering with pleasure. 'I felt sure it was him; will I run up to see if—'

'Naah!' said Angus, with a large gesture. 'Keep your eyes skinned, that's all. I'll give him the dirty heave—if he'll lie.'

'Do you think he'll lie?'

'He'll see me—see the hook and everything. You watch!'

'He's awfully difficult to see, isn't he?' said Kenn, wanting more praise.

'You'll see him better in a minute!' Angus stepped up under the willow bush, and then leapt from boulder to boulder until he had crossed the stream.

His approach to the side of the pool was noiseless. His left foot levered against a stone on the water's edge, his crouching body slowly arched over the water as the stick went out at arm's length and the hook down in a movement so slow that it fascinated Kenn. Like a drooping summer branch with a white leaf at its tip. The leaf drifted to the salmon's side. The salmon never moved, but lay as if waiting to be stroked. The white hook drifted under the ventral fin until it vanished from Kenn's sight. A final movement of delicate poise and Angus struck.

There was a swift boil—and then nothing but a drifting dance of a dozen silver spangles where the salmon had been.

For the second time Angus had missed.

A darkness in his face, he stared at the scales, then at his hook, muttering fiercely, incoherently, out of his hot blood. Arching out over the water, he examined the bottom on which the salmon had lain and found his explanation. Protruding just above the gravel was the leaning edge of a stone (like the first leg of a V), some four inches in length and an inch or so in depth. It had been invisible to Angus. When he had thought his point was under the ventral fin it actually was under the sloping stone and when he had struck, the stone had thrown the point off the belly of the fish on to its back which it had merely scored. It was the sort of odd chance that might happen once or twice in a lifetime.

When Angus came back, he explained exactly what had happened, but with less than his usual exuberance. The darkness was still in his face and his eyes were stormy.

From place to place he went, peering along the shallow edges, getting down on hands and knees, watching for bubbles, staring a long time from the ledge and turning away from it without speaking to Kenn. At last he started stoning the pool. Kenn could see he was forgotten and without a word went and helped in the stone-throwing. When Angus stopped he stopped. When Angus had once more examined all visible resting places, he said shortly, 'Come on!' and Kenn followed him under the willow and away from that place of ill fortune.

They emerged on a narrow flat of grey grass and old bracken. As they went on, Angus began to speak.

'Sometimes a fellow gets luck like that. Once Lachie-the-Fish took three days to get a salmon out of the Serpent Pool—in the height of summer with clear water. He stripped; swam with the gaff in his mouth; tried the three hooks; tried everything; but the fish wouldn't lie. It happens like that. As if the fish put a hoodoo on you. Nothing you ever do is right. You are too quick or too slow; too wild or too careful; and in the end the fish always moves just when you are about to strike. Becomes uncanny. I heard Joe telling about it. The pale mouth opening and shutting, opening and shutting. Wait till you see one swimming like that, up and down, up and down, its mouth opening and shutting.'

'Did you ever see one like that?'

'Yes. The summer before last in the Broch Pool. He was lying by the sloping flag. I got him in the side, but the stone I had my foot on moved and he got off. Alie, who was up on the Broch point watching, could see the white gash quite distinctly going up and down the pool. Took me two days to get him—and the whole world could see you yonder.'

'You got him in the end, though?'

'I did. Lachie got him too. You have to get him.'

'Yes,' said Kenn.

They went on in silence.

'I saw in a book about the Celtic people,' said Kenn, 'they were people somewhere in the olden times. I forget what it was all about, except two lines, and they were something about "the hazel nuts of knowledge and the salmon of wisdom". It made me think of the strath. Funny, wasn't it?'

'Not much sense in it.'

'No,' said Kenn at once. 'Only I thought it was queer at the time.'

'They believed anything in the olden times.'

'Yes,' said Kenn.

They went on in silence until they came to the Smuggler's Pool. There was a shallow cave in the solid rock still blackened from ancient smoke. Angus explained to Kenn about the whisky smugglers, how the men used to meet here and make the white spirits.

Kenn gaped at the cave; climbed up a few paces to its floor level, and saw part of the fleece of a sheep, with white skull and jaw bones lying apart. 'What's that?' he asked, pointing to myriads of brown things like roasted coffee beans in the belly of the fleece. Angus stirred them with his toe. 'Maggot shells.'

A feather of sickness touched Kenn's throat and he backed away. In a small dried water-course behind him grew a bunch of primroses, with four flowers full open. When he saw them, he picked two of the flowers and smelt them, and kept them against his mouth as he followed Angus to the pool and looked up wonderingly at the rock. He nibbled the stalk of one of the primroses. He was not thinking of what he was doing. The stalk was very tender. The yellow petals were softer than any human skin. He crushed them against his mouth, and dropped them, and went forward in a little run of escape, the scent in his nostrils.

Angus was climbing down a crevice to river level. From a precarious hold, he peered into the dark water, but not for very long. He climbed back shaking his head. It was a long, narrow, deep pool. Angus gazed at it for some time. He loved looking at pools.

'You can only work that one with a net,' he said. 'I could tell you ever so many stories about it. In the neck—just there—is a big flat flag. When the water goes down a bit you can see it and stand on it, just over the ankles. They lie under that flag.'

'Is that the flag where last year you progged—and the fish came out with a wild boil and then you—'

'Yes. That chap Harry from Edinburgh was fairly astonished! He thought it was magic! Queer . . . .'

In the middle of his story Angus stopped and said abruptly, 'Come on back.'

He went swiftly and did not speak again until they were at Achglas Pool.

He examined the pool with a concentrated patience. His last move was to reverse himself on the ledge and peer along the base of the rock where no fish normally lay. He even stretched out his cap a foot or two in front of his head for a last glance. And in that last glance he saw the salmon.

'He's here.' There was excitement, but it was almost bitterly controlled. He made Kenn get down, and after a time in a piercing beam of underwater sunlight, Kenn saw the salmon's head, the round eyes, and the pale line of the mouth so distinctly that he started back with instinctive care.

'It's going to be difficult,' muttered Angus. 'You'll keep hold of the line and play him.'

When he had fixed on the hook he brought the line along to the end of the stick and after a double hitch passed the remainder of it to Kenn.

He was lying with his right shoulder against the rock. To strike with his right hand, he would have to lie over on his left side, when the least little jerk outward would land him in the current. It was a delicate position, but the only one. In getting at the fish he also had to crane forward off the narrow ledge, and to make matters still worse the fish was again facing down stream, was in fact staring right into the window of light in which Angus operated. He was lying at a slant against a broken piece of under-rock, which no doubt sent an invisible eddy of water back over the gills. There was no way of getting at him from upstream because of the wall of rock.

But Angus already knew that salmon lying in deep water are not the wary, frightened creatures many make them out to be. That he was directly in the window of the fish's vision he could see for himself. Both eyes of the fish indeed stared up at him through the clear shadow he made with cap and arm. Yet as his stick kept going down, the fish made no slightest move, exhibited no least trace of uneasiness. Angus took care that the stick grounded beyond the head, of course, and then with infinite caution he brought the white visible hook—the water here was two feet shallower than at the other end of the ledge—towards the gill-covers. And the fish lay as if enchanted.

The hook passed out of sight under its head which, although appearing to lie on the bottom, must at least have been two inches clear.

The point, thought Angus to himself quite deliberately, must now be directly under the white triangle of the lower jaw. He knew the spot, knew exactly what it felt like to the exploring touch of fingers. A fish gaffed there is at its least powerful.

But still he was not satisfied, and with the utmost care he brought the stick against the salmon's head until he actually felt its weight, felt it as distinctly as if he had brought his own cupped palm under its chin. And still the salmon did not move.

Then Angus struck straight up.

Because of his position on the rock he was powerless, yet in the first few seconds his instinct made him hang on to the stick. The fish got a grip of the water and his pull was tremendous. Realising that the hook would get torn out, he let the stick go and scrambled to his knees. But Kenn was now so excited that instead of paying out line, he held on as he had seen Angus do. 'Let him go!' shouted Angus, grabbing outward at the line. He caught it and so

increased the strain. 'Let go, you fool!' Kenn let go. From
the whirlpool in the water, the line came away slack and
Angus hauled in an empty gaff.

It was maddening; beyond human power to endure. 'Why
on earth didn't you let go?'

Kenn felt the attack bitterly. It was a dark, horrible
moment, a pit in which the brightness of the day vanished,
in which their lovely friendship was smothered.

Angus's fists were tight-clenched. He looked away. 'God
damn it!' he said.

Very rarely did the boys of that river swear. 'A dirty
mouth' was a reproach amongst them, and a grown man
at sound of even an ambiguous oath would quickly enough
warm a cheek. Angus's expression was thus like the going
out of the sun.

Kenn did not speak. They stood on the rock and stared
at the pool. While they stared the quiet tail-reach began
to undulate. The salmon became dimly visible, his body
moving with a slow waggle like an eel. He nosed the edge of
the green flagstone, left it, came into the outgoing current—
and went with it over the tail-race into a short comparatively
quiet run of water less than two feet deep, with stones here
and there. Beyond were boulders and broken shallows. No
sooner had he entered this place, however, than he turned
towards the pool. He was going back. . . . His head fell off
and with the same slow sinuous movement of the whole
body, he began to explore this shallow of refreshing, running
water.

Angus had Kenn's arm in a strong grip. 'Don't move,' he
muttered, keeping his very lips stiff, as if the salmon might
see them.

But the salmon could find no place to rest. Twice it tried
to wriggle into a comfortable lie, lay for a moment, and
then came away again towards the near side. As its head
got the current it balanced and went slowly forward towards
the pool.

Angus's fingers dug into Kenn's bone. But Kenn kept
the quiver of pain to himself.

The head fell away, and the fingers relaxed.

The salmon began to rub into the bottom and turned half over; the silver under-body flashed rose-gleams through the brown water. In this fashion was scooped the bridal bed.

'Sick!' muttered Angus.

At last it lay still, wholly visible in the shallow water. Slowly the boys backed into the brae, went round some trees and came at the fish from below.

Angus well knew that this was a very different affair from approaching a fish in deep water. Besides, the salmon must be restless, terrified of its enemy. Angus crouched and approached upstream, approached until he could have touched it with the stick at full stretch.

And the salmon did not move.

It lay at a slant to the current, curved like an unstrung bow, sheltering as it were behind its own back, exactly as Angus or Kenn on bare land would shelter from the wind.

Angus's body slid forward again. The stick went out until it overshot the fish, then the hook drifted back with the current and in behind the shoulder. But he could not get the hook under the body, and yet he was fearful of an instant rush back into the pool, when all would be lost, for if the fish went to earth in the deeps now it would never more move.

He must take his chance, he nervously decided. He struck. The hook glanced off the hard shoulder, and now a strange thing happened. Instead of flashing into the pool like a torpedo the fish circled slowly where it was. Quicker than thought Angus gaffed it on the move and walked ashore with it. It hung limp as if played out by a fisherman, and not until Angus was about to deliver the *coup de grâce* did it give a last show of its strength. While they had been watching it, the wound under the jaw had been draining its life away.

Its size was astonishing to Kenn, for even in the shallows it had not looked very big. It was fully twelve pounds, fresh run, blue-green and silver bright, and of all shapes surely the most perfect in creation.

It brought the boys together again. The bitterness, the dumb resentment, that Kenn had felt he would never lose, vanished. The silent laughter, the good-natured friendliness arched in Angus's face even while the eyes glanced hawk-like in the problem of hiding the fish. They stood on a mossy bank against a rock-face some three feet high with scrubby bushes on its brow. Kenn pointed to a triangular recess under a leaning stone and was about to stoop for the fish when there came upon their ears the tread of feet. Angus's face turned and through the scrub saw Gordon and his principal henchman, Stot, swinging down the slanting pathway directly towards them.

The boys sank down, Angus with his back and Kenn with his right shoulder to the rock.

Kenn looked at Angus's face. It had whitened, and playing on it was a weak surface smile.

All the dark proud life was gone.

Doom was in the nervous lips, in the shallow glitter of the eyes. The spirit, netted in the white smile, haunted Kenn through all the rest of his years.

And the footsteps came swinging down, *thud! thud!* treading the reverberating earth, treading on their hearts, down towards them. The boys had made no attempt to hide the salmon. Like Lachie-the-Fish, when Gordon had appeared at the Lodge Pool with his gun, like animals in nature, they stiffened where they sat when it was no longer possible to escape on their feet and while yet there was the last chance, that purely magical chance, that they may not have been seen.

The pathway ran behind the scrub on the brow of the rock. The footsteps came towards the brow of the rock. The iron heels of four boots rang on it; Kenn's shoulders sank under the weight of great hands; vomit lifted to his throat; the clanging on the rock ceased and . . . the footsteps were going away, padding the earth beyond the rock, going away towards the flat, away off, away . . . .

Kenn heard Angus's deep, heavy breathing, saw him wriggle up against the rock, remain for a time peering through the scrub, then slowly slide down again.

'They're gone,' he whispered. 'They never saw us.'

THAT NIGHT KENN RAN his Saturday errands without any grumbling. There was a haste upon him to get everything done. When Angus shouted after him in solemn derision to see that a sufficiency of meat adhered to the sixpenny bone, he made no protest. Indeed he laughed to himself as he sped along.

'Did you see anything, then?' asked his mother of Angus, for Kenn's spirit told her a lot.

'Yes,' he replied, 'we got one.'

'Did anyone see you?'

'No. They were all at the hill today.'

'Where is it?'

'It's up the river.'

'Is it far up?'

'Not very. I'll go for it later on.'

'I don't like you going alone at night in the darkness away up there.'

He smiled. 'I'll go about eleven. After the heavy day on the hill, everyone will be in bed. No one will be watching.'

'I don't like it,' she said.

'Ach, it's all right,' he answered pleasantly.

She glanced at him. He was a finely made lad, tall, and good-looking in an open way. He would yet have great bodily strength. He took to his mother's people. He was a movement of memories for her. She glimpsed dead persons in him. It was a great pity he did not like schooling. That was her secret regret. For she loved the heart of learning. To 'get on' in commerce or business, to become wealthy there, was fine enough, and many a well-doing lad was a credit to his parents, but she would rather have a son a professor

146

than a millionaire. However, life took its own way, and this boy, with his good nature and love of music, was her son, and at the moment she feared for him, thinking of the dark, dangerous ways of the strath.

'You're not going to take Kenn?'

'No,' he laughed. 'He wants to come!' They heard footsteps at the door. 'You needn't say anything to Father,' he added quickly, and went into the back porch where he groped for the potato bag and, rolling it up, hid it outside.

When it was after ten o'clock, the boys were at the far edge of the up plantation, looking into the valley of blackness that was the strath. The night was very dark.

'Ach, I think I'll go now,' said Angus. 'I'll chance it.'

'I want to go,' muttered Kenn.

'Mother wouldn't let you. No use. If I go now I could be back soon after midnight. That's the Sabbath!' The friendly humour was in his voice.

'How will you see?'

'You get used to it. The worst bit is when you're going down the face. Everything is different. You feel—and feel—and get on your knees and grope about as if you were swimming!'

The boys spoke together for a little time, their voices confidential beneath the sough of wind in the trees, then suddenly Angus said, 'Well, boy, I'm off. So long.' In an instant the night had him. Kenn listened for his feet. They faded and the darkness came rushing down. He started running back home and became aware of a body approaching him. He slowed up. The tall body stopped and a man's voice asked, 'Who are you?' Kenn bolted past.

He rested by the gable of his house till his breathing should slow down. His heart was beating very quickly. When he went in his father looked at him. 'It's high time you were home,' he said. 'Where's your brother?'

Kenn hung his head and half turned away.

'I hope he won't be long,' said his wife quietly.

He looked at her, his dark eyes quick under his brows. 'Where has he gone?'

'I think they were up the river the two of them, today,' she replied calmly.

'Has he gone for something?'

'I think so.'

He turned away. 'If he's caught, you know what'll happen. It'll be a court case and disgrace. That's what it'll be.' He rubbed his fingers on his trousers; he stamped about, looking at the fire and the peats as if he had a job of work to do. She paid no particular attention to him. 'Do you hear what I'm saying?'

'I'm hearing you.'

'I wouldn't have allowed it. I would not.'

'You'll maybe take a little of the salmon, should it come.'

He was very fond of salmon, and always told them to lap up the bree. The note of irony in her voice quickened him still more.

'Disgrace on our house, that's what it'll be. How could I face up to the factor or to anyone? I'll be clean shamed yet by the whole of you. I will so. How you could let him go, I don't know. And on this night, too, with the people about, down at the shop from the hills. He'll be seen as sure as he's in it. I wonder at you, woman.'

'I wasn't thinking of the factor or yet the laird or yet the folk from the hills. I was thinking of the dark night and the strath and the boy alone.'

'Yes, and if he fell and broke his leg, what would they think of you then?'

'Oh, man, will you be quiet?'

'Well then!' Turning, he saw Kenn. 'Get to your bed at once!' Kenn hesitated, then shuffled away.

He heard his father go out at the back door. That would be to see the night. He listened from the top of the stairs.

'It's black as tar,' said his father, in a quietened voice.

Kenn now felt the suspense in the kitchen.

'Have you a light there?' called his mother.

'Don't need a light,' he answered gruffly and began taking off his clothes.

His mother wouldn't sleep until Angus returned. If he

didn't come before the morning, she would wake up his father. His father would then come up and question him and maybe go out into the night after Angus.

So he had better not fall asleep. Not that he had the least intention of falling asleep until Angus returned.

His eyes were as wide as the night and his ears heard the cry of the river down below the sough of the trees in the plantation.

How brave Angus was to set off alone, up past the Intake, the Tor, the Broch with its little room, trees snatching his cap, queer sounds, movements, the black tunnels, his hands out, the Hawk's Hol, curlews and peewits on the dark river flats, his foot reaching out to make sure. . . .

Ah, and not these things, as Kenn knew, not the things themselves but—he turned over—hidden in the black night, the awful Thing that might—he buried his face in the pillow—a hand—he crushed thought out of his head and immediately saw Angus, at the foot of a rock-face, his leg broken, rolling on his back in agony, and then beginning to crawl. . . .

His father shouldn't. . . . Never!

In the surge back of the wave Kenn grew half ashamed of himself, for what did all this mean but that he himself was afraid, afraid, afraid? He could have called out he was afraid. I'm afraid!

He would never be able to do what Angus was doing. Never!

Presently from the hollow the noise of the river rose up and he found himself listening so intently that Angus's face came before him, with its white smile of fear. . . .

It touched him on the heart and through his smothered mouth petulantly he whimpered, 'Angus!'

CHAPTER FOURTEEN

HE SAW THAT LOOK again shortly before Angus's death.
Kenn's battery was in position near Mametz Wood. Angus,
who had emigrated to Canada some years before, had come
to France as a private in the Canadian Infantry. Kenn, in
writing him, had done his best to indicate his own where-
abouts by references to the particularly hot time he was
having. Angus replied that he was expecting an equally hot
time pretty soon. In this round about way, helped out with
trench gossip, Kenn felt sure that Angus was due to turn
up in his sector of the line any day. This prospect excited
him. He had a great longing to see his brother.

One evening he was sent out with two signallers to establish an observation post for his battery. In the half-dark of the
dawn, returning from the observation post alone, he became
uncertain of his way. There were many shattered trenches
that his electric torch could not find on his map. Presently
he came to a place where two trenches crossed. A glance at
the map showed a junction at about this point. He had to
go straight on. The grey light was coming strong. The eerie
zero light. The line was unusually quiet. His face, hollow
and frosted from lack of sleep and from hunger, smiled
thinly; no consciousness of danger touched him. When the
two signallers had left him alone, he had fallen to thinking of
Angus. The night, the coming of the dawn—the end of the
poaching foray. He knew this grey atmosphere with a deep
intimacy. So did Angus. The grey dawn on the face like
rime and the stomach flat. A sort of bodiless ease about it,
friendly, with the pleasant humour that doesn't give a damn.
As he walked across the trench junction, he hardly stooped
his head, and when a vicious *phit! phit*! spat behind his ears,

he turned round. From the opposing bank a pellet of earth the size of a marble trickled down, as if some serpent head had pushed it out.

He realised in an instant what had happened. The bullet had missed him by some fraction of an inch. Instead of fear, he experienced a curious feeling of elation, of detachment. The scene of the rabbit snaring, with the marble of earth running down from under the feet of Joe and Angus, flashed upon his mind. That Saturday afternoon he had gone hunting them through the wood. Joe was in the Lovat Scouts. Angus was somewhere about. He was hunting them again. 'I must be getting "hot",' he muttered, laughing to himself, and turned to go on and found a soldier staring at him.

'Is that cross-section under observation?' he asked.

'Under observation! You can bloody well shake hands with yourself!' The man's astonishment was tinged with something like disgust. Apparently no one crossed that trench on his two feet and lived. The sniper up on the slope near Trônes Wood had it taped right to the foot. 'I have crossed it crawling on my bloody guts, but I'm merely lucky.'

Kenn smiled. 'Nothing like having a charmed life. Tell me this. Have you seen any Canadians about?'

The fellow blew his breath out. 'Well, yes, I saw a bunch of them making a road some way back as we were coming up.'

'I knew I was getting hot,' said Kenn. . . .

The following afternoon he got a commission to go foraging in Albert for cigarettes, chocolate, fruit, and anything else his school French would help him to, and ran into the Canadians. They were a set of nice fellows and when Kenn told them that he was hunting his brother, they at once replied that they knew his brother, a crack hand with the mouth organ, all right. One of them volunteered to show Kenn the way, and later led him in the direction of Mametz Wood, and into a strongly fortified trench, which a fortnight before had been in the hands of the Germans. This trench was honeycombed with commodious dugouts fifteen to twenty feet below the ground. Kenn was told to go along until he came to the number he wanted, then to put his head in and shout. Every twenty yards or so there was an entrance with a battalion label fixed to it, and when Kenn came to the right number he entered and went down a step or two until he saw a faint light in the darkness. 'Anyone of the name of Angus Sutherland?' he shouted. 'Yes,' came the answer. He got down all the steps and on to the unevenly boarded floor. The place smelt strongly of mildew. There was no light other than a single candle stuck on a packing case. Beside the candle a figure was squatting on the floor with a canteen of tea beside him. Kenn's heart turned over in him. The candle light made great hollows in the face of the squatting figure. The cheek bones stuck out. The eyes were dark and sunken and gleaming. Kenn went right up.

'Hullo, Angus.'

There was a moment's complete silence, then softly, on a note of wonder, came the voice he knew, 'It's no' Kenn, is it?'

Angus got to his feet. He was tall and thin and the face emaciated. This change from the round-faced healthy brother of the old days struck Kenn strongly. But what lay behind it struck him desperately.

They shook hands. Four or five figures emerged. Angus pointed to Kenn's six feet. 'This is my little brother. When I saw him last he was so high!' He laughed and introduced Kenn all round. Kenn saw that Angus was a favourite. One middle-aged man with grizzled hair was an inquiring fellow, and hospitality was carried along the flood of his talk. Angus's voice lifted in excitement and with a Canadian inflection. But after a time Angus and Kenn naturally enough left the dugout to go and have a talk by themselves. 'We'll go this way,' said Angus, and Kenn observed how careful he was to pick a quiet spot where no stray fragment could possibly get them. He was continuously on the watch, glancing hither and thither. When they sat down, Kenn did not like to look at his face.

'I hope you're taking care of yourself,' were his first words. The Canadian inflection was gone. It was the old home voice, anxious, being friendly.

A queer sad warmth came to Kenn's heart. 'You bet I am,' he answered.

'There's one thing I want to warn you about. Don't take any chances. Don't run any risks. Never mind what they say. If you're asked to do a job, you'd have to do it, of course, but don't volunteer. Remember that, whatever you do. It's a fool's game. Don't you do it.'

He became very eager about this.

Kenn offered him a cigarette and as he held out the burning match glanced at his face and saw the nervous ghostly stranger inside.

'How are you doing here?'

'All right. Pretty safe here.' Angus glanced about him. 'I tell you I'm taking no risks now. I've had enough. And remember—don't you do anything rash. If they want you to volunteer—let them! Don't you. . . .'

'Have you had it rough?'

'Rough enough. I was pretty good with the rifle—'

'Remember the time you smashed the heel of the bottle with Cormac's twenty-two?'

Angus ridged his brows, then remembered the home incident. 'Yes!' The drawn skin on his face crinkled. 'I was good with the rifle, so they made me a sniper up at Ypres. They painted me up all green and then I lay behind a boulder camouflaged by a bush commanding a trench-crossing, potting away at the Germans. It was deadly. God, you couldn't help getting them. Far easier than rabbits. They knew I was there. Their bullets used to come over the stone, fluffing the shoulders of my tunic. They tried to get me in every way, shrapnel and all. And talking of rabbits, man, it was queer at night. You see I had the rifle trained so that I could even shoot in the dark. Not of course that I did regularly. But after a quiet spell I would have a pot shot, when I knew things were moving, and then, boy, you would hear a squeal, just like a rabbit!' He laughed.

Kenn laughed too. He knew the rabbit squeal intimately. A blood warmth went over him.

'Did you stick that long?'

'Yes, a devil of a long time. How they didn't get me earlier I don't know yet. But shrapnel got me in the end—here in the shoulders—look.'

Kenn looked at the patched shoulders of the old tunic. 'They might at least have given you a new tunic,' he said. 'Was it a bad one?'

'Pretty bad. I was in hospital down at Boulogne for weeks. God, it was fine. I was getting on all right, when the telegram came that Father was dying. I thought nothing more on earth would ever move me to feel much, but dammit, man, the old home came over me, so I went to the C O and showed him the telegram and asked for leave. I never had any leave. I was a fool—but never again. Stick out for yourself—or they'll do you down.'

'What happened?'

'The C O said, "Are you fit to travel?" I said, 'Yes'— though I had meant not to be fit for a good long time. And I wasn't fit really. However, never mind. "All right," said the C O, "I'll see what can be done." So I waited, feeling pretty rotten one way or another, but looking forward, too, for I should like to have been at father's funeral. I mean—but what's the use of talking? Next day I got my answer. If I was fit enough to travel I was fit enough for the trenches. That night I was sent up to the front line.'

'Pretty dirty trick,' said Kenn.

'Yes, wasn't it?' Angus went on talking in quick nervous tones. An unspeakable despondency crept upon Kenn. He got the talk round to home and the river.

At first Angus responded with a shallow interest; then all at once went back completely, with a sort of intimate remembering warmth that was almost intolerable.

Kenn felt his own reaction here as quite unreasonable and he fought it down and swapped word for word. But it was no use. Angus began asking after folk. Kenn did his best, laughing and telling, but there was a nerve thread of pain winding underneath that he had to swathe over or he might touch it and jump. It was the old river in a shadowy land. A land it would never flow out of. It was a nightmare in soft pleasant tones. An intimacy that closed over and suffocated. And Angus had no idea of the impression he was conveying. He was being wise, being cute. Take care, do no more than you must, don't be a fool. And all the time the river as pure memory, receding . . . receding . . . until their talk became forced, their occasional chuckles harsh. Kenn was relieved when a friend of Angus's came along.

He was a strapping young fellow, with fair hair, blue laughing eyes, and so clear a voice that the true Canadian accent sounded very attractive. A full-bred Canadian, and the sort of figure Kenn could imagine being picked for a gymnasium exhibition or the Olympic Games. He liked him at once, though feeling a little shy of him. For in some inexplicable way he recognised that not only did this Gus Mackay understand Angus's condition, but looked after him with a delicate reticence.

When they had chatted about their respective jobs for a while, Gus said, 'Oh, say, let us forget it! What I want to hear is more about the old country. My name is Gustavus—after the great Gustavus Adolphus!' His smile lit up his eyes with sunny humour. 'I am a Mackay out of the Mackay country—Strathnaver. I have an ancestor who fought with all the other Mackays—and a few of you—out of the Province of Cat, in the wars of Gustavus Adolphus. Do you know,' he said, turning to Kenn, 'that Angus here didn't know what the Province of Cat meant!'

For an instant the eyes held Kenn, and then the Canadian-born clansman laughed. 'Say, you're not too sure yourself! And you call yourselves Highlanders!'

'The Province of Cat,' continued Gustavus, 'was the Province of Caithness and Sutherland, and at one time it was the roof of Scotland. When this little affair is over, I'm going back with Angus and, from the highest of the granite peaks of Ben Laoghal, I'm going to show him our ancient heritage. That's the one little trip we have promised ourselves. That so, Angus?'

'Yes,' said Angus. But the sound was thin as the expression

on his face, which was concerned with its own problems again.

The eyes of Kenn and the Canadian met—and parted instantly.

'I'll tell you what we'll do,' said Kenn quickly. 'I'll make an offer. We may not know much about the history, but we know a lot about the ground itself. We'll take you up our river and we'll show you all its pools, and we'll poach salmon, and we'll watch the sun rise behind the Orkneys from the top of Morven or Ben Laoghal. How's that?'

'That would be wonderful! Absolutely wonderful! Is it a promise?'

'Yes,' said Kenn.

'Why you smiling?' asked Gustavus.

'I was thinking,' said Kenn, 'about the first time I ever saw Angus land a salmon. It was at a pool called Achglas.'

'Ach-glas—the grey field,' said Gustavus.

'Yes, there is a field below it,' Kenn nodded. 'It was once cultivated, too. You can see the broad swathes still. All that's on it now is the cry of the curlew and the peewit.'

'The curlew and the peewit! The words used to make my grandmother homesick. Hear that, Angus? The cry of the curlew and the peewit. Incantation of the old Druids!'

Kenn turned from this high note and in an ordinary voice, quiet as if he were asking for a fill of tobacco, said to his brother, 'Do you remember that time? They were at the heather-burning. We lay for a while on the Hawk's Hol, and then went on and down to Achglas. There was a fish under the ledge and you made me try to see him in the brown water.'

'Yes,' said Angus, But he did not seem to care about remembering. As if all this talk were now taking up too much of his time. It made him restless. The smile on his face crinkled the drawn skin.

Kenn went deliberately on to relate to Gustavus the story of the landing of the fish, but, when he came to a memory that roused Angus, the effect upon himself was again that of touching a raw nerve. And once Angus looked about him with a sudden start as if in the short absence of thought something might have crept nearer. For there was no reality in the river. There was no reality outside the world in which he was. And the wariness and cuteness served merely to emphasize how inevitable and unending was its maze, with the trapped mind doomed to dodge about for ever.

Kenn got to his feet. Gustavus immediately began making arrangements for another meeting, then shook hands with Kenn and left them.

'Well, I'll have to get along. What are you doing for a bit?' Kenn asked.

'Nothing, but—'

'Come on over to the battery with me now. We'll have a good feed.'

'No, no, thanks. And you're not cutting across that way? There was heavy shelling there lately—and there's no cover.'

'Oh, it's quite safe. Come on, we'll be all right.'

'No, I'm going back. I'm taking no chances. And look here, you should take care. . . .'

Kenn listened, but could not look at his brother. A dreadful awkwardness came upon him, and at the same time a desire to speak. They shook hands. 'I'll come again,' said Kenn, with a desperate smile, and walked off. Out of earshot, he began to curse. He cursed the mud and what came in his way. Disappointment was earth in his mouth.

'Where the bloody hell do you think you're going?'

He looked at the artillery man who was barring his way. He had been about to pass in front of the lean barrels of sixty-pounders. He apologised. The fellow looked in his face. 'Righto, mate!'

Kenn went on. The feeling of being hunted began crawling up behind himself. That's what really happened in life. The fellow who was cocksure got it in the neck while the fellow who was always ill or dying or dodging the issue lived to ninety. Himself and the Canadian might get blown to blazes, while Angus would go on missing the packet that was behind his ear. . . . The mood of fatalism began to settle

on him. His eyes started staring in front. A crash behind him,
however, and he was flat as a rabbit, holding his breath and
trembling. The truth was he was going windy! He swore at
that, in oaths that were unusual in his mouth. His eyes were
now over his shoulders, quick and alert as a hunted beast's,
but with something cunning and malignant in them purely
human.

He no longer cared about Angus's condition. If the fellow
went like that, well he could go, God damn him.

This bitterness stayed with him a whole week and gen-
erated its own humour, a detached, reckless, but human
and kindly humour. He found himself doing things for
the other fellows with an easy generosity. He was skating
on the surface of himself, and discovered an airy freedom
in the exercise. When the skin of ice cracked he pulled his
foot out pretty smartly. Occasionally his whole body would
convulse, and with a thick oath his mind would seize his
body and throw it before thought could come along.

Angus inhabited his mind, but not visually. There were
moments, however, when he saw him without, as it were,
pausing to look at him, when in fact he himself was doing
something or listening to a fellow and ready to answer back
laughing. And the way he saw him was always the same.
There was a great black wood and Angus was moving about
just outside it but in its shadow, with the alert preoccupied
movements of neither the hunter nor the hunted but of an
in-between state. Kenn never paused to think this out. He
saw him anyway from behind, the back of the head or, at
most, the listening side face with its pallor in the shadow.
For the point was that he had forgotten Kenn, had forgotten
everyone, precisely as he used to forget Kenn in a moment
of desperate or defeated salmon-poaching.

Whether in these last days he was thus brushed entirely
from Angus's mind, Kenn never found out. Did the actual
Angus, the living, hunted, miserable figure (and not this
shadowy mythical one) have occasionally his throw-backs to
real intense memories? Sharp bodily convulsions, when the
mind cried out, cried back, cried like the frightened curlew

down the straths of the past? Not a vague memorizing, but like the peewit, *pee-z-wit*, the two-fold wing-beat fierce and sibilant, thickening in the throat, *pee-th-wit*! as it flashed to earth?

When Kenn saw the Canadian coming, he knew it was all over with Angus. Weakness beset him in a warm blood-flushing. The pith melted from his flesh.

Yes, it was over.

'We went through a hellish barrage. He was pretty badly shot up.'

Kenn looked at the Canadian, who avoided his eyes. His features, normally so frank and clear, had a congested shame in them.

'You did not get back then for your rest?'

'No. As you know, everyone was shoved into that last push. We were rounded up and sent back. Right into it.'

'Did he live long?'

'Oh God yes,' said the Canadian. His whole body winced. 'Shrapnel in his back and legs. He was lying out in front of us. We could see him. We said to the officer we would go out for him. He said it meant death. Heavy machine-gun fire. We said we would go. He handled his revolver. He said he would shoot anyone who made a move to go.'

'What sort of officer?'

'Bloody young whipper-snapper.'

There was silence.

'Did he lie there all day?'

'Yes,' said Gustavus. 'We could have saved him. We should—have—saved him. . . . In the dark, I brought him in. But he had bled too much.'

'Did he live long?'

'Another ten hours.'

It was a long time.

They saw sufficient corpses any day to make death common enough. Perhaps the apprehension of this particular death had been drawn out too long.

Kenn slid down through his legs without any feeling of

discomfort. Better sitting anyway. A trifle sick, that was all. He smiled to Gustavus with a sardonic, glancing brilliance. The brilliance gathered into tears that ran down his smiling face.

He was now staring in front of him, breathing heavily through his nostrils, his chest swelling, like one taking ether gas. Then his chin drooped to his chest.

The Canadian looked down at the figure, the tears, the rasping sobs, the hands with their backs to the mud. The head rolled from side to side. 'Ah Christ!' muttered the mouth bitterly.

The Canadian leant back hard against the trench for a little. Then he turned and walked away.

CHAPTER FIFTEEN

SUMMER WAS THE TOP of the year. There was a game little Kenn and Beel and one or two more played in the up plantation that held all the excitement of summer in its daring and delight. It consisted in crossing the plantation from south to north on the tops of the trees. When there was an extra big gap between two trees, then one climbed to the highest possible point on the parent stem and set up a swinging motion from side to side, leaving go of the stem and jumping for the next at the perfect moment.

In this way was possibly born the notion of summer as a cascading down banks of leafy trees that Kenn never quite lost. When Kenn and Beel were in the strath, the steep-sloping face of birches in full bloom would hold their eyes in the sensation of tumbling down, head over heels, through the leafy foliage. They were never so foolish as to try it, of course. They knew how they would be jabbed and gashed by the underlying branches, tough and wet with sap, that could hardly be cut with the sharpest knife. Walking through the woods, the boy in front breasted a thin branch forward and let it whip back into face and eyes.

Yet knowing all that about the real nature of trees, still to Kenn there remained this entrancing notion of standing on the brow of the steep wooded face and stretching out his arms, taking off—whoo!—like a bird, breasting the swaying foliage, turning head over heels as the leafy waves caught his feet, and landing in a delicious, green, breathless tumult on the final mossy turf.

Summer was the only season that gave him this sensation of flight, for at its best it was an actual sensation, not a hopeful notion or aspiration, suggested by the flight of birds.

It moved in his blood. His body quivered and shaped itself, as if some instinct, lost aeons ago, was still in the warm red stuff, as an echo is in a rock.

But this pre-human flight is more dangerous than the one in the tree-tops, though Kenn there got his first awful fright over death. Angus had come upon them, playing their game, and had laughed derisively. Pouf! that tree-road was easy! Then he set out to show them the great jump.

One or two of the older boys could do this jump because they had the weight and reach. Angus set the tree-top swinging, shouting, 'Hup! . . . Hup again!' until the little boys began to get frightened. Wider and wider grew the arc of the swing. The stem bent perilously. They had all been in Pinder Ord's visiting circus. Angus shouted to them to behold the man on the flying trapeze. 'Hup she goes!' He was getting ready to jump. . . . Now! There was a rending crash and Angus landed with a thick thud at their feet and lay still.

They gaped at him. No one touched him. They could see his face. Beel cried out something. His young brother Archie started screaming, 'He's dead!'

He was dead! Kenn tore down through the trees shouting 'Mother! Mother!' His father looked up from the back door, then came running up towards him. 'Angus fell from the tree!' His sobbing voice lifted to a scream. He lost all control of himself. He grabbed blindly at his mother's skirts in mortal terror of being left alone.

She found her husband kneeling by Angus.

'I can't find anything broken, lassie. I think he's just stunned. You watch him till I get some cold water.' He spoke quietly but hurriedly, and got up at once and ran down through the trees.

'My bairn!' said Ellen, on her knees. 'My own bairn!' Her voice broke. She cried to him by name.

There was something in her cry that made him hear it at a great distance. His eyes regarded her blankly, then with roving bewilderment. At that, her cry overtaking her falling tears, she gathered him to her bosom and lifted him like a child, though he was the length of many a grown man.

'Canny! Canny! Ellen,' said her husband meeting her.

By this time Angus was muttering and struggling. She made to lay him down, but Angus wanted to get his feet. He looked scared as a young bull. He staggered, but his father got a grip of him and put him on his back. Then he tilted his head up and made him drink some of the cold water.

By evening Angus was all right, but the fright he gave everyone lay on the house.

When Kenn went out by himself and looked at the half-light in the strath, he felt queer. He had overheard his father say to his mother, 'At first, lassie, I thought he was away with it.'

'God was good to us,' she answered. He had never heard his mother use God's name before except out of the Bible. There had been something in their quiet voices coming from the grey reaches of a last Sabbath of the world.

His mind was hovering in this terrifying apprehension of the end of things, when a voice cried, 'Boo!' and he leapt a foot in the air. It was Angus, his pale face round the corner of the stone wall.

'Boy, you got a fright!' Angus was delighted.

Kenn's heart hurt him with its beating, but the flare of anger died at once. He smiled uncertainly. Angus came up beside him. 'They don't know I'm out!' he chuckled. 'Didn't I fairly get the knock-out today? Complete knock-out, like a boxer! I bet you there is no one in the whole place ever got knocked out before.'

'No,' said Kenn.

'Clean out!' He stretched one leg and then the other.

Angus could always warm Kenn with this sense of the humoured goodness in life. All at once Kenn quivered with relief. The half-light was glimmering now, full of the scents of summer.

Angus sniffed. 'Honeysuckle! Fine, isn't it?'

Summer was the season of scents and yet they were never consciously searched out. For one thing there wasn't time, and for another the picking of blossom was a girl's business.

A boy ran through a drift of scent. There was one scent,
however, hardly noticed, that yet remains, perhaps, most
characteristic of all: the scent of birches in May after rain.
For this is not properly a sensuous scent; it has the tang
of life and growth, pliant and powerful; it is the scent of
briar grown up into the girth and bark of trees; it pervades
a whole strath; drifts on the currents of the air; at its first
waft nostrils tilt up and sniff with the action of a stag. In
the hot emerging sun the trees are still wet and the clean
acrid taste of the bark gets in the mouth; specks of bark and
lichen are spat from behind wet lips, swept off the backs of
hands, finger-combed from the hair, hunted from the small
of the back. The earth breathes upward. The damp is the
sap of life. Young cheeks bloom like petals of the dog-rose.
Glistening eyes are quicker than tits and finches. Slow . . .
cunning . . . noiseless tiptoe movements. Blood on the back
of a hand? The cuckoo. Lips open. *Cuckoo!* . . . *Cuckoo!*
The cuckoo!

Eyes flash to earth to guide feet. Primroses, anemones,
delicate green leaves of the wood sorrel. Bite the leaves;
chew them. Cuckoo's spit. Red bells of the blaeberry. A
good crop. Dead bracken. Violets. Living bracken with
bowed heads. Dandelions. A trickle of water. Orchis and
marsh mallows. Grey grass. Broken sticks and stones. Hazel
shoots—for rabbit snares. Green grass. Young rabbits. Gal-
loping little rabbits. A black rabbit!

'A BLACK RABBIT!'

And back along the wood the answering yell: 'WHERE?'
The sun comes through.

The leaves rustle; bow down with the whole branch; all
the branches bow down one after another along the wood
under the wind, with the grace of ballet dancers under
applause. Then they come erect again and dance the ballet
of green fire.

Under the sun.

This vivid freshness came again with the wild roses, but if it
were noticed it was more by chance, in a glance of the eye,

a momentary stare: the roses are out. The pink roses had a scent but not the tall bushes of white ones. One could pull the petals of a pink rose in passing and take the scent and throw the petals away. Then try the white one. No scent.

'Why isn't there any scent on the white rose, Angus?'

'Just because.'

'Because what?'

'Because there isn't.'

Explanation of the mysteries was generally conveyed in some such formula. It was satisfactory as most formulas, and had the virtue of a mocking friendliness besides.

One late June day, when the sun was at its height and the roses at their best, Kenn met old age and youth. As far as he can now know, it was the first time they ever made him stare or think about them. It was perhaps extraordinary that this should have happened on the same day. All other circumstances attending that day are completely wiped out. Why he was sent to visit the old woman in her long thatched cottage on the crofting land beyond the bathing pools of the Little River, he cannot remember. He may have been sent to her with something in a little tin pail. He can remember the brightness of the curving tin as she did something at the kitchen dresser, but has no recollection at all of carrying anything either to her house or away from it. No doubt the two happenings were in themselves so vivid that ordinary things could not live long in the same light and so faded away and were lost. At mere thought of the old woman, he knows a curious compulsion to go on discussing such detail in order possibly to give the occasion a sort of body or reality or to cover his reluctance at suggesting importance in a meeting so slight, so transitory, so devoid of any action.

She must have been a woman of about eighty, very slim compared with his mother, and stooping slightly, with a finely wrinkled face and grey hair (not silvery or white). The colour of her eyes he cannot tell and yet they remain upon him. When he thinks of them as dark he suspects that he is seeing the feeling that welled in them or the spirit that spoke through them. When the last note of an intimate passage of music has died away, there sometimes comes upon the quiet soul a strange ache, a poignancy akin to pain. Something of this darkens her eyes for Kenn, because in their expressiveness her spirit was revealed, and—this may have been the first astonishing thing—her spirit was shy. Her spirit was shy, her body therefore aloof a little, having the manners that would not come too near, be too familiar with, even a little boy.

As she leant one hand on the dresser, her head was bowed slightly, her flattened breast curving inward under the stoop of her shoulders. He has the distinct memory of entering to her there, of finding her *waiting* in that inner dimmed light.

He had never met so expressive a grace before, so expressive a kindness. Old bodies were usually tired or dull, often stupid and more messy with their food than bairns. This body as it thinned away became the more transparent.

When it thinned away altogether, the spirit would be released in full size, a spirit so sensitive, so kind, that it would remain aloof for fear of intruding, stooping still a little, and attracting with its eyes. Attracting the boy, and the man, and all men—to the all, or the nothing, beyond the veil of the flesh; but—all or nothing—endowing the adventure with a courage, a singing delight, a knowledge so sure of itself that it would, if need be, die fighting God to prove the greater splendour of this its own vision of grace and kindness.

There is something more here, Kenn feels, than the irrational surge of loyalty which more than once in history nearly wiped out his folk from the banks of their Highland River. And if he were to write a modern myth, it would take some such central theme and carry the fight to the last cosmic ridge. For what they would be fighting for would be their own achievement, their own creation, the glory in an old nameless woman's eyes.

As good a gage as the next. And better far than any Helen of Troy, that lovely and wanton bitch—though the thought

of her is bright with laughter. Come on, Helen! Fall in!
And Deirdre, with tragic foreknowledge in her eyes. Here,
Deirdre, never mind these crooners with their Deirdre-the-
Beautiful is dead. It's Conchubar that's dead, the bloody old
rascal. Come on! . . . And that fellow pushing up there—
gode, it's Nietzsche! Let's make him up a squad for the fun
of it. He'll never notice and will go on shouting till the small
stars reel. . . . Napoleon, is it? Ah, to hell with Napoleon.
He can come if he likes. And Caesar, too, if he likes. And
Nero, and Edward FIRST—with his thief's hammer—and the
rest of the old bastard gang. But. . . . What? Who? . . . No?
Is it? Oh, I say, boys, look—Spartacus! The leader of the
slaves, of the nameless! . . . *Spartacus! Spartacus! To the
front!* . . . Where has he gone? Vanished into the upward
flowing river of men. Become one with them. What can we
make of that? What can man ever make of it to the crack
of doom? Enough to bring tears to the eyes. Tears it'll take
more than the brimstone of hell to dry. Take our word for
it. Forward, lads! The river is flowing upward. Behind, see,
the valleys of the shadows. . . .

Ay, all very well, but on the last brink who's going
to do the parlez-vous? Socrates, you say? Cheers! And
if God makes the tactical mistake of listening, He'll be
in for a rough passage! Cataracts of laughter; the spirit
glistening in silver shot with rose gleams through the brown
shadows. And as for Kenn's own quick glances, not Nero
but Copernicus; not Urban but Galileo; not the captains
and the kings but Newton and Leonardo, Archimedes and
Faraday. Quietly there. Forgetting themselves in the River.
Like Spartacus. And the bearded fishermen, quietly hew-
ing away that the River may flow. He knows them from
of old! Sweet death, what a company! Never mind the
murderers and the thugs and the perverts. They'll get
washed, coming behind. Because of the wholesale murderers and the wholesale thieves, they never got a chance
anyway. . . .

Ay, ay, but, joking apart, when we get to the source, who's
going to speak with God? I vote for Shakespeare. After all,

this is an expressive business and we should have the best man for the job. . . .

Speak with God! What an idea! With God, whose power and mystery and terror has been—HIS SILENCE! No, the whole problem is who is to meet God face to face. Who is to stand and look at God? What face may remain unshrivelled when He looks at it? What face may draw God's look and, in the silence, touch God's heart? It's not what we have done: it's what we have become in doing it. For what we have done, to God who knows all, is as nothing. Our philosophers are bookies declaring the odds. Our artists, builders of sand castles. Our poets, noises on the wind. Our scientists, ants balancing on a blade of grass.

On that last crest—where the source is—we'll build a pavilion. This pavilion will take the shape of a long thatched cottage. Inside, it will be cool and dimmed. We will motion God to the door. *Within, You will find the spirit of our River, what has kept it flowing through the ages. By that, we flow on or die. Judgment is in Thy hands.*

God goes to the door and knocks. A voice calls Him to come in. He enters. She is leaning with one hand on the dresser, waiting for Him. He meets her eyes. She is shy, her body therefore aloof a little, for she had the manners that would not be too familiar even with a little boy.

To ask, could not occur to her. To give is her instinct. With this thought for the stranger upon her, smiling, she looks deep into God's eyes and offers Him a glass of milk.

Outside they wait, and the suns, forgotten, stand still.

God comes out. He stalks away from the cottage, head high. He has forgotten them altogether, forgotten the River.

They cry to Him.

God turns round, sees them, waves an arm: FLOW ON!

Little Kenn disliked running errands to strange houses and always crossed a doorstep with reluctance and the resolve to refuse the usual hospitality and come away at the earliest moment. Many of these small croft houses, anyway, were so poor that the usual bread was an oatcake bannock, thick and hard. Kenn and Angus referred to these bannocks as oilcake (winter cattle feed).

But whether he got the bannock or even the milk, he cannot now say—though he knows he got something. Bere bread, thick with fresh butter (this he loved) and creamy milk, possibly. But then, to this day, he does not know even her name. There is a memory of vague but pleasant astonishment at finding she was kin to his father. Probably he never directly enquired, because the whole happening was really so intangible, so momentarily personal, that a secret reluctance or inertia did the rest.

Certainly within ten minutes the sloping flagstones of the bathing pools would have banished her from his mind, for there was always the half-magical chance of a fish being in one of the pools.

There could have been no fish in the pool that day for he continued down the burnside until he came to the flat with the Broch rising above it. This flat was where the wild roses grew.

There was a girl gathering pink petals and at once he knew why she was doing it. Beel and himself had done it last year. The idea was that if you collected a lot of these petals and stuffed them in a bottle, added water and sugar, and shook the lot together, then the whole concoction would in a short time turn to real scent. They had tried a similar experiment last winter with a black stick of liquorice in an endeavour to make beer. The beer had been more successful than the scent.

He knew the girl. It was Annie Grierson. She was on a class above him in school because she was a year older. She had golden hair and a face so fair that it looked cleaner than any face could ever be from washing.

Now being alone, he did not like meeting the girl. It made him feel awkward and shy; and the only way to overcome this feeling was to swagger a bit or walk by without condescending to any particular notice. But it is very difficult for a boy to swagger when not in the company of other boys, and particularly for Kenn who had a shy, secretive streak in him. However, the girl had not yet seen him, so there was a chance, on the mossy turf, that he would be actually past before she would notice. Then he could call, 'Hallo!' and keep going on.

She was stretching for some blooms, when right behind her she heard his footfall on the grass. She had believed herself alone and swung round with a cry. The panic on her face gave its fairness so vivid a quality, so arched her eyebrows, that it stopped Kenn in his tracks and set his heart beating in embarrassed shame.

He might still have been all right, if she had come out of her woodland scare to upbraid him, call him 'A cheeky thing'. But instead, she said, 'Oh, what a fright you gave me!' put her hand on her heart and puffed a long breath through her lips, and laughed.

It was like one grown-up behaving to another. She inclined a step towards him, companionable and friendly, taken up with the fright she had got. What on earth to do, Kenn had no idea, so he grinned vaguely and shifted his stance.

'I know what you were doing,' he challenged.

'What?'

'Gathering roses to make scent.'

'How do you know?'

'Just because.'

'Because what?'

'Because I know.'

'Well—look!' And she opened her pinafore.

'That's a good lot,' he admitted.

'But I want an awful lot,' she said.

His heart certainly was beating now. 'I'll gather one or two then,' he offered with a gulp. 'I'm not in an awful hurry.'

'Will you? That's grand. What a fright you gave me!' She looked at him and smiled. And now her face was a girl's face and its skin all warm and soft. He got from her the strange soft scent that comes from a girl when you are pulling her hair and she attacks you. Only now they were not fighting.

Kenn gathered the pink petals in great style. He was slim and nimble, and showed off, particularly in leaping. He paid the penalty for this by three parallel thorn scratches on the back of his right hand. The blood in all three soon gathered into drops, and, in attempting to flick the drops carelessly away, he merely spread them over the skin. Soon the back of his hand was a fearsome and bloody sight. His pride swelled up. 'Here you are!' he said, coming with cupped palms.

Her eyebrows arched again. The petals spilled from her pinafore to the grass.

'That!' he exclaimed. 'Pouf! Nothing.'

But she got his fingers and held them and looked at the hand. Her concern was real. The blood frightened her. But she had courage and sense. 'Come on and wash it in the burn!'

'What! For that?' He laughed derisively, and snatched his hand away. 'We'll get some more.'

'You will not!' And now the arched eyebrows came together and the blue of the eyes grew strong.

'Ach, don't be a fool!' he said lightly.

'But I will!' she cried and caught his hand.

As they went to the burn together, he furtively looked about him. Wouldn't it be awful if Beel or any of his classmates saw him now? Wouldn't it be terrible? Though he would fight everyone of them in turn and smash them, they would never forget. *Playing with a lassie!*

There was, however, no sign of anyone about. And she held his hand low down and swished water on it. They were on their knees side by side and her hair tickled his face. But he could not stand much of this inaction, so he swished his bloody hand about and stood up and said, 'That's fine,' and walked back to the roses. When she was gathering the petals in her pinafore, he said, 'Well, I think I'll be off. So long.'

She stood up and looked at him, mute. 'So long, then,' she said.

He felt her still looking at him as he went and his legs grew quite awkward. So he started to run to show he was in a great hurry. But very soon he slowed up.

He was now desperately embarrassed. His legs wanted to slow up altogether. There was a white rose, a low bush, growing out of a bank, the emblem rose of Scotland. He sniffed it, expecting to find no scent, and found the most lovely scent of all. He shouted and pointed to the rose. But she was walking slowly among the bushes, and beyond looking at him, paid no heed. He began to whistle and went on to where the bridge crossed the stream. The blood was now not only all over his hand, but running slowly down his fingers. He had known all along quite well what should be done. He should hold his hand up and then the blood would soon stop.

He went down to the river and began washing his hand. She was standing still watching him, half over her shoulder, with the strange expression of a face about to turn away.

Even as he looked, she did turn away and began pulling petals, reaching her hand high up.

He observed that little eels were going up the edge of the stream. He caught one by the head and held it up, and commanded it aloud:

> Eelie eelie ot
> Put a knot
> On your tail
> And I'll let you back
> To your own pool again!

The tiny eel walloped its tail about but failed to tie the knot. He gave it another chance. A last chance. The tail failed to tie. 'All right!' he said, nodding grimly, and, laying it on a boulder, picked up a stone and smashed it to bits. He was very excited.

The sight of the greenish flesh, however, went against his gorge slightly. He always disliked this part of the game.

For the elvers couldn't really understand what they had to do—though some said they did and believed they wouldn't tie the knot out of sheer obstinacy and so deserved their fate. But no boy ever killed more than one or two without throwing the stone away and saying 'Pshach!' and starting to do something else. Angus would just toss one back into

the water and say, 'Ach, you're no use!' and try another
fellow.

> Eelie eelie ot
> Put a—

There was the knot! In a twinkling! He let the little eel go
under the water, when it swam off at once. He spoke out
loud and laughed. Annie was now moving away, her back to
him. She went slowly, concerned with her own business.

The next eel wouldn't tie its knot. 'Ach, you're no use!'
he said and tossed it into the stream. He caught a handful
of them. They tickled his palm. He laughed out very loud.
'Ho! ho! ho!' They wriggled through his fingers. 'Don't!' he
cried. A spasmodic urge came upon him to squeeze them,
to hurt them, to smash them with a stone. He flung them
upon the water. He hit the boulder fiercely, grotesquely.
For two pins, he would smash a thousand of them to pulp.
She had left the bushes and was going slowly up the green
bank towards the high crofting land beyond the Broch.

With great daring, he openly stood and looked back
at her even as she walked. Suddenly his hand waved.
She raised her hand once and let it fall. She kept going
on. He turned and started running home for all he was
worth.

After that at school he did not look at her. If they were
together in a bunch, his eyes never rested on her. She might
have been thinner than the air. Occasionally he would go
as far as the Broch Pool by himself, purely, of course, to
see if there was a salmon in it. Though the water was so
low that salmon could not get up, yet there was always the
chance that one might somehow plough its way through in
the darkness of the night.

The strath exerted a deep fascination upon him that
summer. As far as the Hawk's Hol, Beel and himself got
to know it intimately. Once or twice they went all the way
to the Smuggler's Pool, but these journeys took the whole
day, because their attention was so distracted by the growing
rabbits. Rabbits that went into burrows, they ignored, but

whenever one popped into a crack in a rock or into an old wall, they dug and tore away and poked for hours. Only once did they see a rabbit in a narrow crack of a rock. It couldn't get farther in.

They cut a long stick and tied the barbed salmon-hook (each carried one in his pocket) to the end of it. Beel always had that extra knowledge which Kenn never had. 'What you have got to do in a case like this,' said Beel, 'is to turn the hook in his fur. It then gets a grip. Watch!' The crack was longer than the stick. So Beel had to put all his arm in until his cheek was flattened against the rock. 'I'm feeling him,' he gasped, reaching still farther. 'I've got him. . . . No, he's off!' This went on for a long time. Then Kenn had a go. He had a longer reach. He felt the rabbit. He put the hook over it and struck with a jerk and pulled. The rabbit began to squeal. Kenn heard the rumble of its body against the rock. Beel grabbed it. Kenn was so excited that he did not feel the cruelty much at all. They so seldom got anything of value on their hunting expeditions that the rabbit was a good trophy. As they came down past the Broch, Kenn looked along the flat of the roses, but there was no one there. In the up plantation, they tossed for the rabbit. Beel won. The next one would be Kenn's. They grew hopeful and reminiscent.

'Boy, did you hear him squeal?' Beel's eyes glistened.

'What squeals!'

They laughed.

'Yon was great!' said Beel. 'It was the real thing.'

But in bed that night, Kenn did not think it was so very great. Beel never felt the hurting in himself; never felt the barb going into his face. At odd moments Kenn did. When he thought of it alone, the pain, the squeal, could blot out everything in a blinding flash. Then quivering a little he would draw himself away to keep himself whole. Compared with Beel, he was flawed and uncertain. All the same it was he who had done the deed. There was that abiding satisfaction, deeper even than pain. And he hadn't twisted the barb in the fur. Though it was a queer thing that when you were being cruel you could in a moment be a thousand times more cruel. Queer, that.

The green fire and the white and red roses; but the colour of the long summer days is the glistening yellow in the sides of a darting trout. When the miller screwed up the sluice-board and let all the water rush into the Intake Pool, the half mile of mill-lade was reduced to a series of little pools where a hunt—begun by chance—would last for hours. Absorption in it became complete. The water, which at first may have had a delicious chill, grew warm and soft as the long slakes of green and brown slime. The trout hid under the bank, under stones, and when they darted their sides glistened in the sun.

One day Kenn and Art were in the midst of a hunt, when down upon them came a torrent of water. As they leapt to the bank, they knew what had happened. Someone had deliberately screwed down the board to make fun of them. They set off at full pelt for the Intake. And there, sure enough, was Beel.

'That was a dirty trick!' said Kenn.

'Shut up!' said Beel, and looked about him with a serious air. There was a fine sea-trout in the Intake Pool, and by diverting some of the river water down the lade, Beel had lessened the chances of the trout's escape.

In a moment they were excited conspirators, scouting under Beel's orders. Then they stripped and took to the water. It was deep in the middle, deep enough to drown them. At times no more than the balls of their heads were seen. Beel, with his mouse-coloured hair flattened over his brows and his lips blowing out over his two prominent teeth, looked like a water-rat. As Kenn swam, he turned his dark head to each side like a seal. Art, younger, was the ungainly and timid human child. He came out whenever he could and ran around on the stones, his lower jaw inclined to tremble.

Every now and then all three emerged and hunted round

to see if they had shifted the trout into a place that they could reach with a stick from the edge. For long periods they lost the trout altogether amongst the central boulders. Then they would start him again. They were persistent as otters; and though at that age a few minutes may be as an hour, a day as a week, yet three hours now passed over them in a concentration wherein time was lost.

And this persistence got the trout in the end, for desperation sent it to a stone in the far quiet corner, a tiny arm of the pool. Like beavers, they dammed this arm, so that the trout, even if it escaped their hands, could not get back to the deeps. The leaning stone the trout lay under was some two feet long. Beel put a hand in at each end; they met on the trout. 'I have him,' he said. They watched his face. It swelled out under the holding of his breath. 'He's slippery,' he gasped, and held his breath again. 'I have him.' He smiled. 'He's trying to get off.' Then he cried 'Ow!' as if the trout had tickled him. His face, listening to his fingers, was all alive.

'Hurry up!' cried Kenn.

Beel prolonged his pleasure. 'I wish you could feel him,' he said. 'Ah—now I have him by the gills. I have him now. I can take him out any time.'

'Out with him then!'

'Are you ready?'

'Yes, yes!'

Beel prolonged his pleasure for another voluptuous minute; looked about him leisurely, over one shoulder and the other. Then he drew out the trout and ran in over the dry stones with him and killed him. A sea-trout with faded river spots; a plump excellent trout of about two pounds.

From the feel of the air it was well on in the afternoon. They were very hungry. They decided they would eat the trout.

When they had fixed the sluice-board as they had found it, Beel sent Art to the cave in the rocks with the trout rolled in his jersey. White and purple flowers were on the potatoes in the alluvial soil of the miller's fields. There were rows without flowers—the early varieties, as Beel knew. Through the grass Kenn and himself did a Redskin crawl and coming on the first row of earlies, thrust their hands into the soil and pulled out a dozen potatoes.

The next hour was spent in an orgy of scouting and foraging with the cave as base. Finally little Art was despatched with hens' eggs to Sans' shop. He was so terrified about doing this that he asked for his messages in a whisper, but kind-hearted Sans thought he was shy and chucked him under the chin and told him he would be a man before his mother and gave him a big pandrop to himself. When Art told his confederates of his reception, they roared with laughter. Then Beel took the pandrop from Art's mouth and had a good suck at it and passed it on to Kenn who also sucked hard at it before returning it to Art. When wafts of smoke from the fire under the iron pot stung their eyes they ducked away and wiped them, saying, 'Ding it!' They had found the pot sitting near a henhouse. Hugging the pot to his stomach, Kenn had crushed hurriedly through the nearest undergrowth and almost stepped into a hen's nest containing eleven eggs. When they tried the eggs in water, they sank at once, so they were fresh. Beel returned to the henhouse and ransacked the nests. Now in the pot were the twelve potatoes and on top of the potatoes were the three cuts of the sea-trout. The steam was hissing out round the stone lid. Beel looked sharply at Art and said, 'Don't crack the pandrop with your teeth!' Art at once handed the pandrop to Beel, who examined it carefully. 'If you're thinking there's a nut in it,' said Kenn sarcastically, 'you're wrong.' 'As if I didn't know that!' and Beel popped the hard white sweet into his mouth. Kenn felt sure that Beel would now crack the pandrop out of spite, and his teeth began to water. Beel grew very busy bending down and poking more dry sticks into the heart of the fire; then he looked high up into the cave. 'Ones will be thinking the whole rock is on fire!' he said, as he saw the smoke disappearing in a remote green funnel. He knew that they knew he was trying to divert their attention from the sweet. At this thought, his head being tilted back, the pandrop slipped into his throat and choked him. He rasped violently from the gullet and Kenn caught the ejected pandrop in mid-air. It was the neatest thing they ever saw and they laughed consumedly. Kenn sucked good and hard at the pandrop, Art watching him. Beel thought he would try one of the potatoes with a sharp stick, so he tilted off the lid, and then leant back from the steam, saying, 'Boys, will you look at that!' The skin was lifting from the edges of the cuts of trout and curd showed between the flakes. 'Nyum! Nyum!' Kenn gave the pandrop to Art and told him he could crack it if he liked, which Art immediately did.

After they had eaten the fish, the twelve potatoes, the fresh white loaf, and the pot of strawberry jam, they experienced opulent satisfaction and offered judgment upon the various carvings on smooth rock-faces within the cave. One full name chiselled to tombstone perfection claimed their complete praise and acted as a standard by which all scratching of initials and other linear inequalities were made cause for sarcastic and even jeering comment. Happy in their physical and mental condition, they looked from the mouth of their cave upon the broad world with all the sanguine confidence of freebooters and warriors. The Intake Pool, the grassland beyond, the Tor, the Broch, the strath of adventure to the left and to the right the green flat of the roses. But neither on the flat nor on the braes that rose beyond it to the crofting land could Kenn's secret glances see aught of interest. Nevertheless, these secret glances were to him a cause of mysterious pleasure. Accordingly it was Beel who first saw the woman leading the cow over the rise beyond the Intake. 'Ho! ho! what do I spy?' he cried exultingly. The cow bellowed, its neck out-thrust. The widow in black, a black shawl over her head, pulled on the rope. The cow suddenly ran forward and pulled the woman; then as suddenly stopped and bellowed the pasture fields of the world.

'She's taking her to the bull!' cried Beel in high glee. 'Come on; we'll go and watch!'

They followed him, and from the mouth of the cave

there was a very tricky climb up the rocks. Kenn went last, outwardly with evidence of mirth and excitement, but inwardly with a mysterious reluctance.

When safely over the rocks, they scrambled through the birches and came out on the path that ran by the up plantation. Fields bore away on the left, and beyond their crest could be seen the tops of the steading of the grieve's farm where the bull was kept.

'Look here,' said Kenn; 'I think I'll run off home first. They may be wanting me for something.'

Beel searched him with his greeny-blue eyes. 'Huh!' he said.

'What are you huhhing at?' Kenn demanded instantly.

'Frightened!'

'Frightened of what?'

'Frightened of your mother.'

'You shut your mouth,' said Kenn, 'or I'll shut it for you.'

'Oh you will, will you?'

'Yes, I will.'

'I'd like to see you try it.'

Beel was smiling slyly, but Kenn was white as flame. Beel backed away, sarcasm in his slyness. 'Come on, man!' he cried over his shoulder.

Kenn turned and walked slowly towards the wall of the plantation which he leapt and then found himself alone. For Beel to have said he was frightened of his mother did not anger him very much, because he wasn't frightened of her. He didn't know why he hadn't wanted to go, why he had got into such an awful rage. Miserable, he wandered from tree to tree.

CHAPTER SIXTEEN

AS THE SEASONS went on, Kenn adventured not merely farther up the river but also into a more intimate knowledge of the reaches he knew. Though Angus and himself were unaware that there existed such a thing as a geological formation of their world, they yet could talk of actual rocks and boulders as of a host of acquaintances.

'I saw a fish lie today where I've never seen one lie before. You know the red boulder near the neck of the Serpent Pool. Behind it there's the rock against which they mostly lie. Well, down a yard or so there's the edge of the reef, and behind that again you may not remember but there's a—'

'A low flagstone edge like green slime,' said Kenn, stirring from his pillow.

'Yes. Well, now, you come in from that—'

'Over a little bank of shingly stuff, is it?'

'Yes, that's it. Then there's a deep hollow again, and quite close to the bank a round boulder with sort of black stuff on it.'

'I know it! I remember once saying to myself, "If only a fish was lying there wouldn't I soon nab him!"'

'Well, now, wait till I tell you about that boulder. On the outside of it there's a hole you would never think was there. We had lost the fish and thought of giving up when on a last round of the pool didn't I spot what looked like the very edge of a tail showing—no more. In fact if it hadn't been for the shape of the thing I would never have given it a second glance. You know the shape of a salmon's tail?'

'No, man. What's it like?'

'Oh, it has a distinct shape of its own. I'll show you one sometime. If you throw that pillow I'll nip you!'

This was the precise description that the boys loved. The

recital of the physical details of a pool was exciting in itself. Kenn was absorbed and full of laughter long before Angus reached the climax.

Most of the birds they knew by name and the sight of an uncommon bird made them stand and stare. Behind the birds were their nests and their eggs. There is a mood in which nothing is more magical than to come upon a wild bird's eggs in a cunningly hidden nest. There is a blue of so unexpected and fragile a loveliness that its discovery is held in a hush vaguely uncanny. Little boys feel this. Their eyes widen. And then how delicately their fingers touch the egg. They dare to lift it—and lo! there it is on the palm. 'Boy, is it no' bonnie?' And the whisper, 'Quick! put it back! There's the birdie!' . . . They slip away, glancing over their shoulders. There are birds that will not go back to their eggs once human hands have touched them.

Of the wild flowers, they knew by name only a handful of the most common. Of mosses and grasses, they knew nothing at all—apart from their appearance and possibly their taste.

Rock and bird and plant, grasses and mosses and trees, hollows and ridges, were the world through which their river ran. In this concentration on the river itself, they had no time to learn the names of things.

What they lost here was perhaps compensated in some degree, Kenn now thinks, by a knowledge so physical or real that it could induce a direct response, in which there was an element of pure apprehension or intuition.

If one of the boys had been capable of saying, 'Pouf! the blue is merely caused by the stuff in the shell absorbing all the other colours in the spectrum,' the words might have smashed the blue, much as the stone in Kenn's fist had smashed the elver, for in the superiority that such cleverness breeds there can be a chuckling cruelty.

But where knowledge of the blueness is limited to direct vision, there is born an apprehension of it freed from 'explanation', a reaction to the mystery of its reality purified of the personal emotion of vanity. This reaction may be no more

than momentary, is rarely indeed more than momentary,
but is all the more vivid for that, as a flash of lightning
is vivid.

There is thus caught by the mind a magical perception of
blueness. And if the word magical must be explained, let it
stand for no more than the fact that the moment itself is a
moment of absorption and is remembered with a delight all
the more exquisite for being quite incommunicable.

All this is like saying that there are times when new
knowledge to a child is like a new knife.

But Kenn has an urge to be explicit, even to labour what
is infinitely elusive, because the farther he goes towards the
source of his river the more he feels there is in this very
elusiveness the significance he would like to hold.

For it might well appear that this contemplation of the
magical is opposed by scientific knowledge, that what we
have here are not merging values but antithetical or mutually
destructive values. Yet that would be wrong. The values, he
is convinced, do merge, but they must come in a certain
order. The precise knowledge possessed by himself and his
brother Angus of the physical lay-out of a pool did not kill or
weaken their absorption in the tale of the salmon hunt. On
the contrary, it intensified it, increased the objective selfless
apprehension of the whole in an exquisite way.

And now—to take the matter to a fantastic conclusion—
he feels that if the boulders were to become geological rocks,
the water a chemical compound, and the salmon a polarised
amalgam of tissues reacting to the play of certain stimuli, the
adventure in the pool would be given its cosmic application
and the mirth would break on an abrupt laugh.

For, through his boyhood approaches, he is grounded in a
relationship to his river that is fundamental and that nothing
can ever quite destroy.

And, from his river, the relationship is carried over, in
whatever degree, to every other environment in life.

His greatest friend in Glasgow was a fellow student who
came from a neighbouring village and was studying medi-
cine. After a talk one night on the infernal conditions in

some of the Glasgow slums, Kenn accompanied his friend
to a midwifery case. It was a Saturday night, and the scene,
for Kenn's fresh country senses, one of nightmare horror.
The figures in the dim close, the smash of a fist on flesh,
the sexual oaths, the scurrying feet, the dark stairway, the
stinking common lavatory, the blousy women, the filthy
room with its rags and sheets of newspapers. He had stood
near the door as if guarding it for the doctor, saying to himself
fiercely this is not the time to feel sick or faint, to make a fool
of himself, trying to turn to a boulder against the screams of
the young woman.

The young woman was trapped. She was screaming like
a beast in a trap.

But a trap of nightmare—set within the cage-trap of the
black tenements.

He was intensely aware of the trap, his gorge rising against
its uncleanness, urgent to be off, fearful in a wild way that
something would touch him. And yet fixed there by the door,
his head half turned from his companion labouring away at
his half learned job.

The intensity of his apprehension of the horror around
him thinned it to its ultimate blackened skeleton bones,
gaunt outlines that curved inward like iron girders of a
gutted ruin, with sub-human life in the base of the ruin,
scurrying through putrefying smells. The only thing that
aspired was the girl's scream; it beat up through the bars; it
cried out, O God, on peewit's wings; sibilant in agony; cried
for freedom, for liberation, for the upper air; for the death
of forgetfulness; but could not rise above the flesh clamped
in the trap.

Kenn kept himself still as a boulder, kept himself whole,
endured with primeval cunning, the grey agony on his face
grey as stone.

When anyone talked to him after that about the 'inevitable laws' of political economy, he laughed. That anyone
should attempt to justify such conditions as he had seen
in that slum backland was not so much ethically wrong
as grotesquely hideous. When a politician talked of life's

'glittering prizes', he visualised the politician's face as made of brass, with immense teeth, rabbit's teeth; the modern brazen idol face, worshipped by fear-held folk. There were only two ways one could behave towards it: either laugh at it good-naturedly or—if ignoring it became impossible— calmly, remorselessly, bomb it to smithereens. This grey thread of strength that ran through nature could be remorse-less beyond anything conceivable to the ambitious or ruthless politician. And it would have him in the end.

Man would not endure for ever the horror of that girl trapped in the slums. If not openly, then by secret, violent ways he will destroy the black cage. Kenn, who has never belonged to revolutionary political societies, knows what moves them. Old as the rocks, nameless as the old woman, warm as sunshine, insinuating as the wind, is this river that flows down the straths of time.

CHAPTER SEVENTEEN

IT WAS NOT UNTIL Kenn went to the secondary school in the county town and got his first homesickness that he saw his river no longer as a whole world but as a stream running through time in a distant place. He came back to it for the weekends, straining for hours over the handlebars of his second-hand push-bike along that northern plain where the wind can blow so relentlessly.

Many country boys left the school in a bunch and set off in racing style, heads well down, pacing one another at crackerjack speed, wheel behind wheel, dogs springing out of ditches, bells ringing, hens cackling, ducks quacking, shout and counter shout. On they swept, these new children of the northland, the persistence of sea and rock in them, and an inherited spirit more relentless than the wind.

And nothing can bring the spirit to breaking point more surely than the wind, which legend shows the northern folk have always feared and hated. For not only does it whirl the seas into tempest and wither the green shoot, but drains sea and land of colour and puts a darkness upon them— the shadow of the ancient nameless ones that rode the gale with shriek and howl, or moaned round gable-ends at dead of night. Into a head wind the boys would bore, standing on their pedals, straining at their handlebars, their hearts bursting, until they could have given shriek for shriek and wept in mad rage.

Here and there at village or township a boy would fall out and take the side road to his home, glad to have kept in the race, smiling at being out of it. One by one the lads dropped off until at last Kenn and his close friend Don pedalled on. Then Don dropped out and Kenn was left alone. And alone he kept up the same pace, relaxing nothing, for now he saw before him the harbour and the land that he knew as his own.

The folk knew him, too. 'Hullo, Kenn, boy!' and Kenn, smiling, cried back, 'Hullo!' and beat into the wind, with fine style now. Little boys turned round, following him with their eyes, saying, 'That's Kenn, home from the Academy.'

And so right up to the front door, where he leapt off and staggered a step on his trembling legs, before trundling his machine round the corner of the house and in through the back door. As he straightened himself there was a shy smile on his face. He was home and there were his mother's footsteps.

'You've got back, boy.'

'Yes.'

'You had the wind against you again.'

'Ay, a bit.'

'Come in, come in. I have your tea ready.' So Kenn followed her into the kitchen, grown tall these last few years, his face wind-reddened, his eyes glancing, slim and interesting-looking but with good bone in him.

'And how did you get on?'

'Oh, all right.' His manner was off-hand and pleasant.

'No news, have you?'

'No.'

'Here, then, sit in. Be taking plenty. Your growing body needs it. . . . Is your landlady good to you?'

'Och, she's all right.'

She had a hundred questions to ask him, but feared to annoy him, for he never had any news. He was impatient of news, had no understanding at all of her desire to learn all the things that went on in his lodgings or in the town or at school. She recognised the reticence of the growing man of her race and was never disappointed—except in what pertained to his studies. But there he was least communicative, and after the first few weeks she rarely put a question to him about the results of his class work.

She got to know about these results, however, in many indirect ways. A friend of a friend of his landlady had a niece, who was chief saleswoman in a shop in the county town, an agreeable, mannerly woman of about forty. Having got the chance of a lift in a fishcurer's car one public holiday, she called on Kenn's mother, whom she knew through a maze of kinship very involved and bridged at bloodless gaps by marriage. It was afternoon and Kenn's mother brewed a nice cup of tea in the brown earthenware teapot and offered the welcome that made her visitor feel that life was good as the tea and as gracious.

And then the talk went ahead. Folk in that country never said they would 'have a gossip', they always said they would 'have a news'. The distinction is real, for the visitor brought to Kenn's mother news of what was happening in a distant place, much as a gaberlunzie man or a drover did in the old days. Only the visitor's news had all a woman's intimacy and warmth, and, in fact, Kenn's mother loved each morsel of it, listening with a touch of that wonder which is the native core of good manners.

'Mrs Budge, is it! She looks after her four boy lodgers as if they were her own. She knows all their subjects: Maths, Science, French, Latin, English. You would think she had studied them herself! And she doesn't hesitate, I can assure you, to ask them if they've done their home lessons! Not she! I'll tell you a story about her. . . .'

'She must be a nice woman.'

'She is. She thinks very highly of your boy, Kenn, anyway. You know, when anyone of them does well at school, she's quite proud! Sure as I'm telling you. When Kenn came out top in his class for Maths and Science, she was that prim and pawky you would think she had done the papers herself! Not praising, but just—you know—like a general, nodding approval!'

A deep warm glow suffused Kenn's mother. It was the first word of her boy's success she had heard. Her eyes grew full of light. She smiled, saying quietly, 'Kenn never says much.'

Miss Sinclair looked at her sharply. 'Do you mean to say you didn't know?'

'Well, to tell the truth, I didn't. He wouldn't like to tell me, maybe. There was just the school report.'

Miss Sinclair recorded her astonishment.

'Let me fill your cup,' said Kenn's mother. 'It was so kind of you to come to see me. And I like your news.'

'Well, isn't he a young rascal?' Miss Sinclair laughed, delighted now that she had been the first to bring the news.

'He's all that,' said Kenn's mother. 'This is a poor tea. I wish I had nicer things for you.'

'Indeed,' said Miss Sinclair, 'I'd come twice as far for your welcome, not to mention your tea. It's the best tea I've ever tasted.'

'The little drop of cream does make a difference.'

'Well! well!' said Miss Sinclair, still astonished. 'And what are you going to put him in for?'

'We don't know. But I thought—' she hesitated, then looked with pleasant frankness at her visitor—'well, he got a little bursary from the school here and what one way or another but we managed to send him to the Secondary, though I am ashamed at thinking of the little Mrs Budge gets. She must be a nice woman.'

Miss Sinclair was silent for a moment, then drank her tea.

'We can only do one thing at a time,' said Kenn's mother, 'and it is a mercy he has had this chance itself. I am glad he is sort of doing well.' She paused. 'They are saying,' she resumed quietly, 'that if he got his Higher Leaving Certificate he might get into a bank or something like that. I don't know.'

The impersonality in the last words was not lost on Miss Sinclair.

'They are saying,' she repeated. 'Hmf! Bank, indeed!'

They were silent for a little, their minds in secret accord. 'They would!' continued Miss Sinclair, '—especially if he's clever! What's to hinder him competing for the Highlands and Islands Bursary, I'd like to know?'

'I've thought of that quietly to myself. But seemingly it's

a hard competition and we can't expect everything. And even then—it would hardly be enough.'

'No, but it's for three years. And surely to goodness some of the rest of the family could put together the little extra each year and see him through? Excuse me butting in on what is no business of mine, but if I had a clever boy like your son Kenn—what on earth am I saying?' She laughed, none the less heartily because she had said all she had wanted to say.

The two hours they spent together seemed to Kenn's mother no more than a blink of sunshine, they went past so quickly. And for days afterwards the memory of them kept her unusually quiet.

Neither of them had had to mention the word university.

But affairs did not arrange themselves readily into Miss Sinclair's pattern. During recent years the local fishing had been steadily declining. The young men, seeing no future in it for them, were emigrating or drifting to the cities. Crews got broken up, until the white fishing was being pursued by the old skippers working together in twos and threes on small open boats.

Kenn's father and his old friend Sandy Sutherland had a small boat between them. They needed a third to hold her up against the wind and the drift of the tides while they fished. Sandy's family was dispersed between Glasgow and Vancouver. Davy had no one left with him except his son Kenn, now nearing his seventeenth birthday. Davy's secret hope had been placed in his son Angus, but Angus had gone with other lads to Canada four years before, and so the tradition of the sea was broken. This was a hidden source of regret for him; but outwardly he recognised the stress of circumstance.

Yet it was with deep misgiving that he at last approached his wife and said they would need someone if they were to make anything of the fishing at all.

Long she had dreaded this approach, for she knew what was in her husband's mind.

'Well, we have no one,' she said.

He was silent.

'You cannot be thinking, surely,' she said, 'of asking the boy to leave school?'

'Well, I don't know,' he said helplessly.

'Surely not that! He's in his last year. He'll soon be doing his Orals for the Higher Leaving Certificate. And after that, he'll have the Highlands and Islands Bursary Competition. This will be to ruin everything. All that we have struggled for will come to nothing. It is too terrible to think of.'

'It's not for myself.'

'Is there no one else? Surely there's someone.'

'There's no one, as you know. It's only for a few weeks till we see.'

They were silent, then Davy got up and went out. She sat by herself thoughtfully for a long time.

Nor did they discuss the matter again, but went quietly about their tasks. He felt the silence in her mind far more than any effect absence from school might have on the fortunes of his son.

On Friday evening, as she sat by the fire, the sound of Kenn's grounding feet, as he leapt off the bicycle, went stounding through her. She looked up with a scared expression. Then she rose and smoothed her thought away.

'Did you have a good run?'

'Yes. The wind was in our backs.' He was smiling and fresh looking and hungry. But over their meal, he saw that something was wrong.

'Will you tell him what we are thinking?' her husband asked her.

'You can tell him yourself,' she replied.

Then his father told him quite simply and in a reasonable way the position in which Sandy and himself were placed. 'You would get your share of the takings,' he added, 'if you could manage to get off school for the time. Do you think you could manage?'

Kenn was silent for a little while. 'It's not allowed,' he said, 'but I could see.'

'Would it interfere with your lessons much?' his father asked him.

Kenn took a little time.

'Not much,' he answered.

'What about the bursary competition?' his mother enquired without any stress.

'I could take my books home with me.' He happened to glance up from his plate and met the look that came into her eyes at his words and what they meant; then he glanced down again, a small thrill going through him.

'Very well, then.' His father nodded. 'I'll see Sandy tonight. And you can see the headmaster on Monday.'

And no more was said.

Holding up the boat if the wind was at all strong was an arduous business. One's seat grew tender and arms numb. The oars were heavy and creaked against the thole pins; unwieldy brutes with long narrow blades that raised blisters even between the fingers. The small of the back ached, and every now and then one tried to ease the pain by bending the spine inward and sliding back a little on the thaft until one sat on one's thighs.

'Keep her up, Kenn! Keep her up!'

The two men with beards thrust out, showing the sinews of their hairy necks, and eyes far-sighted, seemed to listen-in through their fingers to the bottom of the sea. They fished with fine skill and a patience that took no account of time. To Kenn they seemed brutally insensitive of his toil, but his pride kept him silent and, when his body was crying out like the creaking oars, he would shift and slither and find some new point of balance. When they struck a fruitful patch, they would make him 'keep her there'.

But when the fishing was over, they would smile to him with that easy good-nature and kindness that came so naturally. However quick their fishing actions or peremptory their commands, the men themselves conveyed this impression always of giving the passing of time the timelessness of the waves of the sea. 'You must be tired, boy,' Sandy would

say. 'You did grand. Give us the oars now.' And with an oar
apiece, the two men would put the nose of the boat on the
harbour and pull a slow stroke that appeared to have no kick
in it at all, the oar seeming merely to rise and fall. In the
stern Kenn gave way to the relief of inaction and found it
good; found it so good that his mood became pensive, and
the company of the old men strangely uplifting.

They went to sea between one and two o'clock on these
May mornings and were in harbour again shortly before
seven. The Higher Leaving Certificate examination over,
the school authorities had been considerate enough, in view
of the special circumstances, to temper the rule that required
regular attendance to the end of the session, so long as Kenn
put in an occasional appearance. Accordingly, on a day when
the weather looked promising, Kenn would come straight
off the sea, wash himself, change his clothes, snatch some
breakfast, leap on his bicycle, and start on the long road
for school. At four in the afternoon he walked out of school,
leapt on his machine, and started back, lucky if at his best
pace he could do the distance in two tearing hours. From this
journey he had no sooner tumbled into bed, than his father's
hand seemed to be at his shoulder. It was one o'clock in the
morning again, and they had to be on the height of the sea
before the dawn broke, for that was the time when the fish
took best.

These few weeks, hard as they were, provided one of the
most enriching experiences of his life. Strength lies curled
in the memory of them, and something of courage travelling
with the eyes to a great distance.

Each Saturday afternoon all three met in a sheltered hollow
within sight of the sea and shared out the week's takings.
Sandy insisted that Kenn should have a full third share. On
the second Saturday, when the money had been divided,
Kenn drew from an inside pocket a half-bottle of whisky
and presented it to them.

They could not believe their eyes. 'Bless me, boy!' said

Sandy. 'What's this?' said his father. 'What?' said Sandy. Their faces shone with wonder.

Life was a glass that brimmed over. As its colour went over Kenn's face, he smiled awkwardly. Rarely has inspiration so perfect, so unforgettable, a moment. He loved the two old men, and felt the comradeship of all the toilers of the world.

Each Saturday after that when he presented his gift, they showed the same signs of astonishment. 'Bless me, what's this I see?' They never took it for granted.

And he left them there sitting on the grass, wet or fine, the black twist going well in their pipes, their voices friendly and quiet, and the bottle passing between them at unhurried intervals.

When Davy came home, his mood was perceptibly quickened and there was upon him a desire to do odd jobs about the house, to take in the peats and fix the stack, to tidy the whole place with a seaman's hands. His wife regarded this mood with humoured tolerance.

'Is he at his lessons?' Davy would whisper.

'Yes,' she would reply in her normal voice, with a large unconcern.

He would nod to that and take care that no unnecessary noise disturbed his son, shut away like a young alchemist amid the mysteries of his studies.

To get his Higher Leaving Certificate, Kenn had to pass in four subjects. He had elected to sit five: Mathematics, Science, English, French and Latin. The certificate would not only qualify him for entrance to any of the Scottish universities, but also would ensure payment of the usual fees by the Carnegie Trust.

The Higher Leaving Certificate examination is one of the fairest in the world, for His Majesty's Inspectors of Schools give personal consideration to all those border-line cases where, for one reason or another, a pupil may not have done himself justice in the actual examination. Accordingly, there is a certain lapse of time before the results are published.

Though Kenn had sat the Leaving Certificate examination

before starting the sea-fishing, yet his recent absence from school had so weighed on his mother's mind that the whole thought of success for him had got shadowed over.

Then the results were published, and it was found that Kenn had passed in all five subjects.

Life is good, too, she thought. Folk are often not grateful enough for the goodness that can be showered on them.

'You have done well,' she said to Kenn.

'Ach, that's nothing,' he answered, dismissing the subject.

She made an extra good supper for the three of them, but Kenn did not rise to the occasion. She could get no warmth out of him. He was awkward and reticent in his manner and gloomed a little when his mother was specially friendly. He left the table at the earliest moment, not hurriedly, but with a preoccupied air.

She did not really mind this. There is a time in adolescence when children often become impatient of their parents. She understood her son; knew that Kenn would hate herself or her husband to boast of his success, would hate it intensely out of all his secret boy's pride.

But in the succeeding days, there were times when she feared even to talk to him other than impersonally. In three weeks he was due to sit the bursary examination.

As the day drew near, she grew so sorry for him that her own mind was freed entirely from its secret hopes. Out of all those who would compete in the northern counties, you could count the successful ones on your hand. How could she expect her son, with far less than no help at home, to be one of them?

A very heavy burden was laid on the poor. To forget it and dream was to ask for the awakening.

The morning came when Kenn left to sit the examination. Her mind in the empty house was like a heavy still day in autumn.

But for Kenn the examination provided a new kind of thrill from science. For the first time he passed beyond the personal, as in stories about men like Faraday, to that impersonal region where facts take on an ordered significance and the whole cosmos is seen opening out like a fan. Balfour Stewart's *Physics* had been a prescribed textbook and from its study he had acquired many facts about such practical things as levers, pulleys, the parallelogram of forces, or old Archimedes' flotation principle. But now, in the excitement of the examination, when he turned over his physics paper, the first question ran: *Enumerate the principal forms of energy and show they are traceable to the sun.*

So different was it from any question he had ever met before that it lay on the white paper like a dark band. It came up against his mental sight like a bandage.

He thrust it from him and tackled the remaining straightforward questions of textbook knowledge. But all the time he was answering these, his under mind must have been doing something about that first question, for when at last he was ready for it, his shoulders squared themselves, his elbows stuck down hard joints on the desk, and his thought, over a beating heart, began to follow the vast revolving processes that go to form such forces as coal and waterfalls and tides. Coal, a carbon from trees and other plant life; green leaves, by the action of their chlorophyll *in sunlight*, remove carbon dioxide from the atmosphere and return oxygen to it, hence carbon assimilation. Forests of dead trees turn into coal. . . . Sun takes up water into clouds; clouds fall and form rivers and waterfalls; falling water directly used for making electricity. . . . The cycles of acction were cosmic wheels, opening fanlike, each spoke glittering in Kenn's mind. The excitement of apprehension made his brain extraordinarily clear; his sentences were factual and precisely written. It was the first time that he had ever consciously evolved out of himself the marvel of the universe, and when he read over what he had written, he was queerly thrilled.

He had to wait about six weeks for the result of the examination. When his mother saw him secretly hanging about the house at the postman's hour, her heart ached and she hoped she had done him no wrong. Then the forenoon came when she heard the postman cry cheerily, 'One for you, Kenn.'

'Thanks,' said Kenn. 'It's a grand day.'

'Oh, grand! Any fish the-day?'

A few more casual words, and she heard Kenn's footsteps going round the house. Then there was silence.

'Be kind to him,' she prayed blindly.

The back-door latch rattled. He was coming in. Smiling awkwardly, he showed some papers.

'It's the result of the bursary comp.'

She waited.

'I've got it,' he said.

She looked at him. 'My dear boy,' she murmured.

Then for the first time in his scholastic career, he volunteered a piece of personal information. 'I've passed first for the northern counties.' He gave a little laugh and handed her the papers.

She took the papers and held them in her hands, her head bowed looking down at them. She made no sound. When he heard her tears fall on the paper he turned away, his mouth opening in a silent, half-derisive laugh.

Outside, the brightness of the day had increased. He hung on the doorstep a minute, held by the look in his mother's eyes when she had said 'My dear boy'. As if she had got the whole world! The wind murmured in the leaves of the tall elm tree. The world was tall and charged with cool radiant light.

He gave his secret smile free play when he got beyond the Intake, and the Tor and the Broch rose in front of him. He saw his father coming into the house and his mother handing him the papers. 'God bless me!' his father would say on that quiet note of wonder. They would sit silent for a little, taking it in. Kenn looked about him, then opened his mouth wide and laughed softly. His father would begin doing little things about the house as if Sandy and himself had just finished the halfie! The humour of all this was irresistible to Kenn. He felt himself drunk with the fun and delight of it. One thing was certain, no salmon that ever breathed was safe on the river this day!

He did not even look at the Broch Pool. He took to the woods. His flesh tingled with power and cunning. No force could trap him, no living thing follow him. In the long trek to the Smuggler's Pool, he rested once or twice to absorb the silence and the feel of the atmosphere, as if an extra sense inside him would be receptive to the most exquisite disturbance. As indeed he knew it would be. His eyes leapt to the bird amongst its myriad leaves; his ears caught the song of the gnat; through his suspended breathing went the surge of the earth. And around him, at his feet, down the alleyways of the wood, were all the things, the dead and living things, so intimate to his blood. The leaves screened boulders in the river, gave him the half-glance of a pool.

With what infinite variety moved the wind in the leaves! No sigh, hardly even a whispering, but a communion ineffably intimate, yet passing away into the austerities, like a quiet wind round the heath of a mountain, upon the grey breast of a planet lifting to the dawn.

To have passed first! *First!*

He remembered how fine it had been long ago when he had come here with Angus, how quiet and caught away into freedom. Angus had been good to him, to have bothered so much as he had, to have been so friendly. It gave life a fine feeling to think there was that sort of pleasant kindness in it; never expressed but there, like a magnetic field. If Angus were here just now, wouldn't he be in great form! What a day they would have! They'd probably go all the way to the Waterhead!

Kenn's eyes glanced hither and thither. His thought was quick in him as the wings of a bird, leaving behind as slight a disturbance on the air.

His mother's eyes soft with light, when she had spoken. 'My dear boy.' A shade too much to bear, that . . . and picking up a stone, he let fly at a tree.

Whereupon, all alert again, his loneliness rushed in upon

him and, hearkening with half-open mouth, he caught the hidden ecstasy. Immediately he got to his feet and was off.

Beyond the Smuggler's Pool, the river wound by rocky ledges with overhanging rowans and bushes. There were some quite good pools here, but Kenn knew that they had been well searched since the water had cleared after the last spate. His only real hope lay beyond the distant ledges where the water tumbled over in a small falls.

Yet he could not resist the temptation of looking in the pools whenever they were sufficiently screened. The fascination they had had for Angus they now had for Kenn.

From pool to pool he went, moving noiselessly as a roe, standing still as a heron, his skin flushed with warmth, his heart beating softly.

The Falls Pool was deep and long and had some great submerged ledges where salmon could hide. He was tempted to strip, but his instinct was against it, and he slid round the last rocky corner and faced the moors.

There now came upon him the third division of his Highland river. The first part was from the sea to the Broch, it belonged to man and was populous with his affairs. From the Broch to the falls was the second part or the strath. Quite elderly visitors would sometimes penetrate here for a picnic and tend to behave as if they were children of once upon a time.

Out of that second part boyhood rose up and faced the moors, where there were no longer trees and hollows, rock-faces and caves, but suddenly an immense bareness, with the soul isolated in a loneliness that could no more be hidden. The secret smile died here—lest it be seen; though now, more than ever, there was no one to see.

Here at last was born the notion of the source.

In thought, this notion gives birth in turn to abstract words, like eternity. This is the desert place into which the prophets went to find their gods. The seers pondered here so long that they conquered their bodies and moved outside them in visions bright and clear as the evening skies beyond the moor ridges.

From the populous place, again and again in the ages man has come hither to find that which was lost.

In between lies the strath of youth.

Upon Kenn, emerging from the strath, this land of bare moors had their austere effect; but he was hunting nothing abstract. The 'salmon of knowledge' for him had real silver scales and a desirable shape; the eyes he feared were the telescope eyes of gamekeepers. Always in life he has sought tangible things. Always he is conscious of having evaded the authoritarian conception of God, of having disbelieved in solemnity. He has never been one of the chosen, of the elect. His instinct is against them. If God is solemn and important, then his instinct is to smile secretly and vanish away like a cloud shadow, a flying gleam.

Far as he could see, no life moved. The shallow depression of the river his eyes followed into the moors until it curved westward behind a long, low ridge. The pools had much greater distances between them now, and they, too, were shallow. It was difficult to hide here.

Kenn went steadily along the river bank, his eyes lifting to the moors at every other step, to distant skylines, to a sudden curlew or grouse or peewit, and as he went he began to feel that he was being received. The assurance that had been with him all day did not desert him now. On the contrary, as with one who has successfully encountered early dangers, there grew in him a feeling of well-being, of a strange and thrilling confidence.

This feeling, he knew, would not be perfected until he had landed a salmon. That would be the test of all the hidden eyes. And there at last stretched the long quiet Peat Pool.

He had hardly reached the foot of it when from before him went a heavy arrow of water. He stood still, his heart beating painfully, watching the arrow as it slowed and swerved towards the bank, and the troubling of the water ceased.

Here even the fish had watching eyes! And it was a heavy fish.

Half an hour later he landed the salmon with his hands, for the hollows under the grassy bank made the use of the gaff difficult. There was a short, sharp struggle in the water before he staggered ashore wet to the neck. A twenty-pound cock fish, with strong nose, and silver sheen discoloured with red mating strength. A splendid brute. He carried it to a peat bank and carefully covered it over with turves cut that May by the flauchter-spade in tirring the bank. Then, taking the bearings of the bank on the hill road, so that he could readily reach the spot in the dark, he went on a short distance and lay down and looked round on the world—in which no living thing moved.

He began smiling, his lips lifting in that half-derisive way he had unconsciously learned from Angus. Slowly he peeled off his wet shirt and wrung it out with all his strength and spread it to dry. Then he took off his trousers and did his best to wring them before giving them to the air. His jacket and socks and shoes were dry, as he had slipped them off before going to battle.

The sun shone on his naked body with delicious warmth. He curled and moved and stretched himself, ran his palms down his skin; looked himself over, then poked his head up and looked over the world.

Here, near the source, body and spirit stirred, but not in strife; in communion rather; in an intercommingling drowsy with pleasure, hazed with desire, but with the sluggish snake in the blood searching, through the aftermath of physical tiredness, for the divine state that borders sleep.

An hour passed.

There came upon him an intense reluctance to put on his clothes and leave this place, as though he had fallen in love with his own body and would take it up the river bank, naked, and in behind the horizon to the river's source, the wind upon its skin. This gentle wind was gaiety's self, with sly finger tips of fun. It carried no code of behaviour at all—except that of fanning one when one grew too hot!

For a time he was tempted to go naked to the next pool,

half a mile away, but decided in the end that he dared not risk human eyes.

Reluctantly he put on his dry shirt and his damp trousers and made for home. From the rock of the falls he turned and looked back.

Quiet and heedless and brown and vacant. Its wind had already forgotten him. A small pang touched his heart, and as he went down through the trees by the rocks he felt like one who for a little had escaped into a world no longer known to those who live on this earth.

A strange thing happened to him that night, when he returned at midnight to fetch home the salmon. For the first time in all his experience, he found that he no longer had any fear of the dark.

A premonition of this had come upon him when his father and mother had tried to dissuade him from the journey. Not that they said much, but he could feel how important he had grown in his mother's eyes. She was afraid that something would happen to him at this last moment that would interfere with everything! His results had been so far beyond their expectations, that this was a tempting of Providence! Life had taught her that the Lord thy God is a jealous God. It was the moment, not for further temptation, but for the offering of thanksgiving.

Yet her son was following the tradition of the men of her race. It was not now the value of the salmon. For that matter she did not need it, did not (in a sudden revulsion of feeling) want, to see it inside her door. Surely it was due to her at last to be freed for ever from uncertainty and fear. Yet the thing was in the very warp and weft of their lives; one with the stormy seas; the dark winter mornings when her husband rose from her side and, with his heavy line on his oilskin back, shut the door behind him and left her listening to the ominous wind. In all that pertained to the outside world, the men made their own decisions. They were hunters, hunting the northern and western seas as their remote ancestors had hunted the forests and the grasslands, as their sons got apprenticed to the hunt by finding the thrill and the fun (as boys must) on river and moor.

Accordingly neither father nor mother directly forbade their son's going. He was a good son and his decision must be respected.

'I am frightened of you going,' was all she said to him, but her eyes conveyed more than a woman's pleading.

He turned away. 'Where's the potato bag?'

Quietly she began to hunt for the bag, but could not find it.

'Did you see the potato bag?' she asked her husband.

'I did not,' he replied shortly. He could hardly keep still, his brows ridged, his eyes quick and stormy. He always disliked this moment, never wanted to have anything to do with it. There seemed a greater fear in him of disgrace falling upon the household than in her. He was old enough, perhaps, to have inherited a fear of ruthless lairds and their factors and an urge to keep clear of them and the powers of court and imprisonment they could move to their ends. To be beholden to no man, to be stigmatised by no institution, to keep his head up and his eyes level, was part of his instinct.

The only bag the mother could find had contained meal and was white and floury.

'It'll do fine,' said Kenn, now impatiently anxious to be off. He rolled it into a bundle and went out the back door. On the corner of the house, he began flailing the flour dust out of it. The back door opened and his father came towards him. It was very dark after the lamp light.

'Look here, boy,' his father said, 'I'll come with you.' His tone was companionable and almost gentle in its friend-liness.

'No, no, Father,' said Kenn at once.

'Yes. I'll come with you. It's so dark.'

'No, no,' said Kenn. 'I'll be no time.'

Kenn rolled up the bag and put it under his jacket. 'I'll be off.'

As he walked away, his smile was slightly warm. He

couldn't help feeling it was nice of his father, all the same—
like the time long ago when he warmed his hands in his
hair! He chuckled silently to himself. He had good parents,
anyway. Hang it, he would do anything for them! How lucky
it was he had passed first!

He felt now in extraordinary good humour, and as the
moors had received him in the day so now the darkness
received him in the night.

In all his life in the city, Kenn missed the darkness of night.
In his student years, before and after the war, he was often
driven to the country to get his head clear and his body
functioning. His resources were so strictly limited that he
had to consider thoughtfully the purchase of a tram ticket
that would take him towards open country. But the rare day
outings were rarely refreshing. Aimless walking on roads
never deserted made him hot and sticky and gave him the
feeling he imagined wild animals in a zoo must have. Gritty
dust and heat in the pads and the passing of gaping humans.
There was no solitude, no loneliness.

But at night, he expected something different; there was
the hope that, unseen in the darkness, he would get so far
away from all other life that he would find himself, and be
able to glance over his shoulders, and look at the heavens,
and smile openly, knowing he was free.

But it never turned out like that, because he could not
get away from artificial lights. However far he went, at
hand or in the distance there were lights always to be
seen; rows of lights marching towards the city, lights on
rumbling tramcars, headlights of motor cars, clusters of
lights that were distant suburbs or towns, lights reflected
in a dull glow even in the heavens.

This affair of city lights became with him a secret obsession, so that, to this day, he finds himself any night in the
open consciously observing light after light, as other men
count stone steps or hit railings, but in his case always with
the feeling of the lights as a tyranny, even a menace; and this
was the more remarkable because he never altogether lost

his country feeling for the magical quality of light or fire. It may have been that these lights had their counterparts in the panthers in the zoo! though that is a depth unnecessary to plumb, for all that Kenn profoundly missed was the darkness of night in which no single man-light shone. He craved this so ardently at times that it kept him walking to the point of exhaustion.

In later academic years, he was introduced one night by Edinburgh friends to the illumination of the Castle on its rock. 'Doesn't it look like some fairy castle in a German legend!' the young woman had exclaimed. He had remained silent, smiling, but inwardly abashed and appalled. The old castle against its night-sky had on occasion caught his mind up into the strength, and the broken strength, of his country's history; hunted men of the Covenant, troopers of the moss hags, the old ballad poetry, the gathering of clans, the pomp and treacheries of courts and kings—the castle on its rock abiding them all, the eternal yea of the Scots spirit. Now become the fairy castle in a German legend. A peep-show.

But it was not so much this illumination, appropriate enough possibly, that affected him in the first instant as his instinctive feeling of treachery to the night.

For the truth was that he loved the darkness. He had loved it ever since that night when with the white meal bag under his jacket he had been received by it. As he passed the Tor and the Broch, their aged secrecies were no longer fearsome. If he had heard a keeper coming, he would have slipped into the little stone chamber and waited till the menace had passed with a feeling of confidence. It was not the place where keepers or landlords would look for him!

Through the laughter of such a thought ran the feet of the folk.

For on this night too—though he did not realise it until he began to retrace his steps by his Highland river with some care—substance was given to his belief in the folk, of whom he was one. This belief has accompanied him with an elusive assurance of power. It explains to him why in history he always found the greatest difficulty in remembering the genealogical trees of kings or the dates of dynastic wars. In a profound sense, they were of no interest to him.

More than that, they contrive to make him feel, in contrast, the value of his own home life. The aristocratic element he discovered in the sea spirit of his father and in the rare wisdom of his mother, for beneath the manifestations, crude or delicate, of their material living, is always a responsiveness quick as delight or pain. Accordingly he finds it difficult to understand why men of genius of 'humble origin'—nearly always, however, of artistic genius—have so frequently craved recognition by the leaders of society, and is inclined to put it down to an early environment vitiated by unnatural social conditions. Robbed of a background of their own, they aspired to one which would most readily permit the free exercise of their fine gifts of recognition and response.

But how tragical the aspiration so frequently proved itself to be, not merely because of the inevitable defeats inflicted by snobbery, but because the greater the genius the more certain the failure of finding the desired background where it was looked for. Tragical finally to his gifts.

These men did not come out of the folk; they came out of bodies tied to the million handles of a million wheels, thwarted bodies giving birth now and then to the dream of freedom that so mysteriously haunts them.

If kings and nobles and millionaires did not specially attract Kenn, he believes it was because he had no particular need of them, not out of pride, inverted or otherwise, but simply because all the more subtle elements of human intuitions, the sap and health of life, came naturally out of his heritage from the folk. Whether in this he was exceptional manifestly did not matter, because, scientifically considered, a solitary exception is good enough! It is difficult to be solemn or assertive about it. Nor would the whole subject be permitted to destroy reticence by more than a smile, were it not that in this belief in the fundamental value of his folk experience there is for Kenn a haunting augury of the future. Indeed if he were to probe deep enough he would probably find here one of the reasons prompting his mind to acceptance of the modern anthropologist's belief in the existence once upon a time of the golden age!

This may provide the speculative pleasure of an amusing idealism; may evoke even the laughter of fantasy—bitter a trifle before the horrors of the life of the poor, before the realism of sociological novelists or the crime and disease statistics of official records. But Kenn strives to distinguish the accidents of life from life itself. The life of an atom is as unpredictable as the life of a man. An atom of uranium may blow up at birth or live for a million years. But that does not deter Kenn, in his work on nuclear physics, from charting the radioactive principle through milliards of years.

If only one could chart the radioactive principle of mind! What a piece of research would be there! In comparison, how trifling the utmost limits of the physicist's knowledge: the scratchings of a few meanings on a photographic plate, like the beginnings of some primitive ogham script.

It would certainly be an exquisitely intricate piece of work to chart the reactions of Kenn's mind to the darkness of that far river world when the last crofter's light sank into the heather!

It is the sort of thought that makes him dream dreams and see in his tubes and tiny electric currents and recording apparatus the flint arrow heads and stone drawings of his brothers who travelled before him into the straths of darkness.

The cry of the peewit is the cry of the living human, anxious, swift, flashing to earth. The long cry of the curlew passes overhead, disembodied and unearthly. Once the crying of curlews in the night had made him think of the men and women and children burned out of their homes in Strathnaver more than a century before. The spirits of his people, the disinherited, the nameless, the folk.

Threading the darkness towards the Falls Pool with the twenty-pound salmon in the white bag on his back, he certainly was one of them! And the knowledge gave him so sure a power that he could smile with speculative humour at thought of keepers and bailiffs, and feel kindly disposed towards them, and even grateful for the extra thrill they provided!

Above him, as he left the falls behind, he saw the cemetery against the sky. The tombstones, showing over the wall, were tall and short, broad-shouldered and slim, as humans are. But the older stones inside were flat to the grass, as he knew, and the names and the dates half eaten away. Once Angus had said to him that he, too, would pass the place at midnight. And here he was, not frightened at all. A vague apprehension, perhaps—sort of dynamic potential: but no fear!

When he saw what appeared to be two of the tombstones move, the supernatural did not even flick him. Instantly he knew that here in very fact were the two keepers.

His thinking must have been extremely swift, for in the very moment that he saw their dark heads and shoulders move against the sky, he swung the bag from his back and threw himself down, not on the heather but on the bag, lest its whiteness be seen. The whole of him must certainly have been in some extraordinary state of harmony to have worked so flawlessly without conscious thought.

He heard their footsteps on the moor road not twenty paces away. He buried his face in the heather and dug his hands deep.

And then a new sound began to come at him with a dreadful stealthiness; a soft swishing of the heather by infinitely careful feet. Nearer, nearer still, like spirit feet, until quite distinctly he heard a release of breath in nostrils. Directly towards him, towards his vulnerable head, with the cautious movement he himself would adopt towards a crouching hare.

There was a slight pause, a suspension of action above him, and then a wet substance was thrust into his ear, with a sniffing and hissing of breath.

Kenn lay as one dead.

A sharp whistle came from the road, and the swishing through the heather receded. A keeper's dog is too well trained to bark or make any fuss. Presently, lifting his head, Kenn saw nothing move against the sky. Picking up the bag, he slipped down round the cemetery and made his way home through the hollows of the night.

CHAPTER EIGHTEEN

'ELEVEN O'CLOCK. It never gets quite dark now.' Radzyn turned his dark-grey, close-cropped head and looked out of the high western window of the laboratory. It was the last night of June and the roofs and spires were clear cut against a green sky. The light in the green made Kenn imagine the East, deserts, a remote stillness in thought. The quiet tones of his chief's voice did not seek an answer and both men remained in an easy silence.

Radzyn was a Pole whose brilliance was held in leash by an unremitting conscientiousness. This quality of thoroughness was also Kenn's. In both men it was an implacable force. Radzyn on rare occasions gave utterance to a philosophic phrase. Kenn perceived it as a use of invisible irony, and from the moment Radzyn surprised the shadow of derision at the corner of his lips, there began to grow between them a delicate friendship.

Not that Kenn always understood his chief's references. He recognised the irony, but too frequently missed its bearing. For his education, he regretfully realised, had been too circumscribed, directed too purposefully to one specific end. Radzyn's range of knowledge, on the other hand, was wide and deep, so deep that it was of the stuff of his silence.

He had been driven, Kenn could see, by an innate need 'to find out'. Something disturbingly beyond even love of learning for its own sake. Whereas he, Kenn, had started out with no more than the narrow Scottish idea of 'getting on', of making the conquest of a certain limited knowledge subserve the material need to establish himself.

There seemed a profound distinction here in their respective approaches to knowledge. And Kenn certainly did a lot of private reading to try to meliorate the harshness of his ignorance. But the more he read the more he realised the distinction was not really so profound as it seemed. Radzyn, for example, had a far keener personal ambition to excel as a scientist than ever Kenn would have, however complex the motive behind. In flashes, Kenn saw this in him, and admired therefore all the more the infinite patience of the man, his incorruptible integrity. But it meant, at odd moments, that expression of quietude, which Kenn instinctively felt was a holding of restlessness in iron fingers. Kenn realised he was spared those personal stresses and inner conflicts, but whether because of the narrowness of his knowledge or of something native to his character, he could not be sure.

'I suppose', Radzyn added, 'in the far north it hardly gets dark at all.'

'Practically not at all,' said Kenn. 'The red of sunset and sunrise merge. They play bowls at Thurso at midnight.'

'And what will you do with yourself?'

'Oh, I'll knock about and fish and that.' He paused. 'Though actually I have one small idea—I intend to walk a certain river to its source.'

Radzyn turned from the window and looked at him.

Kenn's eyes brightened in humour. 'It's a thing I have wanted to do for a long time. That's all really.'

'Not a pilgrimage?'

'Hardly!'

'You mean that it is—slightly?'

'Well, perhaps, slightly.' And pin-point gleams in his eyes held a certain challenge.

'Very interesting.' Radzyn never nodded. His dark eyes had at certain moments a just perceptible Mongol cast. Kenn had early been attracted by this, though why he could not say. Possibly from some irrational feeling that Radzyn belonged to a folk, had a native background or thickness rather than a European or continental polish. Though his social manners were indeed exquisite. 'Nothing like that Yogi's pilgrimage to Lake Mānas?'

'Not exactly!' said Kenn.

'What, by the way, did you think of that?'

'I really don't know what to think of it. The details of the early part of his journey were recorded quite precisely. But that at the end of it he sat without moving for three days and three nights on a frozen lake high up the mountain in a snow-storm and then had his vision and came away—I begin to wonder how he checked his time; I am assailed by our Western scepticism.'

'And yet you have a feeling that things may have happened as he said?'

'I just—don't know.'

'You have been thinking of this pilgrimage up your river for a long time?'

'I suppose I have.'

'However elementary, unconscious, you too therefore must have a vision?'

'Yes.'

'You admit that?'

'Well, yes.'

'You smile—but the psychologist might find something here.' Radzyn smiled, too, in the way that subtly composed his face. But Kenn saw that he was restless a little, wanted to probe, out of the mood induced by the evening, or by some temporary wash of loneliness at thought of parting, possibly. 'I have observed the way some of your Celtic poets have lately been inclined towards the East. You had better be careful.'

'Oh I know pretty definitely what to expect.'

'You mean you expect, at the source, to find something?'

Kenn held his eyes. 'I do.'

'What?'

'Nothing.'

They continued to look at each other in the dimming light. Then into Radzyn's expression, without perceptible facial change, there came a politeness of profound derision.

'That sounds very philosophic.'

'It's quite literal,' Kenn answered simply.

'I think I look for too much.'

'I think, perhaps, you do.'

'How old are you, may I ask?'

'Thirty-seven,' said Kenn.

'I am fifty-five,' said Radzyn. 'Perhaps when I look now I look for something. It is age.'

There was silence for a short time.

'By nothing I meant no vision.'

'I understand,' said Radzyn. 'The scientist has no beliefs: he has only his eyes and his brain. He has nothing else.'

Here was the moment of enigmatic humour that Kenn sometimes found difficult, yet rarely to the point of being unresponsive to its essence or colour.

'Of all the creeds—how it is the most difficult.'

'I suppose it is,' Kenn answered quietly.

'You suppose.'

Kenn darkened slightly and kept silent.

'How much more entertaining for us if you had been going to be *enceinte* with a vision.'

Under the irony was often a slash of cruelty almost savage, and yet—as Kenn felt now—utterly impersonal. Not directed against him, but against the bitterness of the unknown withheld, of the dark, and at the same time against the soft assurance of religions, of visions, of satisfying philosophies. In a sense it hardly touched Radzyn at all, so much at home was he to the state of mind.

'I suppose it would,' Kenn answered, with his pleasant, shy smile. 'But—when I think over it—I have never had any vision. Nor any belief. I don't think, perhaps, many of us had where I was brought up. Don't think we ever really believed in our church any more than we believed in the sort of clan landlord we had, though they were the two most unavoidable of realities. That's the sort of thing that becomes clear to me when thinking of the river.'

'It's a good sort of vision to get.' Radzyn turned to the window again and his eyes grew still. 'Yet some sort of living or working belief you must have.'

'I don't know that one bothers trying to formulate it much.'

'Supposing you try now.'

'Without thinking, I would say at once that the work you are doing is the most important in the world. Nothing can be equally important with investigation into the nature of things. It is also the most difficult. It is also so infinitely slow. The greatest step any one man can take into the unknown is almost negligible. There are no spiritual rewards or divine assurances. Not even the sensuous pleasure that artists presumably get. And if a man is fortunate enough to make some critical discovery, the thing is not his creation, it is the discovery of what is already created. I mean he cannot hang it up on his wall or stick it on his piano.'

'I have rarely heard you so eloquent. You would think the scientist was the modern saint. And you dismiss the artist and literary men—sensuous pleasure.' It was clearly a point.

'That's the worst of talking.' Kenn tried to smile away the embarrassment that comes from talking too much. But he had a point to make. And it was not any statement of his own belief but a need, quick in him, to reassure this man for whom he realised, in the quiet of the evening, he had so deep a respect. There was no such need to reassure himself. He was not subtle and various in knowledge; he was not given to any internal doubts and stresses. To himself he was simple and obvious. But this man's use of the word saint was somehow extraordinarily suggestive and potent.

'We have to do a little talk sometimes. And your point of view is refreshing—perhaps because, in religion and the arts, if I may be permitted to say so, you are not weighted down with knowledge.'

Kenn smiled in sheer relief.

Radzyn looked at him and his eyes glimmered in friendliness. 'Tell me,' he said, 'what you really think of the arts.'

'Do you mean modern theories—words like surrealism and so on?'

'Well, even these?'

'It's silly my trying to say anything about it. But from what I can gather it's pretty much a case of the old trinity again.

There is the purely objective and the purely subjective. They marry and externalize the offspring. Most of the argument, as far as I can make out, is a matter of where to place the emphasis. The purely objective is photographic. The purely subjective is incommunicable. How to give form to the fusion so that the most arresting communication is made? And so on. Now all that is important, no doubt, but it is really social. It is decorative; it is cultural; in a million years it would never get us anywhere—that is from the point of view of apprehending the real nature of the universe in which we live. It's the same with literature. If poetry is the highest expression of literature, how is it that the modern age has produced no great poetry, no poetry anyway that dominates intelligent minds, holds them with a sense of being an absolute—as it has done in the past? It must be surely because its principal attributes of wonder and curiosity and the thrill of new forms or new beauty are today to be found in science. The way in which science has opened out the universe is the real saga or drama of our day. New words, exciting and strange, and yet more exact than words in the starkest ballad. The scientist is the discoverer. It's he who is on the peak of Darien. But I'm afraid I'm not getting my words very exact!'

'You do not seem to consider much the value of the social effort.'

'Well, if it comes to that—what effect has any of man's pre-occupations had on life compared with science? Take away scientific discovery and consequent mechanical invention and what would our age be like? The last time I was going home I crossed the Forth Bridge. No one whom I asked knew the architect's or engineer's name. Like the great cathedrals of the medieval age. Already a sort of nameless communal effort. The work of the folk. I felt there was something rather fine in the idea. I got, I suppose, a sort of vision!'

'You have the folk idea strong in you.'

'That may come out of our past, for we were a fairly communal folk until we were thoroughly debauched by predatory chiefs and the like. A feeling lingers that the poor have always been wronged. It goes pretty deep. And anyway, deep or not, it's time they were freed—as far as freedom is possible to the animal. And ultimately science will free them.'

'That seems a piece of dialectical materialism rather than what one would expect from the Celtic—fringe, is it? Are you forsaking your Twilight?'

'I never had any experience of this Twilight. An old woman in the old days in my country knew the nature of what grew around her quite precisely. She gathered her roots and her lichens and out of them made the vivid dyes you see in tartans. That was what happened in fact. It is clear, too, that they achieved in their way a very tolerable communal life, and worked to the rhythm of their own music and that sort of thing. In fact if a Scot is interested in dialectical materialism or proletarian humanism, it seems to me he should study the old system in order to find out how the new system would be likely to work amongst his kind. It might help him at least to get rid of his more idealistic wind.'

'Possibly! But how can you compare the complex Marxian dialectic with the social simplicities that obtained amongst your primitives?'

'That's one thing I have wondered about. The use of this word primitive—I am not so sure. How would you define it? They were primitive only in their lack of machinery and therefore of a complex industrialism. But they were not primitive in their humanism or social recognition of one another. For example, where in English we have only the one word, man, and a few adjectives to differentiate all the kinds of men, they had scores of exact words in their language, each one of which at once evoked a different kind of man. In this matter they were much more complex than we are. Our lack of capacity for precise verbal discrimination here shows us as primitives to them.'

Radzyn's smile flashed a gleam from his dark eyes.

'I like your simplicity. Whether it is great—or merely

naïve—I am not so sure. You do not appear to have experienced the pressure of great systems of thought. Possibly you are too naturally pagan to be worried. But that apart— and perhaps I am glad it is apart—are you not avoiding the pressure of life around us today? In our laboratory here, are we not secluded and safe? While outside—every newspaper has its records of human slaughter. Foreign wars, civil wars, and steady preparation for another great world war. And beneath that, the pits of human misery, with communism— the new creed of your folk—recognising with a sort of religious fervour that there can be no hope for the folk except by revolution. Not only that, but what little we as scientists find out is being used instantly and with diabolic cunning to perfect the art of universal slaughter. And you believe we are important. Well, in that diabolic sense, I suppose we are. But it is hardly one which at the moment I think we can afford to stress. Do you?'

'I hardly see it like that. Everyone who reads a paper knows the facts. But I believe that the scientist is the one man who with certainty is going to make war impossible. The golden age of Pericles went down before the black death. So did the Mayas before yellow jack. Typhus, malaria, smallpox, diphtheria, leprosy, have been more terrible in their time than any number of armies with banners. But science has beaten them all. The scientist cannot work in his laboratory today and at the same time be outside trying to chain up the predatory animal. He can leave that, I think, to the slow but sure emergence of the folk. It must be their job anyway. They must of themselves make it impossible for the predatory animal to function—on any large scale, at least. And they will. I am quite certain of that. Why? Because I am one of the folk myself. I know them, because I know what moves me.'

'And so you see your job now, your job as a scientist, as being a great contribution to the folk, as being the new faith that will liberate them? By its means they will for the first time really inherit the earth? And they will inherit not only its wealth but also some knowledge of its true nature, and out of it all make their new art and their new literature. And all this will be charged with dynamic joy and with splendid loyalties. These loyalties will generate their own morality. And for religion there will continue to be, as always, the Unknowable—to provide us with our search for truth.'

For the first time Kenn used hidden irony against his chief. 'I admit,' he said, smiling blandly, 'that you make me shy at so much ideal speculation.'

Radzyn looked narrowly at him, at the smiling unwavering eyes, and saw deep in the eyes the indissoluble hard core, the native, inalienable residuum, saw it with the surprise one might come on a face in a mirror or a still adder-head in a pleasant bunch of heather.

Radzyn experienced a sharp and exciting shock. The sort of shock a stranger might have in a strange land when suddenly one of the people of that land comes near to him, nearer to his spirit than could one of his own blood.

Radzyn got up. So did Kenn. The hour certainly was getting late. But now Radzyn showed no sign of preparing to walk away with Kenn. He held out his hand, his manner very polished, very precise.

'I have enjoyed our talk. I wish you a pleasant holiday.'

Kenn thanked him. Their hands fell to their sides. They bowed. 'You have been very good to me,' said Kenn. Then he turned and walked away.

On the pavement, Kenn felt himself tingling with pleasure. 'Hang it, he's a nice fellow!' he said aloud. What the conversation had been about did not much matter. Too often in fact a lot of talking left the feeling that what really mattered had got smothered. Making a point of view or upholding an attitude was so often a sententious exercise.

The thought now was good fun. For Kenn knew that somehow he had achieved his purpose of complimenting Radzyn; and not only that but of bringing conviction to the man's own lonely convictions. Without having said anything at all to the point really! Perhaps this bore out his idea about the complexity of the Highlander in the matter of human relationship! Folk did say the Highlander was two-faced! Kenn would have liked to have laughed aloud on the street because it appeared so good a joke. Like the saying, too— once whispered to him very privately by a Highland divine— that the Highlander had no ethical basis. There was so much acute observation in both sayings that to appreciate the lack of the slight extra penetration necessary to permit the turning of the corner to revelation required the sort of mood he himself was in at the moment!

And Radzyn, too: he had some of the divine's conception of the ethical. Not the same at all really—yet parallel. Radzyn's gravity or solemnity had something in it of black chasms in a fair earth. The nearest thing to it that Kenn had struck was a certain period of the Renaissance when thought had pushed itself by infinite refinements to a sort of face-to-face with death. Only in Radzyn's case there was no refined sensuous artistry. The thing was sheer— the scientific visualization! Radzyn's quietism of the East was flawed in this way.

And it wasn't as if he had practised a fraud on Radzyn. On the contrary, he hadn't conveyed anything like the sincerity of assurance he should have liked to have conveyed. It was the sincerity, the glimmer of ultimate integrity, *and nothing else*, that now induced his mood of fun. And he knew it; but knew also that if Radzyn saw his expression, with its broad grin, he might well get the shock of misgiving!

For the truth of life to Kenn was that at its core there was a wise pagan laughter. Behind importance and solemnity, it lay in wait. It was cunning and evasive; it was charming and amusing; it was hard as a tree knot; it was perhaps the old serpent myth that his folk had forgotten how to interpret. The serpent that stuck its tail in its mouth to suppress its laughter!

The folk—and goodness and kindness and loyalties. True, Herr Radzyn!

A girl, sauntering past, looked into his face, but did not speak. The words of sly invitation faded on her lips; the brightness that came to her eyes faded also, slowly, into a half-bitter envy or regret. When she had gone a little way, she turned and walked back, her steps quickening but then falling slack again, for he had passed from the streets.

CHAPTER NINETEEN

THE OLD HOME was now occupied by strangers. He looked at it over his shoulder. Already he had seen the harbour deserted of fishing craft. How typical he was in himself of countless Highland lads who came back to the scenes of their boyhood! How many had returned after the Napoleonic wars to find that even the ruins of their homes had been obliterated!

The speculation produced no more than a momentary dry smile. His father had died a short time before Angus had been killed. There had been between these two a curious dumb relationship that one could understand but not express. It had always been there. He could remember—very early in his own life it must have been—seeing his father going apart to talk to Angus who had committed the terrible sin of playing truant from school. His father had stooped down and talked to him. That was all of the action he could remember, but it still held a mysterious significance. Angus had thrown over the sea, that was his father's life, and emigrated. Then he had come back to Europe and been killed. His father had never seen him after he had left for Canada.

On all the little grey-granite war-memorials of the north, how often was that story told!

Six years after that his mother had died. Not before he had got her south to see him capped Master of Arts and Bachelor of Science. At least he had had the wit to do that!

During the capping ceremony, she kept her countenance. When he walked on amid the learned gowns, there was perhaps a moment's difficulty, a slight stress, but she did not lower her head.

During her visit, in a way he had never foreseen, he

was extraordinarily proud of her. There had been a supper celebration with two or three friends at an expensive restaurant. But the array of knives and forks merely made her smile. She smiled upon them all out of a good nature that enjoyed the perplexing abundance with a quiet humour. Life was good. 'Well, well, bairns!' she said and prepared to have every good thing that was going. 'A little more of the wine, Mother.' 'Thank you,' she said, and added, 'I think it is going a little to my head.' They all laughed, moved to pleasure by her wise naïvety. She looked around the room and then at her plate and ate modestly. To her, the room was full of ladies and gentlemen. She would have had no desire to be reminded of the grey, hard north. She would have had no sentimental illusions about the homeland. She knew its grain too well. Here at last life blossomed into its flower.

And if this was her illusion, it at least sprang out of some very deep instinct, some need for brightness and happiness, for the primordial goodness that so persists in haunting the minds of the children of women.

He took her up to her bedroom himself. 'Goodnight, Mother!' and he kissed her quickly, laughing. For a moment, she had nearly lost herself in a deep mother-surging of the body towards him, for this exhibition of southern manners had taken her by surprise. 'Have a good sleep,' he said and turned from her hungry eyes. Before going downstairs he had paused to fumble with his tie, smiling to himself at thought of her emotion—and of his own.

A moment worth remembering—together with that other moment when he had had the wit to bring the half-bottle of whisky to his father and Sandy.

Strangers now in the old home. Well, what of it? The thought of his father and mother being dead brought no sadness. Some conception of fulfilment rather, and of, on his part, an acceptance not at all stoical but at the moment full of a wise, bright pleasure.

And here once more the river. How small it had seemed when he had returned after the war! Everything had shrunken.

What had been to him as a boy great journeys, were now short distances for a forenoon's stroll. The forests had dwindled to decaying woods. The paths were little broader than sheep tracks and in places were overgrown, broken down, or eaten away. Even the little round house in the wall of the Broch, perfect in his boyhood as it had been for two thousand years, had now a breach in its side.

But in the years before his mother's death, he had quite conquered this obvious grown-up reaction to childhood's conception of size or even of importance, and the river had once more established itself, with values arising out of the old, but with a new intensity and meaning. Since his mother's death, there had been no direct need to visit the homeland, had possibly been an underlying reluctance to visit it, and vacations for the most part had been spent on sea trips or in the cities of the Continent or in other parts of Scotland. Until in recent years, the simple fact that he had never actually gone to the source of his childhood's river had quietly taken possession of his mind, and by a slowly growing impulsive need had started it on this long, intricate quest, a quest of lost times and places, but not for the mere sake of evoking them, or of indulging pleasant or sentimental memories, but of capturing, of isolating, a quality of awareness and delight in order to provide the core of life with warmth and light.

A careless happiness, derisively touched, thus sat at his heart as he took the path by the river, by the Intake Pool, to the Broch promontory where he paused to throw a glance up the green flat. The roses were once again in bloom.

When he had seen Annie Grierson six years ago, she was the mother of a young family and settled to the soil. She had been pleasant but perfectly matter of fact. He had laughed to himself afterwards, recognising his own male romanticism— as if he had expected to find a certain shyness, a veiled remembrance! Absurd! Yet what absolute guarantee had he that she did not remember?

None, for she possibly remembered all right—only not

with an airy grace! There was a delicious humour against himself in this. For the truth no doubt was that Annie saw him as the young man who had had a notable career, who, amongst the learned, would have forgotten his boyish pranks and, in any case, would scarcely want to be reminded of them. Yet Annie had oddly disturbed him for a year or so; and almost certainly had been the unknown factor that had so mysteriously interfered with the expedition to see the bull! Out of what strange deep in the mind does such early romantic idealism spring?

While his mind swithered in this vague debate, his legs suddenly decided to carry him round to the right. Yes, the white rose of Scotland was growing here still. And the scent—it improved on his memory, as it always did. No rose in the world had so lovely a scent. He had tried all the roses he had ever met and no scent was so fragile and so deep. Time breathed up warm from its yellow heart. The youth of the world, cupped in fragrant quietude forever. Upon the restless soul, a benediction and a wild cry.

He came away with a couple of blooms, a sun-warmth the colour of old ivory in their white petals. For he had sent the five petals of this rose to the nurse whose ear had, more or less inadvertently, touched his lips in Leicester—'to prove to you that all the roses of England—and how many have I to thank you for!—may not compare with this wild rose out of the heart of my native country. Simply that—and nothing more.' The 'nothing more' being designed (sweet youth!) as the obvious thorn that may not go untouched. As it hadn't!

He regarded the roses in his hands, his eyelids quivering in amusement. Then he pulled off the petals and put them flat as shillings into his pocket book, and looked around and laughed silently, as he used to laugh to himself when a boy. He would give them to her when he got back. The blue in her eye that she had carried over from an Irish ancestor would be worth mocking for a moment. Such sweet havoc they had played with the English roses!

He did not go up to the Broch, but held by the river,

passed the white house, came in sight of the lodge, and at last climbed up on to the Hawk's Hol. From the heather, he arose and went along the wooded crest and down to Achglas Pool. Not a very large pool but still dark and impenetrable in the centre. And there was the ledge, too. Could he balance his six feet on its tiny shelf? It was not very easy, but he managed to do it, even to lean out over the brown foam-flecked water and peer down. He leaned a long time, his elbow bent out, his sleeve in the water, and when he looked up it was as if at the ghost of someone present, the trickle from his forehead unheeded. With silent care, he got off the ledge and, standing on the rock above the pool, stared all around him and listened, his mouth slightly open.

Spink! Spink! came from the trees above. Coloured bubbles, light as thistledown, tumbled from the branches. The summer sunlight was shafted by the clouds. All he knew in the world was that the large trout he had just seen must in fact be a salmon of twelve pounds.

Weakness beset his leg muscles. They grew tremulous and he sat down. When he found his hands searching through his pockets for a hook, he smiled. But the smile was fugitive and pale, and the ghost of his brother Angus looked through his face.

I'm in it now! he thought.

By the time he had passed the Smuggler's Pool, the burying ground, the Serpent Pool, the falls, and reached the place where twenty years before he had lain naked in the sun, the river ran through him with all the ancient potency.

The excitement in this was deep because it was surprising. Somehow he had expected it would all, in a sense, be a looking back, or, at best, an effort to recapture something of the past in the present. Nothing altogether nostalgic or sentimental, because he was prepared for that, but still a certain deliberate use of the past to enrich the present.

And lo! he had entered absolutely into the present itself.

The sweat and sun on his face made the skin smooth and oily. His nails and knuckles were seamed with earth. He took off his shirt—after a look around—and bared his chest to the sun. Lord, you're white! he muttered. As white as leprosy. This is good, boys! A chuckle rumbled in his throat. Lord, it was good, this! What! He was in complete command of the situation. He could imitate Angus imitating the show-man in front of Pinder Ord's circus. Walk up, gentlemen! Walk up! Lions and tigers, elephants and bears! Angus's solemn boasting, his solemn eructation-with-variations, his less reputable variations, his fecund play-acting, rich and warm with laughter, warm as your face smothered in the pillow lest they heard you downstairs.

Life was flowing through him, thick with health. This was the health out of which one looked, as brown eyes out of a curled furry body, but with the understanding in the eyes that the wise call humour.

All the little lewdnesses and sexual movements of early boyhood are seen with a friendly chuckle, as young lambs racing and mounting one another in a field. What merriment they could arouse—often to the point of utter, of helpless laughter! Out of the simple game of seeing who could squirt his water the farthest, what a row of serious intentions, what 'accidents', what mirth! And even the more intimate little acts that one would have been so ashamed of—worth a humoured thought now!

Lying naked at seventeen. These pale idealizations of adolescent love, romantically conceived, hotly imagined. Even these—for understanding darkened with something akin to pity.

This feel of the earth, of the body; this goodness of health that flowed from the body over the mind, adder-cool, sun-warm; this thick richness of texture, for a laughing mouth to threaten.

No evil here; only immemorial good; life a centre-knot that draws individual consciousness out of eternal absorption, before letting it go again, soon or late.

He had only to stick his head up over the edge of the bank to see the eternal absorption, to see the moors, the dark brown rising to far low ridges, and passing over them the wind, and the cry of a hill bird. The wind touched his parched city skin to velvet; the bird-cry sounded the depth of silence that he had forgotten was in the world and in his soul.

Knots of mist gather and fade, but this moor-world remains, detached and unexpectant; so detached, so unexpectant, that nearness and urgency may rush the conscious soul to a listening that hears the flowing of the river under the ultimate silence.

What more may one expect? How acquisitive the personal gluttony that must hang on to everything! In the welter of the unclean that is evil is it not something to be certain that this will remain? That into this one may sink?

And as for the rest and the hereafter—if any (Kenn stretched his pagan legs)—what more certain than that only in proportion as one apprehends this now will one apprehend that hereafter? Perhaps this is why the folk have always seen something of divinity in the work of the artist. For the divinity consists in this: that he observes here and now. Precisely as the scientist observes; if working with a different set of values. The religious who is always trying to see hereafter is like one trying to occupy the last stance in a mathematical regression.

Or assume God. Assume God sets a paper in the final exam on the nature of His Creation. Will the religious who saw little but evil and engaged in little but sycophantic prayer. . . . A deep drowsiness was washing in upon Kenn from the upheaving moors; the smile on his face grew faint in pure beneficence; grew fainter still until it passed quite away, and left upon his features, the mouth fallen slightly open, the forewriting of death.

His eyes flashed open in frightened bewilderment; then his spirit came back into his face. I must very nearly have fallen asleep! he muttered, knowing even as he glanced at the sun that he must have been asleep a good hour. This gift of an hour's sleep from the moor is very handsome, he thought, as his face came smiling through the neck of his shirt. Inside his clothes, his body, cooled by wind and cloud, rustled in lightness and ease.

As he stepped away, the quiver of humour in his eyelids was an answer to all the social voices of the world. But he did not debate with them. He heard no single disputant, for no single voice could come through to him now, no single voice of all the voices drowning far back in their own solemn concerns.

He was arisen right enough! Not difficult to understand why no traveller ever returned across the bourne!

The last of the birches were now behind him. The strath was flattening out. The heather came down to the grass. He passed over a rise and saw before him a wide shallow dip in the moor in which was a shepherd's house. This was the last inhabited house on the way to the source, and, though he did not know the family's name, he knew that the shepherd was employed, no longer by the estate, but by a club of crofters from round his old home. Was this the first step in the coming back of the folk to their own?

The rolling ground here was all green grass, acres and acres of it, clumped at wide intervals by grey ruins. It extended beyond the other bank where further heaps of ruins were visible. On an old large-scale map of this region that he had studied he had seen the words *Picts Houses*, and had been oddly moved, as by some pictorial reminiscence that cunningly evaded being focused by memory or eye.

When he saw a golden-brown caterpillar on a twig of heather, the rich hairy body seemed to have something to do with Picts Houses. So much for environment! But beneath the humour was the evasive magic. An exotic, lovely, crawling thing out of the heather. Not smooth; but rich and hairy and deeper in its gold than honey. It curled upon his palm, tickling his skin to the incipient panic that wanted to drop it.

At the first mass of ruins he saw a thing that pleased him instantly. The bulk of the ruins represented the ordinary rectangular croft houses, manifestly occupied in recent centuries. But at the head of the straggling cairn was the round building of one of the Picts Houses of the map, its thick prehistoric stone wall still almost as tall as himself. It had clearly been used as one of the gable walls of a rectangular house, and this effect of intimacy between old and new hit him strongly. Its dumbness was eloquent of the continuity of the folk. It solved for him in a flash the interminable debate as to the identity of the Pict. I am the Pict! he thought.

When he turned and looked at the river and saw it winding far on and leftward through this pastoral land, the effect of Stevenson's 'vanished races' came full upon him. He had always been secretly affected by the poem.

> Hills of sheep, and the howes of the silent
>   vanished races,
> And winds, austere and pure.

The whaup-cry from Vailima! Out of the marrow of the bone! 'My heart remembers how.'

Stevenson had known the 'influence' all right! Sonorous or poetic or *mot-justely* as one likes, but there! The golden caterpillar warmth beneath the heart.

And his face—a queer vanishing face. It vanished before Kenn as he looked, and left his own heart touched to a dark embarrassment.

The pools were now new to him. The old red sandstone was no longer broken into boulders but thrust its strata through the river bed, through the hide of the earth, like elbows—running into smooth skin. As with a connoisseur of period painting, each new pool to Kenn was a new piece, full of its fascinating delights and judgments. He knew where the salmon would lie, to this side or that, resting at the bottom or ready at the neck.

Beyond the shepherd's house, a large tributary entered. This occupied his attention for a long time. He was now in the spawning land.

From here onward the salmon in the autumn consummated their journey from the dark ledges of the Atlantic. How many hundreds of miles they travelled to this stream that wandered more lonely than any cloud! The glimmer on

Kenn's face held a friendly satire browner and older than a peat bog.

For he was at home here. He was drawing back into his own. He could feel the pull—as the salmon felt it—if to no such fruitful end!

The laugh could come through his nostrils in soft gusts. There was no one to see; and as for that inexplicable sensation of there being an eye about somewhere, a non-human eye, a peat-hag eye under heather tufts, he appreciated so well the sheer illusoriness of it, that—well—he could outstare it.

Turning, he saw the shepherd's house away behind him, set in the green land of the vanished Picts. It was inconceivably lonely, its life so strange an intrusion that it emphasized more than anything could have done the static eternal quality of the scene. At such a moment, eternity was felt not as a dimension in time forward in the way the mind usually feels it, nor even as a dimension in time backward, but as the point of meeting where the circle starts and ends. Time held in suspension or poise and losing all dimension in an eternal now.

His mind became so held with correspondent mathematical speculation, that when he turned again the house was gone, and looking down and ahead he saw that the river had grown smaller, that the banks were hollowed peat, that flowing directly down upon him at last were the heather moors, with the mountain-tops riding beyond them to the west, and that this place—where he had never been before—no, he would not say it was familiar—that would be too obvious a paradox—besides, it would be wrong, because he had never been here before.

His mind trifled with itself, amused and happy. Time was gone. Human relationship was gone. He had entered into the non-human, not only in the moor but in himself. Perhaps it was this that was familiar!

The familiar strangeness he would take in his stride, not letting his mind dwell upon it. There were certain things one kept down, not out of fear but for the extra enjoyment of that healthy normality that holds all things in its sway.

One played with the queerer forces of the mind as one played with kittens. Lovely things they were—that turned all claw only when one lost the power to play, when sadism or masochism or other perverted fear craved the filthy abomination of cruelty, craved it in a paroxysm that turned the blood acid and squirted saliva about the fangs.

Almost any one of the small pools now was a good spawning pool. In the stalking season the gillies often saw the fish ploughing up the gravel beds. A great commotion they made. One would sometimes think, said the gillies, that they had gone mad or that an otter had got in amongst them.

Their love rites. Well, they had come a long way for them! thought Kenn. A fellow feeling made him hope that the emotions would match the strength and beauty. And certainly the strength was spent magnificently, utterly, almost to the point of death.

Lovely fish! So worked upon was his mood that the killing of them seemed a sad business.

But the whisper of this was far under his mind and soft as the wind. For a moment, without thinking the problem out, he held it sanely in the glimmer of his eyes. Then he passed away from it and from himself, as the wind passed, and the sunlight.

In the inconsequent way that images will come upon the mind when one is walking for a long time in a solitary place, Kenn saw an immense stretch of ocean with his father's boat upon it, black buoys, and the thin dark line of a drift of herring nets. Morning, and they are hauling the nets, when a salmon leaps high in the air, all gleaming silver, his tail curving over in the pride of strength as he takes the water again.

His father's voice comes clearly to him: 'It was a fine morning.'

The calm, reminiscent voice and the leagues of the sea and the sun rising; the voice concerned leisurely with exact detail, and particularly with this detail—that they were fifty miles from land.

Those who wrote about the salmon, judging from the

books Kenn had read, would be glad of a detail like that. How many of the salmon followed the herring shoals? Were they chance raiders, fellows who set off on poaching forays? . . . Only once in his lifetime had his father caught a salmon in his nets. Many skippers never caught one. At fifty miles out, the land—

Kenn smacked his neck violently and smashed the horse-fly and threw it to the ground with fierce disgust. A cleg! He had forgotten the loathsome, the silent-footed brutes. One thing he had never understood—would never make any effort to understand—why insects had been created. Of all forms of life, surely the most vile. The cleg was silent, the colour of old horse manure, a sort of living ghost of evil. The tenderest skin never felt him land. Not content with filling his belly with one's blood—for which he might have been forgiven in a difficult world—he must go on to leave behind him a filthy poison to swell the flesh in maddening irritation for days.

Kenn abhorred them, and now looked about him with malignant wariness. There were Junes and Julys in the Highlands of Scotland that would be pure paradise but for these moor-emanations of some diabolic intelligence. They certainly gave pith to the belief in an evil principle in creation. The blister was already beginning to rise.

Sufficient for the moment to dispel imaginative images anyhow! Bringing a rough rake to the throat and sinking the heels solidly in the earth, hang it! with a wry laugh, the brutes!

This business, he considered, of finding background for thought itself went pretty deep. Perhaps it explained his reactions to some modern writers who would build up human life into the social complex of the beehive. How appalling! Quick-stinging insect intelligences creating an insect philosophy, an insect social order. Efficient to the nth, within their surface pattern. Made one think of the bees that sting the mouse to death and wax him over in a pale aseptic mausoleum. How dreadful, how sterile a nightmare!

Had his abhorrence of this started with boyhood's experience of the cleg? Blue bottles laying their eggs on the hidden
salmon; an attack by wasps; clouds of midges eating the
eyelids. . . .

For what if one gained an insect world but lost one's own
soul? There was the idea, juggle with it as one liked. Any
particular creedal significance was neither here nor there. A
man had to find himself, had to hold himself with a solitary,
lonely integrity. That always; and more imperatively than
ever, when the mechanics of bodily sustenance—food and
shelter—were themselves being elevated into a whole way
of life, a religion. Good God (said Kenn to his multiple
disputant) this business of political economy is at bottom
a matter of pure animalism, a matter of arranging the
production and distribution of the admitted abundance of
what we as animals need. Because we make wars and commit
social cruelties of incredible hideousness in its name, that's
not going to make me forget that it's animalism, not going
to make me talk of high ambition and holy endeavour and
glittering prizes. That sort of sentimentality is surely beyond
being borne, is surely the sin against any holy ghost that may
inhabit the body. Oh, to hell with it! A cleg had landed on
his thigh. He hit it a terrific welt and it rebounded to the
ground.

Invigorated, he went on happily.

Since entering the barer country, he had been noticing
the wild flowers. Eye-bright, butterwort, milkwort, cuckoo-
flower, lousewort, stonecrop, tormentil, orchis, forget-me-
not, scabious, trefoil, and a pink vetch were fairly common.
Now the heaths and the lichens of the moor were drawing
his attention. The bell heather proper clustered in deep
blood-red, but the bells of the cross-leaved heath (*erica
tetralix*) hung pale pink, so delicate and soft to the eye
that they seemed to have an added bloom, like the peach
or the blaeberry. The basic tone, too, had a wide range,
now almost campion red, now fading away in moonlit pallor.
Rushes grew in clumps along the green ways. Apart from
sudden bends, where the peat hags directly overhung the

water, the stream never lost the generous borderings of rich grass. Occasionally they widened into fair pasturage, into what old folk called 'the leans'—a term that at once evoked the ancient shieling days and the summer herdings of cattle far from the townships or villages. How many centuries had slid down the peat water since the folk of the Picts Houses had pastured their small black cattle here where the rushes grew?

Crossing a boggy tongue of ground at a bend in the stream, Kenn came on a sundew. It immediately evoked the sensation of having something of the sea about it, as though allied to certain marine plants that filled the rock pools of his boyhood. This sort of subterranean linking of sea and land in his mind had its own strange potency, though precisely how or why he could not say. Possibly it was little more than a long subconscious enriching of what he had read in early days about the beginnings of all life on the sea beaches. He was prepared to accept that—were it only to avoid the exquisite difficulty of attempting further analysis—with a possible direction of speculation towards conclusions too utterly fantastic. In any case, thought of such analysis did not worry him now, for, alongside the sundew with the elongated leaves, he saw—what he had never seen before—a perfect specimen of the round-leaved sundew, shaped like the face of a small clock, with minute hands radiating at equal intervals and carrying on their tips their round hairy leaves.

Standing up, he looked about him, at the far, slow-rising moors, and beyond to where the shapely peak of Morven was half-veiled in mist. He saw the shower coming from the mountain towards him, a thin curtain trailing its lace along the heather, and going down under an overhanging hag he squatted on his heels and suddenly felt hungry. He looked at his watch. It was five o'clock.

As he munched his sandwiches, the fine rain drenched the air and the earth and drew small grey insects to their whirling dance. But it was too early in the year for the stinging midge to be really troublesome and, beyond wetting his face in absent-minded swipes, he was not inconvenienced greatly. He had nothing to drink, so chewed away at the sandwiches as he stared at the water at his feet, until the mood of communion with the sodden black earth—too often an imagined mood—became a mindless reality, with physical points of discomfort where the sweat was drying to a chill in the small of his back and the rain was wetting a knee and a shoulder. But he could not be bothered shifting the knee or the shoulder. Once his eyes glimmered in the humour that might have said, 'This is fine,' but his lips remained soundless and the glimmer passed.

The small pool in the black peat at his feet became a world of its own. It was separated from the stream by a green bank. The reflections of the rushes seemed more vivid than the rushes themselves, more intricate in their patterns. The end of his hazel crook stirred the pool and bubbles came to life on its surface. The bubbles had an attraction for one another. When two drew close together they rushed into a violent embrace and became one. The one sailed about for a time, then burst, and from the place where it had been went out an uncountable number of close concentric waves, as if the skin of the pool shivered. Idly the stick created more individual bubbles. They united; they died. Some never united. But they all died. The shadow of his stick lay on the pool. When a bubble crossed it the shadow at that point disappeared and the stick was broken. The bubble vanished and the shadow was made whole.

There was scientific knowledge in him to explain all this. Possibly an odd heap of symbols lay about somewhere as well. That the reflection of the rushes was more vivid than the rushes themselves had doubtless a meaning for art. He was beyond caring. The inertia was too profound. The objectivity absolute.

So still was he now that two birds came tumbling down the air in front of him, flirting in twists and spirals. They were smaller than skylarks. In a detachment finer than excitement, he realised that they were heather linties, the singing birds that an older generation had snared for the cage. Half-fabulous birds to him; yet all in a moment endowing the earth and air about them with attributes of home. Their home. His perception of this was clear as the sunlight that came after the shower and poised the birds in air in a ruffle of under feathers and threw a rainbow in the sky.

As he went on the chill passed from his skin and his emptied mind began to fill with emotion. He knew the emotion before it quite arrived and his lips parted in their friendly, half-derisive humour.

From heel to toe his body moved with a cool tautening of muscle as if about to race, to jump; and this explosive energy was held in check, as laughter is held in check, behind glistening eyes. For inside this buoyancy the emotion he smiled at was very familiar, very old, very ordinary, ordinary as the poised fluttering of the birds, full of kindness, of affection, affection for the beauty of the birds, the coloured arch in the sky, for earth and air, for life. And this affection, held coolly in the extreme buoyancy of his body, pervaded him with a feeling of inexpressible well-being.

Coolly he recognised that his body was purged of the passions of evil and fear and hate; was for the moment reintegrated and made whole.

And the expression of the eyes, admitting this, was a subtle challenge to all the forces from the world behind him, the world he had left. A subtle but not unfriendly challenge. For he recognised his own strength. The heather root, the wind, the running water, the undefeatable strength of the moor, the hidden eye. Delicious as a chuckle of laughter in a pool's hidden throat. Nothing could ever throw this strength. And nothing could even approach an understanding of how to attempt to throw it—except in the spirit of a game, in the spirit of that excitement that is the pulse of the creative act.

But always with the instant power to step back into the detachment that makes the lid of the eye tremble in speculative primordial humour. A humour ready to smother sententious thought in a shout of bright fragments.

And consciousness of the mood to pass quietly, in an instant, into the quiet of the moor.

So quiet was this remote, twisting valley of the ever narrowing stream, that when he rounded a bend and saw the herd of hinds, he involuntarily stood still. The three hinds farthest out had their heads up watching him. They made no move. The hinds in the hollow had their heads down, grazing. As he stood looking, the whole scene took on the mood of arrested enchantment.

As he broke out of this mood, the farthest hind trotted a few steps, then turned its head again in that high flat-browed ear-pointed look that has something memoried about it out of some leprechaun world. The other two trotted and looked. More heads were lifted. Movement began in hesitant starts and pauses; rhythms taken up and broken, yet ever running together. The last to see him was a mother hind with her calf beside her. She wheeled round and was off, but holding herself in, too, her head thrown back and riding above her body with a lovely grace. He looked for the others. They were gone. The calf was pale against the golden tan of its mother and ran eagerly at its mother's side. In no time they were gone also. In the soft ground there had been no sound of hooves. There had indeed been no sound at all.

The valley kept changing and was ever the same. The stream dwindled slowly. His thought wrapped him about in a half-dark oblivion, a half-dark sea on which two craft fell away and came again. Their names were Aristocratic and Thoroughbred. The meaning of their names had the virginal freshness of white sails in a burst of sun. The names had been degraded. He saw how far they had been degraded. The whole historic social process was apprehended by an unanswerable intuition.

The hinds would run through his mind, would run through the mind of the world, for ever.

Of that he was certain.

His eyes were abstracted but with a deep glow in them. His features paled a trifle in sensitiveness. When the spirit of man recaptured the grace of the hinds, the two words would once more have meaning. Not until then. Only occasionally now was the meaning amongst men. Radzyn. Though in Radzyn—he saw it now—there was something for ever tragic. Could not one hand to Radzyn this lightness and positiveness, this sun-brightness, this beauty of health. . . . His hands had begun to move forward but instantly relaxed and fell to his sides. His eyes quested about him with an odd, sardonic humour, as if they were not quite his own eyes. There was nothing one could do with the tragic conception of life except acknowledge it.

Bow to it, giving nothing away, and pass on the moor like sunlight, like shadow, with thoughts hesitant and swift as a herd of hinds. In this way one is undefeatable—until death comes. And as death is inevitable, its victory is no great triumph.

The stream narrowed in places to no more than a foot. The source could not now be far away. The sun was behind a bank of cloud that hung low over the horizon in the north-west. The shadow of evening gave a darker texture to the moors in the distance. The mountain of Morven that had been hard and bright all afternoon, its screes and growths clearly defined, was now gathering about it an imponderable blue. The mountain was retiring within itself. All mountains did this at night. They withdrew. They folded their shoulders and drew their mantles about their feet, like gigantic prophets. But once in the West he had seen them like gigantic beasts, immense squatting brutes, mammoth figures moulded by some cosmic youth already touched by the tragic brooding of mind.

A band of mist lay high up along the mountain's shoulder, not settled to it, held in an immobile grace. The blue summit rose above it and in this way height was given to the mountain and a serene detachment.

Not the beast there, thought Kenn, but the prophet! His eyes glimmered, for there were two aspects of mountains that always either excited or drained his mind. This was one of them. The other was what he called their planetary light, in the dawn.

Suddenly, before his very eyes, the stream vanished into the earth.

His dismay was vague and ludicrous. From his map-gazing he knew that his river should rise in a loch. He could not have been mistaken. This loch was to have been the end of his journey. Like the yogi in his pilgrimage to Lake Mānas!

And here it was coming out of the earth itself. The realism mocked him. He had actually thought of a loch with shores of sand and water grey in the evening light.

Coming out of a black hole in the earth like life itself. A hole that was like death. Life and death in ooze. He poked into the dark hole with his stick.

He climbed over broken ground. Remembering how they listened-in to the earth when boys, he lay down and put his ear to the ground. Faintly he heard the surge of the stream away underground. So it was not lost! But listening more acutely, he realised that what he heard was the surge of the river of his own blood.

He went on over the broken ground and came to a round still pool. There was no sound of water running underneath. He leant over and thrust his stick out of sight in this navel-hole that was black as a death tarn.

About him the ground was broken and hag-ridden, but he could see he had not yet reached the crest of the watershed. There remained the suggestion of an upward hollow. He came on another small pool like the first. Then another. A primeval no-man's-land of outspewings like waterlogged shell-holes.

The touch of uncanniness began to get lost in an earthy zest. The pale sands and the wan water would have been a bit too poetic anyhow! His own, his native land; the quagmires and mosses; the deathly oozes and shivering tussocks: a place of such utter disillusion that, fighting from it, one's laughter could never be defeated. And then all at once before him again was the tiny stream and lifting his eyes he saw the far half of the loch, Loch Braighe na h'Aibhne, the water-head.

A deep humour flooded his sight as he stood still, and his

tongue came out searching his lips. His expression was half shy as at the unexpected sight of a loved woman. Then he went on, looking at the streamlet, until presently its water grew quiet, seeming to flow neither way; and when he came to the loch he saw that its shores were not of dove-grey sand but of pure ground quartz, paler than any woman's face in any old poet's dream.

He realised precisely the joke that had been played on him. Nature had a sly way of behaving like this occasionally. The goodness of it sank deep into his heart. He walked along the shore. He lifted handfuls of the ground quartz and let it run through his fingers. There were no footprints anywhere. The wind had fallen with the evening. The clegs had gone with the sun. There were no midges, no life of any kind. Perhaps no life ever came here. In front of him he saw marks on the white sand, delicate hoof-marks—of the hinds that came to drink.

He sat down, for he was tired now, suddenly tired. The surface of the loch before him was divided; on the right reflecting a turbulent glory of clouds, red and pearl and dark; on the left reflecting nothing, a grey shield, a mere, too wan for thought to gaze at.

He lay over on his side. He realised that it was some excitement in him that made him tired and unequal to the scene. He closed his eyes and let the place come about him. This it did with a caressing wash softer than any wind. But every now and then his eyes opened stealthily to set it back, and through his lashes the grey water receded to an infinite shore.

A strange fret ran along his bones. A surge from all the ways of life behind him pressed up, unvisualized and unresolved. Into what was around him he could not enter. He was not equal to it; or it was not equal to the ways of life, to the humoured flesh, the sardonic awareness that may never be imposed upon.

Unheeding, remote, without fret or passion, it waited, and would wait through aeons of time.

The suns died in it and rose again.

It was greyer than the marrow in his bones.

The familiar note that had haunted him all day—its excitement was now passing along his laboured flesh as in the preliminary pains to some creative act.

Giving birth to a vision! He felt his humour going nihilist, felt himself on the verge of some awful and irrevocable denial. For it was writ in his nerves that he could have no vision, that no figure could appear to bless or to fulfil.

He was a solitary.

That was his destiny. He saw its meaning in his people, even in their religion, for what was the Calvinist but one who would have no mediating figures between himself and the ultimate, no one to take responsibility from him, to suffer for him.

It was not pride—unless it was the pride of austerity.

Responsibility; the inexorable search for truth; the vision that came to the scientist, not of personal salvation, but of an unending spiritual drive into the unknown. Man's greatest of all poaching forays: leading him to what inconceivable water-head?

The gathering clot of moody denial dissolved like tiredness from his flesh, and his body lay to the sands lightly in a desire for sleep. As his eyes looked across the water, they smiled. Out of great works of art, out of great writing, there comes upon the soul sometimes a feeling of strange intimacy. It is the moment in which all conflict is reconciled, in which a timeless harmony is achieved.

It was coming upon him now.

An hour later, he left the white shore and encountered two or three tiny lochs, called dubh lochs. The inland moors were full of them. He had heard stories of their treacherous depths. The one in front of him was barely six feet across, its water hardly a foot deep. When his stick touched bottom in the middle it went sinking into the soft, dark ooze under its own weight. With his finger tip and the slightest of pressures, he sank it its full five feet. He had only to take one step forward and not all his struggles or clawings at the bank would save him from being sucked to death.

He was aware of an irrational pleasure, arising out of an absolute absence of fear. He had once thought of Radzyn's mind as a remote place with chasms.

As he looked back at Loch Braighe na h'Aibhne, his lips moved in their characteristic humour, but in his eyes was a deep, secret tenderness.

The intimacy was very close now. In the last few moments before he had risen he had seen himself walking towards the mountain, much as, in the last year or two, he had seen the little figure of the boy Kenn adventuring into the strath. What older mind, in this curious regress, was now the observer might be difficult to say, for its apprehension seemed profounder than individual thought. Pict, and Viking too, and Gael; the folk, through immense eras of time; sea and river, moor and loch; the abiding land: of which the departing figure was a silent emanation, more inevitable than any figure in any vision.

From the high summit, the solitary figure would watch the dawn come up behind the Orkneys; would see on the mountain ranges of Sutherland the grey planetary light that reveals the earth as a ball turning slowly in the immense chasm of space; would turn again to the plain of Caithness, that land of exquisite lights, and be held by a myriad lochs and dubh lochs glimmering blood-red. He could then bow his head and see what lay in his heart and in his mind.

Kenn withdrew his eyes from the source of his river and, turning, saw about him here and there on the moor the golden spikes of the bog asphodel. He picked one and found it had a scent. He searched for the name of the scent and remembered the taste of a golden candy Sans used to sell out of a glass bottle. At that, little Kenn's face vanished goblin-like across his mind. He could not all at once throw the flower from him nor could he put it in his buttonhole, so he forgot it in his hand as he went over the watershed and down into the valley that lay between him and the base of the mountain.